A Wife from the Ancestors

Books by John Chitakure

The Pursuit of the Sacred: An Introduction to Religious Studies. Eugene, Oregon: Wipf and Stock Publishers, 2016.

Shona Women in Zimbabwe: A Purchased People? Marriage, Bridewealth, Domestic Violence, and the Christian Traditions on Women. Eugene, Oregon: Wipf and Stock Publishers, 2016.

African Traditional Religion Encounters Christianity: The Resilience of a Demonized Religion. Eugene, Oregon: Wipf and Stock, 2017.

The Audacity to Dream: Stories from an African Immigrant. USA: Amazon Kindle Direct Publishing, 2018.

Things That My Father Forgot to Tell Me. USA: Amazon Kindle Direct Publishing, 2019.

A Wife from the Ancestors

JOHN CHITAKURE

Amazon Kindle Direct Publishing
USA

A Wife from the Ancestors

3718 Southern Grove
San Antonio, Texas 78222
USA
jchitakure@gmail.com

First printing, November 2020
ISBN: 978-0-9998339-3-3
EBOOK ISBN: 978-0-9998339-4-0

Cover Design: Mufaro Sean Chitakure

*This book is dedicated to couples in
intercultural marriages.*

Contents

Prologue 1

A Difficult Conversation 7

Let us Start from the Beginning.................................30

An Intercultural Encounter...49

The Winds of Destruction...80

The Wedding 102

A Trip to Zimbabwe 152

A Time to Confess..212

A Glossary of Foreign Terms and Phrases 231

Prologue

Having lived all my adult life in an almost monocultural society in Zimbabwe, except for the two years, which I had spent in Chicago, there were two significant issues about my cultural identity that I took for granted, before my family and I migrated to Texas, in 2012. First, I was not quite conscious of my ethnical otherness as a black person, and I was ignorant of the fact that my ethnicity could be conceived by people of other ethnicities as inferior. I took it for granted that all human beings were equal and must treat each other with equal respect and dignity. Even though I knew something about the racial discrimination in pre-independence Zimbabwe, and had read about the notorious apartheid in South Africa, I did not believe that there were some people in the world, who still had the same mentality. I had not personally experienced racial prejudices, stereotypes, and discrimination all my life, and I did not have a reason to imagine myself being a victim. For instance, I was not aware of how insulting the "N" word was to people of black origin until I started living in the United States. I knew that the word existed, and that it was derogatory and demeaning, but its mention did not raise any emotions in me then than it does now.

Second, I was not conscious of my cultural identity and integrity except that I was a Shona person from Zimbabwe. I did not quite value my culture, and was ready to trade my cultural identity for anything foreign. I did not care much about maintaining my cultural integrity by speaking my indigenous language, eating my traditional foods, and observing my traditional code of ethics. I erroneously thought that European culture was better than my Shona culture, and if I had an opportunity to adopt European culture, I would have done it without giving it a second thought.

In America, my cultural consciousness had a rude awakening. It was like a baptism by fire that destroyed my cultural naivety and innocence, and forced me to think of my cultural identity in relationship to other cultures. I shall share three incidents that awakened me to racial stereotypes and prejudices in America. The first incident happened when my family and I had just arrived in San Antonio, Texas, in 2012. Both my wife and I were frantically looking for jobs, and soon, we both realized that in spite of all the "we are hiring" posts that littered the internet and institutions' notice boards, it was not easy for us to get jobs. When I did not get a job as soon as I expected, I reached out to a friend in Chicago, who knew someone in San Antonio, who could connect me with prospective employers. After a few calls, which triangled my good friend in Chicago, the gentleman in San Antonio agreed to meet with me at a certain restaurant, where he told me, in no uncertain terms that he would not be able to assist me to get a job. Why? He said that since I was black, very few employers in San Antonio would want to employ me because of the stereotypes that people had about blacks.

When I asked him to elaborate on that, he said, "Some Americans believe that blacks are lazy, and use the color card to avoid performing their job responsibilities. If you give them a job, you should be willing to pay them for doing nothing. If you reprimand them, they are likely to accuse you of illtreating them because of their skin color. So, I am sorry, my friend, I will not be able to assist you. However, I wish you the best." I thanked him for enlightening me, and our conversation ended on that note. I never saw him again. I was devasted and disillusioned by what he said. I wondered why no one ever told me about those stereotypes before I relocated to America.

Although it took me almost five years to land a full-time job, I discovered that what he said was not completely true about all the American people because my wife was later assisted by a white American supervisor to get a job. My sons have not struggled to find summer jobs here in San Antonio, despite most of their interviewers being white or Hispanic.

The second incident occurred when I was being interviewed to participate in clinical pastoral education at one of the local hospitals, here, in San Antonio, Texas. I had been undertaking the chaplaincy training for about six months at a different hospital, and as per the tradition of the health system in which I was enrolled, I was supposed to transfer to another hospital site for the remaining six months. The transfer was not a straightforward process because I had to be interviewed by the chaplains working at that new site. It was a panel interview, which went on well, until at almost the end of the interview, when one of the panelists asked me an unexpected question. He asked, "John, with that heavy accent of yours, don't you think, you are going to make our patients worse, while straining to understand you?" I thought that it was a good question except that it contained some unfair ethnical overtones. His colleagues, who might not have expected such a question, were startled a little bit. I thanked the chaplain who had asked the question, and answered him as best as I could because my life depended on it.

I said, "I will try to listen to my clients more than I speak to them. Sometimes, there is more therapeutic and transformative power in listening and silence than in talking. Also, I understand that some of the patients whom I shall minister to will not make it back to their homes. In that unfortunate event of their demise, some may end up meeting their creator in heaven, and they are likely to thank me later. Who knows the accent of God? Maybe God has an accent as heavy as mine, and those patients who would have encountered me, are likely to understand it, and may even interpret the creator's message for their family members."

Everyone laughed, and they gave me a place to complete my clinical pastoral education.

The third incident happened at the same hospital as I was doing my rounds as a chaplain. One day, I received a call from one of the wards to visit a patient who was in great distress because of what was happening in his life. I immediately visited and ministered to him, and we built a professional connection. At the end of my visit, I thanked him for the conversation, and I started walking towards the exit. The client called me, and I stopped in my tracks.

"My brother, where do you live?" he asked.

"On the South East side of the city," I responded.

He looked at me quizzically, and shouted, "Why did you follow them? My friend, why did you follow them? Now, they are already busy trying to sell away their properties to run away from you. Why did you follow them?"

I was puzzled.

"Who are you talking about?" I asked.

"The whites," he responded. "Here, in America, you don't just buy a house wherever you want. You should purchase a home, where your people live. You, as a black man, your place is the East side of the city. That's where your *amigos* are found. You better sell your home, and move to where your people live."

"I didn't know about that, but thank you for the advice." That was the other conversation that awakened my racial consciousness in the United States. I had never heard anything like that before. My wife and I thought that we could just purchase a home wherever we wanted if we afforded it. It never crossed our minds that Americans lived in their ethnical "clans" just like we did in rural Zimbabwe.

Apart from the above-mentioned incidents, I had many other encounters in which I was conscientized of the ethnical stereotypes and realities in the United States. As my struggles to achieve the American dream, here in San Antonio, continued, I never ceased to think about the above incidents of racial differences, stereotypes, and realities in the United States. In my nine-years stay in the United States, I have experienced both subtle and direct racial discrimination from people of other ethnicities. However, I have also encountered people of other cultures who have transcended the racial divide, and have helped me and my family, in ways that black people have never assisted me. I should mention it here, that there are white and Hispanic Americans, who are deeply emersed in intercultural living and respect, and are always ready to lend a helping hand to anyone, irrespective of one's culture, skin color, sexual orientation, religious affiliation, and gender.

I have also discovered that I am not innocent of this racist mentality because I have my own racial prejudices, stereotypes, and discrimination against people of other cultures. In other words, I am also a racist in my own way, and I also need to acquire intercultural competencies just like everyone else living in the United States. It cannot be denied that we are all still enslaved by unhelpful racial stereotypes, biases, and prejudices against each other. My only difference from other Americans is that I do not have the power like some of them have because power adds weight to racism.

It is true that it has become increasingly more difficult to stay away from people who are different from us. Therefore, we need to find a way of living with each other, respectfully and peacefully, since we may not be able to run away from each other. Globalization has taken the universe by storm, and it is becoming almost impossible for one cultural group to avoid encountering people of other ethnicities because they are found everywhere—at the church, hospital, workplace, airplane, classroom, conference, bus, stores, park, weddings, graduation ceremonies, and many other places. Even if one succeeds in evading intercultural encounters here on earth, one may not be able to escape them in the hereafter. I do not think that God will create different compartments for each ethnicity in heaven.

This global community is here to stay, and people should be prepared for intercultural living. Our ethnocentric mindsets must be transformed, and our provincial worldviews enlarged, if our communities are to benefit from this cultural diversity rather than being destroyed by it. People should acquire competencies for intercultural respect and living, and this learning starts from humble beginnings. One of the initial stages of learning to live interculturally is the willingness to take the risk to encounter the other, however discomfortable it may be. This encounter will eventually lead to the mutual cultivation of intercultural respect and integrity.

This novel is about an intercultural encounter, and an eventual integration that happened in an imaginary interracial marriage. For an interracial marriage to even begin, there is a need for mutual cultural respect, and a relentless pursuit and attainment of intercultural competencies that may be acquired through marital experiences and hard work. In an interracial marriage, the learning and attainment of intercultural competencies may be easier for the spouses because they may have come into such a union well prepared for the challenges of living interculturally, but might not be easy for their relatives, who are sometimes reluctantly dragged into such family relationships.

This novel narrates the fictional story of two young people who decided to set aside their cultural differences because they were willing to encounter each other, fall in love, and get married. Of all the romantic places in the world, they met on a garage elevator, and it was love at first sight. The fact that they belonged to ethnicities, which espoused different worldviews did not deter them from opening their hearts to each other. The next thing on their menu was marriage, but the success of that plan depended on the approval of their parents, who in their different ways, were stuck in unhelpful cultural prejudices, biases, and stereotypes. It took some doing for the man to prove that he would be a good husband to his wife, and for the woman to prove that she indeed was "a wife from the ancestors."

The novel explores the Shona and white American cultures as they are understood and practiced by the fictional spouses and their families and friends. For the benefit of the readers who are not privy to ethnic groups in Zimbabwe, the Shona are one of the two major linguistic groups in Zimbabwe, which comprises about eight ethnic groups, each with slightly different cultural practices and language.

It should be declared that the names of the characters in this novel are fictitious, and any resemblance of the names of the characters, with names of living people is merely coincidental. Although some names of real roads, cities, and countries have been used, they have no historical connection to the fictional events narrated. However, the intercultural biases, prejudices, and stereotypes explored may have been experienced by the writer, although without any connection to the characters and places mentioned in the novel.

November 10, 2020

1

A Difficult Conversation

Eventually, I realized that I had to break the news to him by myself. I also felt that dillydallying or shillyshallying would not help me at this time as it used to do in the past. Procrastination had helped me buy some more time in the past, but it was not going to be useful now. Sooner or later, he would come to know about it. And perhaps, he would confront me, and accuse me of hiding from him important issues that had an impact upon the family. I dreaded it, but I had to do it myself. That is what grown men are expected to do. They should speak their mind fearlessly and stand their ground unwaveringly. If I were still a teenager, I would have relied on my mother conveying my messages to him, but I am a grown man now. I should do my own things, and earn my own victories, or face the humiliation and criticism that come with failure.

Even if I had tried to coax my mother for support, she would have flatly refused to be my advocate. Not again. Not anymore. She was tired of being my middleperson, and at times, taking some hard blows on my timid behalf. At some point, she had told me, "You are a grown man now. You need to man up, and learn to stand on your two feet. Learn how to have a manly conversation with your father. Talk to him like a man would talk to another man. Firmly, but with respect. A man-to-man talk. Look at me. Look at me, my son. I am your mother. I am a woman. I cannot be in the crossfire for you all the time. Take your chances." She paused as she continued cutting her vegetables. "Your father is not a very difficult man. He is not a lion. You know it."

I looked at Mother, and opened both my mouth and eyes in disbelief. I did not say a word, but she understood what I meant. Both of us had learnt that there were many things that were better left unsaid.

"It's true. You know, it is true. I cannot lie to you about him. I have lived with him at least one year longer than you have. Before that, I had known him for many years. I know him through and through. He is an ordinary man. There are a few things that your father does not like—lying and being illogical. When you talk to him, be truthful. State your case as clearly as you can. Answer his questions coherently and prudently. If he defeats you in an argument, accept your defeat. If you are wrong, apologize. If he gives you advice or a gift, show your gratitude. That is all. That is all you need to do. And that is what a grown man does."

She was right. I had to learn to fight my own battles and to earn my own victories or defeats. I had to experience the sweetness of winning a battle, and the bitterness and shame of losing one. You must get me right; I am not saying that I was afraid of my own father. Maybe a little. He could be so scary if he chose to. Sometimes, it is wise and prudent to be horrified by the fearsome. Of course, he could be very difficult, if he deemed it necessary. I had no doubt about that. I am not saying that Mother was wrong. She was right from her own perspective, as his wife. But I saw Baba from a different angle; that of a son. I knew what a son could only know about a parent. Nothing more. Nothing less.

Not that he was an unreasonable person. Never. But who says reasonable fathers are not bothersome? Yes, Mother was right. He was a very logical man. He was very difficult to beat in an argument. I am not saying that he was unbeatable. Or that he would refuse to accept defeat if beaten. No, he would calmly listen to your argument and would occasionally ask a few questions for clarification. At the end, he would shred your line of reasoning into pieces. Even before he opened his mouth, his line of questioning would give you a cue of what was in store for you. My father was like a hunter, who would place a long rope around an animal's neck, and the animal would erroneously celebrate its short-lived freedom, only to discover its predicament. Have you ever witnessed your main line of argument being shred to pieces? It is not only embarrassing, but also humiliating. You begin to think about how your teacher used to comment on the weaknesses of your arguments. You begin to believe them. You begin to teach yourself a new logic. Sometimes, it works, at other times, it does not.

Experience had taught me that, sometimes, when dealing with Baba, timing and context were the key to escape his scrutiny. Each conversation had to be carried out at the right time and had to fit our cultural context. I say "our" because at most times, I was dragged into some Shona cultural practices whose significance I did not know. On that day, I felt that it was not the right time to break the good news to him. I say "good news" because that is how I perceived it. However, I was aware that Baba could perceive the same news as bad news. Maybe the best could have been to hide this issue from him, like I used to do when I was in high school and college, but this was not a matter to conceal. *Rine manyanga hariputirwe.* Sooner or later, he would know about it, and would chastise me for keeping him in the dark.

I had vowed that if he were to know about it, it should be from me. Certainly, not from the grapevine, and not from my mother. I knew that, if he did not like what I had done or was about to do, there was no way I could ever convince him to give me a blessing. Not that his blessing mattered a lot to me at this point in my life. Maybe, to some extent. I knew about parental blessings. But I did not rely on his approval to be myself. I would not beg another man for permission to be a man. No, men are men because they are men, not because another man makes them men.

I was my own man now. I had my own manhood. I had a job—a very good job. I had a nice home—my own home. I had friends. I was a man. After all, it was my own life. It was my decision to make. As a matter of fact, I could not say this to his face. The first time I had tried to challenge him, it had not ended well. He nearly got a heart attack. No one wants to be blamed for having caused his father's death. That is witchcraft. Fortunately, or unfortunately, the imagined heart attack was mild, and it did not harm him at all. As if the imagined heart attack was not bad enough, he challenged me to a boxing match. I was shocked that he had mistaken my verbal outbursts for a boxing challenge. I do not think he meant it. Of course, I declined the offer. I guess that was not good enough for him, for he continued shouting at me threateningly, and I decided to appease his demons. I knew what they wanted—an apology. I apologized, not because I could not have stood my chance against him in the boxing arena, but because he was my father. You do not try your fake *karateka* moves on your old man. That is sheer stupidity. If you were to win the fight, you would have lost a father and your *hunhu*. If you were to lose the fight, he would beat the stupidity out of you. Either way you lose. You do not start a fight in which you can either lose or lose.

Yes, he was difficult to beat in an argument. Not that he cheated. Never. At times, he was a little bit arrogant, but he never boasted. I am not saying that he was not kind or loving. He indeed was the kindest and most loving person I had known. Although I had not lived a long life at that point, I had never met a man as gentle, kind, and as loving as Baba. Maybe, I am biased. Of course, I should be.

I am not certain about his understanding of other people's feelings. I am not saying that he was not empathetic, for being too empathetic was his weakness. He never watched an emotional movie without shedding a tear or two. Of course, most people cry easily, but he somewhat overdid it. He had the ability to stand in another person's shoes and could feel what it was like to be in that person's world. That made him a better person; a person who could look at every need through the concerned person's lenses. It made him a kinder and more generous person.

He never boasted about his impressive academic achievements. I am not saying that he was oblivious of them. He was not. He talked about them a little, without making us feel less talented. He was a prolific writer too. Unfortunately, he never made much money out of it. In fact, the academic prowess and effort he put into his research and writings were not proportionate to the little remuneration he got out of it. I think that most people in his professional area faced the same scourge. Whenever he was not working in his field, he would be writing something. It was odd to see someone in his context writing that much. There is no time to write in the rural areas, but he still did.

I believe he could have been a proud man if he chose to be, but he did not. He had done everything that would make a man proud. He had a plethora of academic achievements, but his greatest setback was his failure to get a better paying job. It humbled him. It somewhat drove him to self-pity and early retirement. In a way, it was good for him. There is always something that a man misses if he has everything. There is always something lost, if a man has academic intelligence, wisdom, a beautiful home, sound health, a wonderful wife, moral uprightness, excellent kids, and a well-paying job. Some deficiency in an area or two makes a better man. It makes a man human because human beings are not perfect and self-sufficient. It makes a man considerate. Sometimes, when the world looks bad, it is not because of imperfect people, but it is because of perfectionists who do not understand why other people make mistakes in life.

There were times when I felt that Baba wanted to win every argument. I am not saying that he did not have the mental stamina to win an argument. He did. He won arguments most of the times. His logic was impressive. I cannot remember witnessing him losing an argument although he did, sometimes. It could be that he never argued if he knew he would lose. I guess that is what smart people do. He did not cheat. He earned his victories, which may have cost him his humility. He was still humble though, but not as humble as he might have been if he had lost half of his debates. A humble man needs to lose some of his arguments occasionally to prove his humanity. Only gods do not lose arguments. Humans do, at times, if not all the time.

You may think that Baba was old fashioned, but he was not. Not at this point, but maybe, later. He was still young, for he was 48 years old then. Perhaps a little bit older, for he claimed not to know his exact age and would put up a strong argument for that claim. We somehow believed him, but I do not think his friends did because he looked exactly his age. He was a handsome man too. Not very handsome, but still handsome. He might have been more handsome in his youth. I am not saying that he cared much about outward looks. He did not. At least, that is what he repeatedly said in some of his conversations with me. He relentlessly told us that the beauty of the face was useless because of its temporality. He was a strong believer in the beauty of the heart.

Baba would say, "When you look for a woman to marry, my son, don't be deceived by outward looks. Outward beauty fades away. Looks can just be cosmetic. Hunt for the beauty of the heart because it never fades away. The facial looks of a human being are affected by time, but the human heart becomes better with time." I think he was right.

Baba had his fair share of struggles in life. He freely and openly talked about them. I found some of them very sad, but still inspiring. They were the type of struggles that would choke the life out of an ordinary person. Not him. In fact, they strengthened him. Now, that I am older, and have my own struggles, though incomparable to those of Baba, I understand his struggles better, and how they shaped the man he became. His were insurmountable struggles, which he fought and won. When he was young, he bought his own clothes and school uniforms. He worked and earned his own school fees. He struggled to get an education, which most of us take for granted.

I never cried when I listened to his sad life stories, and I still do not know why I did not. Perhaps I was not empathetic enough. Maybe, the stories were too emotional for me to be able to cry. Maybe, I cried. Yes, I did; inside. I shed invisible tears deep down in my heart. How could people not help such a gifted and strong-willed young man? I believe that if anyone had assisted Baba to get an education, that person would be proud for having done so. Baba would treat that person like a king or queen, but nobody had the insight to help him. There were people who could have assisted him, but they did not. Whenever I listen to the stories of his struggles to get an education, I always feel that he was a self-made man. Of course, he flatly denies it. He appreciates the assistance he received from every person he met along the way.

He would say, "My son, there is no such thing as a self-made man. Never. We depend on each other in one way or another. If you give yourself enough time to reflect, you will see what you have benefited from other people. The people who claim to be self-made are only too proud to acknowledge the help that they have received from others. Look beyond yourself. A person can never be a person without the assistance of others. No one is completely self-sufficient, not even the wealthiest of people. Beyond others, there are the creator and the ancestors."

Baba had a talent of always finding a silver lining in every cloud. When things went wrong as they sometimes did, he focused on the positive. When I lost something, or had my cellphone stolen, Baba would advise me to be grateful for the time I had it in my possession. When someone lost a job, Baba would encourage him to be thankful for the time he had that job. In times of drought, Baba encouraged our relatives and friends to work harder while being thankful for the past good harvests. If his friend's daughter failed an examination, Baba would remind him that there was more to education than just passing an examination. I am not saying that he was too optimistic; no. In fact, he was a pessimist, but once something went wrong, he would focus on the positive.

Baba was the most grateful person that I had ever known. He always paid tribute to all the people who assisted him in life. He remembered all of them by their names. He narrated even the minute details of how each of them assisted him. He also tried to pay back the good they had done for him. Of course, his gratitude and generosity bordered on prodigality. There was nothing wrong with that except that he sometimes, tried to drag me into it. I am not saying I hated it, but there were times when I felt that my father was overdoing it. Yes, I enjoyed paying school fees for some of my nephews back home. I also enjoyed sending them Christmas gifts. It felt good except that some of them were never thankful. I know that if my father had enough money, the world would be a better place. I have no doubt that he would donate some, if not most of it, to those in need.

To get back to my story, my intention is not to bother you with my father's struggles, but to tell you my story. On that day, I kept telling myself that I was going to tell him what I had wanted to tell him for some time. I kept reassuring myself of the uprightness of my decision, and convinced myself that it was my life, not his, and that it was my decision to make, not his. But that did not make it easier for me to break the news to him. What made it so hard for me to share my story with him was that he was a traditional man. He loved his Shona culture. He loved his Shona food. He took pride in Shona wisdom. For him, to maintain one's cultural identity was a big deal. He was quick to castigate those who he thought were deliberately deviating from the Shona cultural norms. He did not spare the parents of the kids who were born in the diaspora and were never taught the Shona language. He respected other cultures, and unequivocally asserted that all cultures were equal, though different. He condemned cultural imperialism. He advocated for intercultural sensitivity and respect. Baba strongly believed that for one to achieve intercultural competencies, one had to be firmly grounded in his own culture. My issue was difficult for me to share with him because it had everything to do with culture or the violation of it.

Perhaps, before I get into the issue, which was troubling me, I need to tell you a little bit about my mother as well. She was different. She was one of the coolest mothers one could ever ask for. She was calm, intelligent, and beautiful. Her beauty made Baba's talk about hunting for inward beauty in one's spouse, almost seem like hypocrisy. How could he encourage other men to not be concerned with facial beauty, yet he was married to the most beautiful woman in the world? Who would listen to him?

Mother was a woman of few words, but in a good way. She hardly expressed her affection or anger, verbally, for us or anyone else. She never used phrases like, "my son, my baby, I love you, I don't like that. You are wrong," and so on. Regardless, I always understood that she loved us a great deal because her eyes radiated her love for us. Her gaze was gentle and kind. Her voice was gracious. Yes, she loved us immensely, and there was no question about that. She talked a little, whenever it was necessary. She never raised her voice even when she was upset. She laughed. She worked. She cooked. She never complained about anything. What else can one look for in a mother?

Mother and Baba were great friends and inseparable companions. I also think they were deeply in love. I guess that time had failed to diminish their love for each other. If you heard the two laughing together, you would think that they were a pair of clueless teenagers. All my life, I never heard them shouting at each other. I never saw them fighting. I never witnessed them disagreeing with each other openly. Maybe they did, secretly. They knew each other's every story very well, but they still laughed whenever those stories were retold. It was like they were hearing each other's story for the first time. Amazing parents. I would not have asked for any other.

Back to the issue, which was troubling me. That day, I kept reminding myself that it was my day to share my story with Baba. I had informed my mother about the wonderful issue. I had also instructed her not to let the cat out of the bag. I feared she had already told Baba. I could not imagine her hiding anything from him. I sensed that she had already told him because when I finally gathered enough courage to narrate my story to Baba, he did not appear shocked. He did not panic or freak out like I expected him to do. He remained calm like a man who had rehearsed how to react. I felt that he expected the news.

"So, you got married without notifying us?" My father asked, rhetorically.

I did not respond, for I did not think that it was a question.

"Answer my question," he demanded.

"Not quite. We are not married. We are merely engaged. It's not considered a marriage in America. We just live together. It's common over there."

"But you already live together?"

"Yes, Baba, but we are not a married," I tried to convince him.

"You live with someone's daughter. You sleep with her, and you say, it's not a marriage? That is wrong. It's unethical, my son. Real men don't treat women like that."

I ignored his question for I felt that it was too personal. I had told him that we lived together, and there was no need for him to bring in the "sleeping together" issue. I knew that it was used to embarrass me, and to make me feel bad. Baba and I had never talked about sleeping with women before, and we were not going to start it then.

"We are engaged. We are planning our wedding, Baba. Her parents are making the plans and they will be paying for the larger part of the wedding," I explained.

"Do they know that you live together?"

"They do."

"And they approve of that?"

"I don't know."

"Are they Zimbabweans?"

"No."

"Who are they? What's their ethnicity?" Baba was becoming more energetic about the issue.

"She is American."

"African American?"

"No. White American, Baba."

"You married a white woman? Is that what you are telling me? A white woman?" There was concern in his voice.

"Yes, Baba. I did. She is white. I will show you her photos. You will love her. She is a little angel," I tried hard to convince him.

"She is white, my son." It was not a question. "Wives come from the ancestors, not America," he added.

"I know. But I love her, and she loves me. What else does a man need from a woman?" I asked.

"Have you already paid bridewealth for her?" He asked.

I laughed. Baba, with all his education did not know that whites do not know anything about bridewealth.

"No. Whites don't know about bridewealth, Baba."

"So, you are telling me that you just take someone's daughter, make her your wife, have children, and you don't pay bridewealth to her parents, and you call that a marriage?"

"You are right, Baba. It will be a marriage. She is American. She has her own culture. I can't impose my culture on her parents."

"What do her parents say?"

"About what?"

"Do they like you? Remember, they are white, and you are black? And we know about racism in America. We know that American whites do not like blacks?

"I am not marrying all American whites, Baba."

"Don't talk to me like that. I know what I am talking about." He was a little offended.

"Yes, there is racism, but not all of them are like that."

"They discriminate against blacks, and you want to marry one of them?"

"Not all whites are racist, Baba. Ninety nine percent of whites in America do not hate blacks. Yes, there are a few who are racist. Maria's parents are not racist. They know me. They respect me. They know that I am black, but as for our marriage, it is not their decision to make. It is Maria's decision, not theirs. I am marrying Maria, not them."

"No. I don't agree with that. She is their daughter. They raised her. They educated her. They have everything to say. They should. They have the right to have a say in who she is going to marry."

"They don't."

"If they don't, then, who will accept bridewealth? At least, they should accept bridewealth."

"No, Baba. They won't accept bridewealth. It's not their culture. Maria is not up for sale."

"Don't be stupid, Peter. Who said that bridewealth is buying and selling of women? Is that what you told them?"

"No."

"Please, don't distort our culture."

"I don't."

"Don't forget your culture, my son." It was more of a threat than advice. "Bridewealth is a token of appreciation given to the parents of one's wife for their part in raising and educating their daughter. It is not the purchase of a woman. You cannot place some monetary value on a human being. Even after bridewealth has been paid, she remains their daughter. Please, don't tell me that any parent can refuse to accept a token of appreciation."

I knew he was getting agitated, but this was my time to educate him. I had an ace in the pack in that I had two worldviews. I knew both the American and Shona cultures. He was not going to win this one. I was not going to give him a chance to win it. Not on that day.

"Baba, cultures are different. You cannot impose your culture on other people. They do have their own cultures too. You have to respect other people's cultures."

"You are right, my son. Cultures are different. That is why I think that you should not marry a white woman. It is complicated. We are so different."

"I love her," I said.

"How dare you try to lecture me about love? What's love? Tell me. Love must be prudent. Love must be disciplined. You cannot go around the world loving people who don't think that you are as human as they are. People who enslaved our ancestors for over three hundred years, yet still see nothing wrong with it. People who continue to discriminate against blacks. People who do not hesitate to shoot a black person. No, Peter, my son. You cannot do that to us. What would other black people think about us? You have to discipline your feelings."

He looked aside as if he no longer wanted to talk about it.

"It's none of other people's business."

"What about us?"

"Well, I don't know."

He paused, shook his head slowly, and continued to talk. "We have so many beautiful Zimbabwean girls here. You can find one that you love. Your aunts can help you find a beautiful Shona woman. There are many educated women here. They speak good English too. Why a white woman? What will the ancestors say about us? What will the people say? Don't do this to us, my son," Baba pleaded with me.

"Baba, I don't see where you come in, in all this. She will be my wife, not yours. If you don't like her, it doesn't matter. After all, we will be living in America, not here. You may keep it a secret, if you are worried about what your friends will say."

"What did you just say? You said, she will be your wife alone? You, alone? That is very selfish of you. She will be the family's wife. She will be the mother of the clan. She will be the ancestors' wife. In our culture, you don't marry for yourself, but for the family. That is why your wife's parents must accept bridewealth. Marriage is a family thing, not an individual affair."

"You are right, Baba. She will be the mother of the clan, but you have to go over your prejudices against white people."

"It's them who are prejudiced against blacks, not me."

I looked at him, and frowned.

"You are no better than them, Baba."

"Who are you to stand there and judge me?"

"Your son. Have you forgotten me?"

"How dare you talk to me like that? I am not your son?"

"I am sorry, Baba."

"At least, they should accept *roora*. There is no marriage without bridewealth."

"I told you, Baba, they don't know anything about bridewealth."

"They will learn. You will teach them. If they want us to accept their daughter and culture, they too should learn about our culture, unless you say, they don't have a culture."

It looked like he was conceding defeat. I was enjoying the show.

"I will teach them if they want to learn, but they have no obligation to learn our culture. I am only marrying Maria, not the whole family. They may refuse to learn it."

"I hope they will understand. A marriage without the payment of bridewealth is not a marriage at all. We call it a *mapoto* marriage. If you do not want to use your money, I can sell my cows, and pay for your bridewealth. You do not just grab a woman, and start living with her, and then call her your wife. That's *mapoto*, my son. If she dies, who is going to bury her? Who is going to mark her grave?"

"Baba, it will be a marriage, not *mapoto*. You should get over it. If she dies, her family and I would bury her. I can even bury her alone. There is no big deal about it. You do not have to worry about marking the grave because it's not their culture. They don't know about it."

"You want her avenging spirit to haunt us? We don't want to invite an avenging spirit into our family. How can you mark the grave of a person who is not your relative? If you do that, we will be haunted and decimated by her avenging spirit."

"I will tell them about bridewealth, but there is no guarantee that they will accept it."

Baba looked indifferent. He stared at the cows that were busy chewing the cud as if oblivious of my presence. I looked at him, but it seemed his mind was far away. He was annoyed because he could not have his own way. I had achieved my goal. I had told him.

He suddenly gave me a piercing glance, and asked, "What's her totem?"

"Who?"

"Your wife."

I laughed. I looked at him, and laughed again. My father looked more puzzled than irritated.

"She is a white American, Baba."

"What is that supposed to mean?"

"She doesn't have a totem. White people don't have totems."

"Why not?"

"I don't know. Who says they should have totems?"

"My son, you see what you are doing to the ancestors? How are we going to present this woman to the ancestors of the family? A wife without a totem? You are creating problems for us, my son."

He started walking back to the homestead. I followed behind him. From the way he walked, I knew he was upset. He went straight into the round thatched kitchen, and sat on the stool, closer to where Mother was sitting. Mother never said a word. She just looked at him and continued with her never-ending kitchen chores. She knew that I had told him.

"Did he tell you about his wife?" This question was directed at Mother.

"Girlfriend, not wife, Baba," I corrected him.

"How can she be your girlfriend when you already live together, and her family knows about it?" He was becoming impatient. "Peter married a white woman, and he is planning to have a wedding," he explained.

Mother froze for a moment as if hearing the news for the first time. "I have never heard about it. How could I have known about it before you did?" She flatly denied it. She did not want to be accused of having encouraged me or hidden the news from him.

Father did not respond. He just made an inaudible guttural sound, which Mother ignored.

"Congratulations, my son. We will have more food, Sigauke! Can she cook *sadza*?" Mother asked while smiling.

"Cooking? You talk of cooking, Mai Peter? She doesn't even have a totem. Her parents don't know anything about bridewealth. Even if we offer them a little, they are not going to accept it. Is that a marriage? Is that the daughter-in-law we want?" He complained.

"She will learn. I will teach her how to cook *sadza*. It's easy to cook *sadza,* Baba Peter." Mother looked excited. "So, who cooks *sadza* for them? Don't they eat *sadza*? *Nhaiwe,* Peter, don't you eat *sadza* in America?"

"No, we don't. Maybe, occasionally. We eat potatoes, spaghetti, bread, salads, and many other foods."

"How do you survive without *sadza*? Truly, white people are in trouble. How can they survive without *sadza*?" Mother was perplexed.

"They don't know what *sadza* is. They do have their own foods, just like we have our own."

Baba jumped in, "They also eat salads and ice cream, Mai Peter."

"What is salad? What is salad?" Mother asked.

"Uncooked vegetables such as lettuce, spinach, or even cabbage," I explained.

"Raw vegetables? They eat them straight from the garden like animals do," Baba chipped in.

"Raw vegetables? How is that possible? Don't they have fire and pots? Don't they suffer from stomach acids? Your girlfriend also eats raw vegetables?"

"Salad, Mother," I corrected her.

"Where are we going to get lettuce and carrots for her? This year, she will eat *nyevhe* for salad."

I giggled.

"These are harbingers of evil things, Mai Peter. What sort of a wife, does not have a totem? A wife who can't cook *sadza*? A wife who lives on raw vegetables, chocolate, and ice cream?" Baba was scandalized. He was already panicking.

"Baba Peter, not everyone has a totem, even here in Africa. We should not worry about her not having a totem. *Sadza* is not the only food in the world. The lack of education is your greatest challenge." She paused. "White people eat light food. They love nice foods; ice cream, rice, potatoes, and raw vegetables. That's why their skin is white and smooth."

"Who is not educated? Me? You must be kidding." Baba was annoyed.

There was silence for a moment.

I had to take a stance. "In fact, I am not asking for your permission to marry Maria. I was just notifying you. Plans for the wedding are already at an advanced stage. When I get back to San Antonio, next week, I will purchase air tickets for you to come over. I want both of you to attend the wedding. That will be your opportunity to board a plane, and to visit the United States. You will stay with us for a couple of months if you want."

I had rehearsed this moment for several times.

Before they recovered from the shock, I continued. "If you do not attend, my in-laws would think that I don't have parents, which is not a good thing. White people take family support seriously. You must show your support. The trip will cost you nothing. In fact, the trip will add value to your status quo here in the village. When you come back, every villager will come here to listen to the stories from beyond the oceans. I would like you to sleep over it, and let me know your thoughts tomorrow."

Nobody answered. I did not expect them to answer.

I stood up and bid them good night. No one said a thing. Baba just looked at me as I walked out of the kitchen. He was sad. I cared about his concerns, but there was nothing I could do about it. I really wanted both of them to attend the wedding. It was their opportunity to visit the United States. And maybe, to learn about other cultures. It was a lifetime opportunity that one could not afford to miss.

The following morning, Baba looked happy, happier than the previous night. I knew that the night had done a lot of good to him. It always did.

He told me that after an all-night meeting with Mother, they had decided to attend the wedding. He even seemed excited about it. I knew that the "all-night" part of it was exaggerated. No one would need an all-night conference to decide on a trip to the United States.

"Your mother and I agreed to attend the wedding. What can we do? An ancestor that permits you to get hurt, has given permission to the flies to feast on your wound. We will come. You should give us directions before you leave for America. We don't want to get lost on the plane."

"Thank you. You will love America. I will give you the directions before I leave," I responded.

"No. We are not coming to see America, but for the wedding." It was Mother.

"I know," I responded. "I guess you will keep your eyes closed until the wedding day."

No one responded.

We never talked about my wedding again with Baba, until I left for Texas. I did not want to give him an opportunity to change his mind or criticize me. However, I had several conversations with my mother. She was excited about the wedding. She liked her daughter-in-law to be. She even started polishing up her English skills in preparation for the encounter. Not that her English was bad; it was good. She was well educated, and had attended a very good high school. Before her retirement, she had worked as a teacher and an accountant. Her only concern was about her heavy accent. It was not that her accent was too heavy, but that she was concerned about it. She was afraid that Maria would not understand her accent. I told her not to worry about it. Americans were used to listening to accents of people from all over the world.

When we were alone with Mother, we talked about Maria, but whenever Baba was around, she avoided the topic, and I appreciated it.

In a couple of weeks, I was back in San Antonio, Texas. Maria drove all the way to George Bush International Airport, in Houston, to pick me up. I was happy to see her. She too was ecstatic. She gave me a big hug that lasted almost forever. I think it was mutual. As we took the elevator back to the car garage, she could not wait to ask me about what my parents had said about our forthcoming wedding.

"No problem at all. They are coming to America. They all love you, and are looking forward to meeting with you," I lied a little bit.

"I thought you said your dad would be difficult?"

"At times, he can choose to be. Not this time."

"I am so thrilled that they are coming, and that we will be going to Africa," she said.

She blew me a quick kiss.

"Not Africa. It's Zimbabwe. Of course, Zimbabwe is in Africa. Yes, we may visit other African countries as well," I corrected her. "I have never visited any other African country myself, and we can do it together."

"I meant Zimbabwe." She corrected herself. "We shall visit the Victoria Falls, first, and Great Zimbabwe Ruins, later."

She giggled. She was excited.

"Who else from Zimbabwe will be attending the wedding?" She looked at me. "Remember, we can't afford to host the whole clan."

"You are right. We will not have the whole village coming to Texas. I will purchase only two air tickets—for my mother and father." I paused. "Even if I could afford air tickets for the whole village, they wouldn't be awarded visas to travel to the United States. Even now, I don't know if my parents will get visas. My mother applied for a visa twice in the past, and was denied on both occasions. It's very frustrating."

"What did the consulate give as a reason for denying her a visa? I guess they give a reason for denying a person a visa," she wanted to know.

"Yes, they do, but the reasons are sometimes illogical. The first time she was told that she had never traveled outside Zimbabwe. She had no history of traveling. Her passport was too new for the American visa, which I thought was a lame excuse. She then decided to remedy the situation by traveling to South Africa before applying for the visa for a second time."

"Did she get the visa that second time?"

"No."

"What did they say? I guess they didn't talk about her not having traveled outside Zimbabwe."

"Well, they told her that they could not give her a visa to visit the United States because she had just been to South Africa. She needed to rest a little bit."

"Are you kidding me?"

"For real."

"But that's contradictory."

"Who cares?"

"Did she go back for a third time?"

"Not yet. This will be her third time. They will go together with Baba. One of them may get it."

"Do you think they are going to get visas to attend the wedding?" She looked worried.

"I hope so," I responded hesitantly.

"They better get the visas because if they don't, my parents might think that they don't care."

"You should explain to them about the challenges of getting United States visas in Zimbabwe. They will understand. It is not easy to get a visa. One of my friends from Zimbabwe who was studying in Chicago, on a full ride scholarship, was denied a visa last year. As a student, he had a two-year visa, which was about to expire in four weeks' time. He went back to Zimbabwe to visit his family, and to renew his visa. They denied him. He had two more years to complete his degree program, and all his papers were in order. He applied for the renewal of his visa for a second time and was denied again. A third time and was denied. He was devastated. Since he still had a few days on his visa, they confiscated his passport to prevent him from coming back to the United States. He got his passport back after it had expired."

"Very sad. That was very cruel."

"Indeed. He wasted two years of his time studying for a degree that he would not get. People who had offered him a full scholarship also lost their money."

"What did he do?"

"He did the unexpected. He went to South Africa under the pretext of studying at one of his church-affiliated universities. In fact, he enrolled with that university, paid fees, and attended classes. Life was difficult for him. Very difficult. He called me, and I advised him to apply for a United States visa from there. At first, he was hesitant, but I convinced him to do it anyway. He finally did, and got the visa. He went back to Zimbabwe to bid farewell to his family, and came back to the United States. He just graduated from a university in Chicago. That is how difficult and unreasonable the United States consular in Harare can be. Later, his wife applied for a visa to attend his graduation, and was denied. The consular said that they were frustrated to learn that her husband had got a United States student visa from South Africa after they had denied him."

We got into the car, and started our journey to San Antonio. We talked about work among other things. I was driving. Maria fell asleep. Within four hours, we were home, in San Antonio. Home, sweet home. Maria woke up just before we exited Loop 410 South to get into Highway 87 South. We decided to stop at Taco Cabana to get some *fajitas* for supper. As we opened the door of the restaurant, we were greeted by the usual delicious aromas of Mexican food. We bought baked chicken and beef *fajita* tacos (with no toppings), bean, chips, cheese, and guacamole. The waiter helped us carry our food back to the car. Soon, we were home.

"We are already home. You were flying." Maria pretended to be scared.

"No. It's eight o'clock. It's already been four hours since we left Houston, and there was little traffic on the freeway."

I parked the car in the garage. We got into the house. There was silence. There was no one at home. Maria helped me carry my suitcases into the house. I was too tired to unpack, and I decided that I would unpack them the following morning.

"I am excited that you are back. I really missed you."

She hugged me and sat on my lap.

"Me too."

"By the way, what's your mom's name?" She asked this as she sat on the sofa beside me.

"What makes you ask? You don't need to know it."

"Sweetheart, is there anything wrong in knowing and calling people by their names?"

"Her name is Tendai, but please, never call her by that name in her presence."

"But that's her name?"

"Yes."

"What does it mean?"

"It's a command to people to be grateful. It is like, "you must be grateful." In our Shona culture, we don't call married and older women by their first names."

"How do you refer to them?"

"It's complicated, sweetheart. As soon as a woman gets married, she is called by her totem or sub-totem. For instance, my totem is Shumba, which is the Shona word for a lion. So, if my sister gets married, she would be called Masivanda. Every married woman whose totem is Shumba can be referred to as Masivanda."

"Throughout her life?" She interjected.

"Wait. Be patient. Yes, as long as she lives. However, she acquires another name as soon as she gives birth to her first child. She is called by the name of her first born. My name is Peter, and I am the first born in my family. So, my mom is called Mai Peter, which means Mother of Peter."

"Now, she has three names?" Maria was curious.

"Which ones?" I tested her.

"Her original first name. Her totem or sub-totem. And her firstborn's name."

"You got it. She gets a fourth name," I hesitated. "When any of her children gives birth to a child, my mom can be called by the name of her first grandchild. Suppose we have a kid, and we name him, Mike. My mother becomes Mbuya VaMike, meaning, the grandmother of Mike."

"Four names?"

"Wrong. She acquires a fifth one, her husband's last name. For instances, my mother is also called Mai Masika, which literally means Mother of Masika. That's Mrs. Masika, in the Western way of doing things. She may have a nickname, which she doesn't have yet."

"Where does the nickname come from?"

"The nickname comes from some repeated behavior by a person, or her favorite phrases. For instance, if one likes using the word "story," they may call her, VaStory. A gossiper is usually nicknamed, Madenyaya, meaning, the one who likes gossip. A drunkard can be nicknamed, Musiyadzasukwa meaning someone who does not leave a beer party until all beer is gone. A greedy person can be nicknamed, Mugezarichakwata meaning someone who washes his hands before the food is ready."

Maria nodded. She was fascinated.

"How about a crazy woman?"

"She is nicknamed, Marujata or Haruna."

"So, what happens to a married woman's original first name? She just forgets about it?" Maria was concerned.

"No. It remains on her personal documents. She may use it at work if she is employed as a civil servant. Of course, her own relatives may still use her original first name if they want. But generally, calling a married woman by her first name is considered disrespectful," I explained. "A married woman's name is so sacred that even her own children may not know it until they are in the fifth grade. Even when they know it, they pretend that they do not. You have no business knowing your mother's name."

"What about me? Are you going to give me four more names?" She sounded both curious and frustrated. I knew that the conversation would take that direction.

"No and yes. They will call you *muroora,* which means daughter-in-law. When we have a kid, some may call you by her name, for instance, Mai Sarah. But they will not impose it on you if you don't like it. They may call you Maria if you insist."

"Nickname?"

"You don't just get it from the onset. They must watch and observe your mannerisms and behavior, first. Once, someone decides to give you a nickname, she may give you a token called *rupfumbidzo*. It's difficult to translate the word into English. It comes from the Shona word, *kupfumba*, which refers to a well-marked and traveled path. So, the *rupfumbidzo* token makes the nickname official, and signals that the community can use it publicly."

"I feel like I already have a bachelor's degree in Anthropology," she said.

I laughed.

"This is only the beginning. You have a long way to go. Learning a new culture takes some real doing. There are no shortcuts. I have been in the United States for almost six years now, and I still learn the culture," I warned her.

But she was not yet done.

"How about Shona men?"

"What about them?"

"How many names do they have?"

"It's just the same as women, but a bit more flexible. My father's name is David Masika, but they call him Baba Peter, meaning father of Peter. When we get our first kid, he becomes, Sekuru VaMike. He is also called by our sub-totem, Sigauke. He is also VaMasika, which means Mr. Masika. He may have a nickname as well. I just don't know it yet."

"What do I call your mom or dad? I mean what names or titles do I use for them?" She wanted to know.

"Good question. You call my mom, *amai or mhayi,* which means *Mother.* You call my father, *baba,* which means father. You never use their first names. Of course, if you do, they will forgive you. They know that you come from a different culture, and everyone will be patient and gentle with you."

I had jetlag, and was tired from all the driving. We went to bed early that night.

That night, I had a dream. I was in Harare, and I had accompanied my parents to the visa interview at the United States embassy. I was denied entrance into the embassy by the security guard manning the main gate, and I had to wait outside, across the road. After about an hour, my parents emerged from the embassy. My father was in front, and my mother following behind him. It looked like my father was talking to himself. He looked angry, and was throwing his hands about. The moment I saw them, I ran across the road to meet them. Before I could ask what had happened, I woke up. I was relieved that it was just a dream.

That was in August. Many more conversations about the Shona culture between Maria and I followed. Of course, that was not the first time for us to explore the Shona culture, for we had been doing that for some time. Maria was learning a lot of the Shona culture. She learned to prepare Zimbabwean dishes except *sadza*. It was difficult for her to learn how to cook *sadza*, not because it was too complicated to do so, but because I was not a good teacher. I am not sure if my recipe was good.

Cooking *sadza* is a paradox because it is both a simple and complex process. You need maize or corn meal, which was plentiful at Walmart and H.E.B, here in San Antonio. You need a medium-sized pot, depending on the amount of *sadza* that you would like to prepare. If you cook more *sadza* than you can consume at one sitting, you may store the remainder in a deep freezer, only to warm it when you want to eat it later. You need a round cooking stick, whose bottom end is flat. You need some water.

The process is simple. You boil the water in a pot. Just before the water reaches the boiling point, you add a little corn meal into the water while stirring. It should be the right amount of corn meal, lest the *sadza* becomes too thick prematurely. Once the *sadza* begins to simmer, just like porridge would do, you begin to add more corn meal, and keep stirring. Intermittently, you close the pot with a lid. When the *sadza* is ready, you remove it from the pot, and put it in a plate. You eat it with some tasty relish because *sadza* is tasteless. Although you can use your fork and knife, the best way to enjoy *sadza* is to use your own bare hands. You get a morsel of *sadza*, then dip it in the relish. The relish gives *sadza* its taste. It should be noted that *Sadza* is addictive. Shona people eat *sadza* for lunch and supper every day, and they never get tired of it. The only thing that changes is the relish. My mother taught me how to cook *sadza*, but I never mastered the skills. I thought it was no big deal until I tried to cook it by myself for the first time, and it was *mbodza*. *Mbodza* is *sadza* that is not properly cooked.

Among my people, the ability to cook good *sadza* is one of the competencies expected of a good bride. A bride who does not know how to cook *sadza* is not considered a proper bride. A bride can be forgiven for almost anything, but failure to cook *sadza* is unforgiveable. I just hoped that my parents would be patient and lenient with Maria. With time, my mother would teach her to cook proper *sadza*. Shona people expect a wife that comes from the ancestors, and there is no wife from the ancestors who does not know how to cook *sadza*. *Sadza* is the food of the ancestors, which in the past was shared from one plate as a communal meal.

At that time, I was not going to worry much about teaching Maria how to cook *sadza* because there were better things to worry about. The wedding was in December, and my parents had not applied for their visas yet. I was excited about my parents visiting the United States for the first time. However, deep down, I was praying that my father be denied a visa. Without him at the wedding, there would not be any cultural complications. My mother was easygoing and very forgiving, and my father was the opposite. He was a very sensitive, pensive, and observant man. No single mistake or slip of the tongue would escape his scrutiny. He would talk about that mistake for days, and making it sound as news every time he referred to it.

2

Let us Start from the Beginning

In my last year at Mudarikwa Secondary School in Masvingo, Zimbabwe, most of the senior students and some of our teachers talked about going to study abroad. For most of us, the most popular and favorite oversees study destination was the United States. This aspiration was surprising because Mudarikwa was a poor rural secondary school, but we too had dreams just like students at the prestigious boarding schools. We called such dreams, the American dream, as they are known in America today. I do not know who had brought that term to Mudarikwa, for it was already in use when I went to study there. Most of us had no idea about the tedious application process involved in getting admitted to a college to study abroad, and we hoped to cross that bridge when we came to it.

We did not know much about the realities of the American life and educational system except the few exaggerated, and sometimes, imagined stories of the American splendor. We were fortunate that a few former students had managed to obtain scholarships to study at American universities, and a couple of them had graduated and come back to Zimbabwe. Occasionally, some of them visited Mudarikwa Secondary School just to hang out with friends and relatives, and of course, to greet their former educators. The previous year, we had a couple of former students who came to our school on career guidance day to talk to us about the American dream, which we had already embraced without much persuasion. They told us about America's beautiful and advanced universities, job opportunities, availability of power and clean water, the good food, kind people, and many other nice things. Hence, most of us dreamt of landing some scholarship opportunities to pursue undergraduate studies in America.

It is not that we did not like or trust our own institutions of higher learning. We did. The main hurdle for us concerned the unavailability of jobs after graduation from such institutions. At that time, we were told that Zimbabwe's unemployment rate was above 90%. Things were hard for everyone, except for the members of the ruling class and their friends. Most people who did not belong to the Zimbabwean aristocracy wanted to leave the country as soon as they could, for Zimbabwe's economy held no hope for them. If Zimbabwe shared a border with the United States, many people would have crossed it, but there was none except thousands of miles of water. For many students, the solution lay in getting into America via a student visa, with the aim of not returning to Zimbabwe after graduation, except for visiting. Already, there were many Mudarikwa's former students studying in South Africa, China, and the UK.

At some point, I shared my American dream with Mother, who, instead of supporting me as I had expected, showed no interest in me studying abroad at all.

"It's too far away, my son. Who do you know in America?" Mother asked.

"There are other Zimbabwean students there," I responded.

"You can't just trust people. You don't know how they got there. Their parents may be wealthy, and you can't equate yourself to them."

"I don't need to know anyone in America to study there. I just need a college to go to."

"What will you eat? Where will you live? Are you crazy?"

"I will apply for a scholarship, Mother."

"Who will give you a scholarship?"

"I don't know. There are many universities in America. One might offer me a scholarship."

"Do you know any of the people involved in awarding international scholarships there?"

"No."

"So how do expect to get a scholarship? You think they can give you a scholarship just like that?"

"Mother, America is not Zimbabwe. They don't have corruption in America. They treat every application according to its merit."

"How do you know that American universities are not as corrupt as ours?"

"That's what Americans tell us, and we have every reason to believe what they say."

"Do you think that they are going to admit to corrupt activities just like that?"

"Why not? They are honest people."

"My son, corruption is everywhere. It's not easy to get a scholarship anywhere in the world. Don't be naïve."

"Mother, I know what I am talking about. I know students who got full-ride scholarships in America. I am not talking about something that is impossible."

"Don't they have poor kids who need scholarships in America?"

"I guess, they don't. Or they want the cultural diversity that international students bring."

"Peter, you are too optimistic. Why would America need diversity? Don't they have enough diversity right now? You must think, my son. Use your brain."

"I am using my brain, Mother."

"Okay. Let's say you get a scholarship to study in the USA, who will buy an air ticket for you? Does the scholarship also provide for that?"

"Some do, others don't. It depends on the kind of scholarship one gets."

"What if it doesn't cover transport expenses, food, and board?"

"Mother why are you so pessimistic. I thought you were a Christian who believes in divine providence."

"Don't judge me. My faith is between me and my God."

"I am sorry. It was just a gentle reminder."

"What if you get sick over there? Who would take care of you?"

"Mother, they have hospitals in America."

"I know. I am not a fool. But do they treat people for free?"

"It's America, Mother. Everything is almost for free."

"How do you know that. America is a capitalist country, and cannot just give free healthcare to everyone. Don't forget that you are not an American. The best for you is to go to a university here, graduate, and become a teacher. It's a good profession. You will have free housing, and sometimes, free water and electricity. They earn a decent salary too."

"Who earns a decent salary? Teachers?"

"Yes."

"Maybe in the past they did. Things have changed. All of them struggle to make ends meet. They complain every day."

"Even in America, workers don't earn enough money, my son. Someone told me that some of them have two jobs because what they earn is not good enough. What is important is to budget your earnings, and try to live within your means. I don't think it's a good idea for you to go to America. If it were South Africa, I would understand. It's near, and we can come over to see you if something happens to you. America is too far away."

Mother and I had this conversation on numerous occasions, and I never managed to convince her. My strategy was to convince Mother, first, so that she would be my advocate to Baba, for she always found a way of convincing him. She always had a way. But on this matter, she was not on my side. I was quite certain that approaching Baba directly would be a waste of time.

There are certain times when one must do things that he has never done before. There are times when one must do something despite the paralyzing fear gripping him. For me, this was the time. I had relied on Mother to advocate for me for too long, and this time, I was on my own, and I had to learn how to fight my own battles. I spent a few days gathering enough energy to approach Baba, and rehearsing how I was going to present my case to him. Then one day, I braved the winds and talked to Baba about my intention to study in America. I did not know what to expect, but I felt that I could make him see the other side of the story. Like always, he listened to my request carefully and thoughtfully without asking any question or commenting. When I was done explaining and justifying my intention to study abroad, I was surprised by his response.

"You are a man, my son. You can go anywhere in the world in pursuit of your dreams. Life is not easy here in Zimbabwe. There is no future for young people. Our economy has collapsed, and it seems that there is no viable plan for an economic turnaround by our government. If you want a future for your children, please, follow your dreams. But you should know that nothing in life is easy."

"Thank you, Baba. Thank you, very much."

"Are there any scholarship opportunities in America?"

"I have been surfing the internet, and it's not easy to get one. I have sent out applications, and I just hope to get a scholarship. In addition to that, I should take an English language test called TOEFL."

"What does that stand for?"

"Test of English as a Foreign Language."

"Foreign to who? You don't need that. You have been learning English for the past fourteen years. What more English do you need?"

"American colleges require it, Baba. They want all international students who speak English as a second language to pass a standardized test before they can admit them into their colleges, or soon after admission."

"Why would you want to go to America to study at a college? Why not go to a university?"

I smiled. "In America, people refer to universities as colleges."

"Ok. But I don't understand why you should take the English language test."

"It's one of the requirements, Baba."

"I understand that, and I am saying that you don't need it."

"I know, but they won't offer me a place in their colleges unless I pass the test. Once I pass the test, and get a study place, I can then apply for scholarships."

"I see. Why do Americans always want to complicate things? Someone was telling me that they drive on the wrong side of the road. They use miles instead of kilometers. They talk of pounds, not kilograms. They make things so difficult for people who don't understand their system."

"There is nothing wrong with that."

"Maybe. But this TOEFL thing drives me crazy. Or is it that they have a different version of English?"

"Americans have their own way of doing things. Since the test is mandatory for most students who speak English as a second language, it should be useful."

"You do what you need to do. Where are you going to take the test? In America?"

"They have a testing center in Harare. I need to register for the test, and do some reading in preparation for it. A friend of mine who already took the same test told me that it's not an easy test."

"Please, let your Mother know when you are ready to register for the test."

"Okay. Thank you, Baba."

I was glad that Baba was not difficult like Mother had been. I waited to hear what Mother would say after discussing the issue with Baba. Of course, he had not told me that he would discuss it with

Mother, but I knew that he would. He did because Mother started the conversation a couple of days after my conversation with Baba.

"Baba told me that you still have plans to go to study in America?"

"Yes, I do."

"I don't think it's a good idea, my son."

"Mai Peter, you are taking us backwards. There is nothing wrong with him going to study abroad. There is nothing for him here in Zimbabwe," Baba said.

"Don't interrupt me, Baba Peter. Let me speak out what is in my heart. I think that America is too far away from home. Peter is just a kid. We must make decisions for him. We can't just allow him to go to a place where no one in our family has ever gone. Just like that. If he becomes sick or even die over there, how would we bring his remains back home?" Mother complained.

"Please, don't talk about death. Death is everywhere. In life, one needs to take risks. Sometimes you win, at other times you lose. But he can't just sit here doing nothing. Other kids of his age are going abroad to study. Mr. Jere's son went to the UK to study, graduated, got a job there, and is now supporting his parents. Last week, Mr. Jere was bragging that by December, this year, he will be driving a car bought for him by his son. He is already building a big house for them. If he had not risked by going into the unknown, he could be still here wallowing in poverty like all other graduates." Baba was doing just fine.

"So, what are you saying?" Mother asked.

"I am saying that he should go if he gets an opportunity. We should support him, and hope that things will be good."

"You do what you want, but my heart is not in it. If anything happens to him, don't say, I didn't warn you."

"Good. Life is not simple. You don't speak like that about our son because you invoke evil spirits. We are in this together. You should show your support."

Mother was silent for a moment, and then asked, "What would you like to study in America?"

"Business studies."

"Commercials are good, my son. Once you graduate, you will get a job." It was Baba.

I thanked them both, and continued doing my studies, and sending more applications to American universities. Later that month, I registered for TOEFL, wrote the test, and passed with flying colors. Baba, my brother, Ben, and I celebrated, but Mother was not quite in it. She was glad that I passed the test, but did not want to be dragged into celebrating it.

I continued applying for study vacancies at American colleges, but I was not quite lucky. Several colleges rejected my application letters. Many others just did not respond.

By March, our Advanced Level examinations results were out, and I had twelve points out of the fifteen possible points. I intensified my search for international scholarships to no avail. All my classmates who aspired to study in America were still sending out application letters, but none had been successful.

Then my fortunes changed, as they sometimes do. I got a place to study business administration at a private university in San Antonio, Texas. However, the university did not offer any scholarships. I emailed the registrar who told me that partial scholarships would be available, and would be offered to students on a merit basis. Since I had matriculated at a non-American high school, my grades were being evaluated to see their worth as compared to American standards.

I was also told that if I wanted to start college that Fall semester, I had to quickly apply for a student visa at the American embassy. Later, I discovered that I could only apply for a visa if the university that had offered me a place had issued me an I-20 form. This form would state my source of college funding, among other things. I learnt that the school could not offer the 1-20 form until I provided them with the evidence that I could finance my studies. They wanted me to provide bank statements or affidavits of financial support from my guardians. Baba and Mother had some money in the bank, and they got bank statements to vouch for me. They also asked some of our relatives working in the UK to vouch for me, though without any obligation to assist me financially. In other words, it was a scam. They all vouched for me, and the university issued me with the I-20 document. I was so happy because I could now apply for a student visa.

I did apply for a student visa, and I got it, but there were still other hurdles. I needed to purchase an air ticket, and secure some scholarship. All the idealism I had about studying abroad was being challenged by realism. It was real that I would end up going to America without having any money for tuition, accommodation, health insurance, educational supplies, and food. Indeed, I had been told that I could find a student, twenty-hour per week job, at the university where I was going to attend, but the wages would not be sufficient for my upkeep. The university could give me a little money for scholarship, and that would be all they could offer.

My parents had no money. There was no way they could finance my studies abroad. At times, I felt like giving up the American dream before it was too late. Something within me said that Mother might have been right, but I kept the faith. I hoped that things would be alright. This was my only opportunity, and I could not just allow it to slip away through my fingers.

The time for me to leave for the USA arrived. My parents sold a few of their cattle to purchase my air ticket. They also gave me a few thousands of dollars to help me begin my studies in the dream land. As my departure drew closer, I knew that there was no way I could escape a lecture about good morals and cultural integrity from Baba. The unsolicited lecture took place one Wednesday night, after supper, and it did not end until midnight.

"Peter, you are now going to America. Your mother and I have never been there. We have never been outside Zimbabwe. So, there isn't much that we can teach you about America and its culture. What I can talk about is our culture because that is what I know. Do you hear me, Peter?"

"Yes, Baba."

"Don't get lost on your way to America. Whenever you get confused, ask for directions. The best people to ask are police officers and other uniformed airport workers."

"I won't get lost."

"Peter. Peter. Listen to your father. He is not a fool." It was Mother.

"When you get there, keep your manners, my son. Greet people politely. Respect elders and your teachers. Show your gratitude to people who will assist you in any way. Never forget to thank people."

"I know, Baba."

"I know that you know. But let me just say it again. Don't forget to thank people. Blessings come to people who show gratitude to other people. Gratitude will give you the food you eat, and a place in which to sleep."

Mother jumped in. "Don't fight. Don't take advantage of women, my son. Don't take anything that doesn't belong to you. Better die of hunger than steal, my son. Do you understand what I am saying?"

"I do."

"Do your studies seriously. We can sell everything that we have; every cow, every goat, and every chicken so that you receive a decent education. Things will not be easy, my son. People may not like you, but do your best to always do what is right. Don't ever do anything that you would not do here."

"Okay, Baba."

"Don't forget to call us. We will be worried about you if we don't hear from you frequently. Call your mother if you don't want to call me."

"I will call both of you."

"Good, *mwanangu*. Find some work. Send your mother and brother a little money if you can. Don't chase after women. Do one thing at a time. Study first, pleasure later. When you want to find a woman for marriage, come back home. We don't want to talk about this all night long. You know what we have always taught you. You know what your teachers taught you. Observe that, and you will be good."

"Thank you, Baba. Thank you, Mother."

"Be safe. Stay out of trouble, my son. We want you back here in one piece. You understand what I mean?"

"I understand, Baba."

"Don't do drugs. They say that there are drugs in America. Don't ever try them. They are addictive, and they destroy your life. Do you smoke tobacco?"

"You know that I don't."

"Don't start it. You will not be able to get out of the habit even when you want to quit."

"Don't tell people that you are going to study in America. You will be bewitched," Mother said.

The instructions went on until midnight. Whenever I thought they were about to end either of them would bring up something else. I had to pretend to be falling asleep for them to stop.

"Peter. Peter. Are you already asleep?" Baba asked.

"No."

"You are lying. You were snoring."

"Maybe. I think it's time to go to bed. I have heard all what you said. I will be good."

"Do you have any questions?" Mother asked.

"No. I am good. I am going to sleep. Good night." Nobody responded.

My flight, aboard the British Airways, was from Harare international Airport, via Johannesburg, with a short layover in London. It was a smooth flight, which I had dreamt about many years before it happened. In about twenty-four hours of being airborne, we landed at George Bush International Airport in Houston, Texas. From Houston, I got into a four-hour bus ride to San Antonio, Texas. I got a taxi from the Greyhound bus station in downtown San Antonio to the university where I was going. That was at the beginning of August.

I checked in at the university, and I was allowed into the dormitory after paying part of my tuition, and half of my housing fees. I told the administrators that my parents would be sending more money for the arrears. Even though I hoped that they would, I knew very well that they had nothing left for me. They had used all their savings and investment on me, and expecting any more money from them was not being realistic.

The following week, the orientation began. I felt relieved when I got a student job in the university library. Although the money I would get from that job was not sufficient to pay for my tuition, it would help me with accommodation and food. It was not a surprise because the university had forewarned me, and also calculated my budget for me before I came to the United States.

Soon after, I applied for several scholarships, and I got almost half the tuition that I needed that semester. I was grateful that I was set for the semester.

Classes started by the middle of August, and I met a few hurdles in the American educational system. First, we were required to read a lot of books and online articles for each course. It seemed that each professor was oblivious of the fact that we were taking other classes, which also required us to read. There was also homework. The amount of work they piled on students was more than I could comfortably handle. Indeed, education brings about change, and all change comes with discomfort, but there is a vast difference between transformational and destructive discomfort. It felt more of the latter, than the former. I read and studied like I had never done before. The subject matter of all my courses was doable, despite the insurmountable required reading. Other students who were privy to the American type of education did not seem to struggle much with their readings like I did. Perhaps, I had not yet mastered the gimmicks of using my brain to scan the material and get the most out of it. My second challenge was with technology. I had to type my work and use some online resources, which were huge academic blessings except that I had never used a computer before. I mean, using it in the sense of relying on it for almost every academic exercise.

There were many other technical things about computers, which I did not understand. For instance, I did not even know how to turn a computer on and off. I did not know how to save my typed work properly, which cost me a considerable amount of time after losing some of my valuable work. I did not know how to type, and it took me ages to type even a single page. Despite these few pinpricks, there were blessings in the American education system. The library was replete with relevant books, computers, and journals for students to use. Many students had their own laptops, which left the library computers free for me and other poor students to use. The professors were punctual, smart, and most of the time, respectful. Unlike at home, where I used a candle as the source of light when studying at night, in America, electricity was available all the time. The rooms were clean and spacious, and furnished with huge desks. There were writing centers to assist students with essay writing. In fact, students were given everything that they needed to succeed. Hence, the semester went on smoothly. My library job turned out to be the best student job on campus because when the library was not busy, I could read a book. My end of semester grades were excellent, and I felt really proud of myself.

As the Fall semester was about to end, I started thinking about how I would find tuition fees for the Spring semester. If I were lucky enough to get more scholarships, the scholarship money would be covering about a third of my tuition, and I had to find a source for the rest. I also needed money for rent. I needed money for food. I needed money for educational supplies. I started talking to friends about my impending financial constraints, which was not easy because it was hard to find a willing listener. American students mind their own business, and rarely talk to strangers. I was fortunate to find someone who told me that if I moved out of university accommodation, I could rent a cheaper apartment elsewhere with other students. I talked to a few students from other African countries, but they were not interested. I was then referred to some men who I thought were undergoing a time of financial instability just like me. They were renting a one-bedroomed backyard house about some fifteen minutes' drive from college. The duo agreed to take me in so that we could split the rent. I do not know for how long they had been in that backyard house because I never asked them. The three of us shared that huge bedroom, each with his own twin-sized bed. The house was self-contained with a bathroom and a small kitchen.

I still do not know what the other two guys did for a living since we only met at the house in the evenings, and rarely talked. When I asked them about what they were doing for a living, they were evasive, and I gave up. I know that they were from Kenya, and spoke Swahili, which they often used in the house, most probably to gossip about issues that they did not want me to overhear. Indeed, there were a few Swahili words that I could understand since they had the same meaning in Shona. I never told them that I understood some of the things that they were saying, until one day, I burst into uncontrollable laughter after hearing one of them describing a beautiful woman he had met in explicit terms. After that incident, they became more careful about what they discussed in my presence. That being said, they were indeed good men.

Although it was a one-bedroomed house, and our personal spaces were sometimes violated, we were independent of each other. They cooked their own food, and I cooked mine. They bought their own drinks, and I bought mine. We had a house cleaning roster, which we observed strictly. Even though I did not have a strong bond with them, I knew that I needed them as much as they needed me. Fate had brought us together, so we needed to stick together.

At first, I did not quite trust them, and I guess the feeling was mutual. I was afraid that they would steal my belongings when I was at school, but they never did. It is not that they looked suspicious in any way, but I had never shared a room with a stranger in all my life. Also, they were like brothers, for they knew each other, spoke the same language, and came from the same country. They could easily team up against me if they wanted to, but they proved me wrong. They were good people, and had great respect for me and my dreams. In fact, they treated me like a brother. At night, when they were not working, they allowed me to use the kitchen table to do my studies. I thought that was kind and generous of them because all of us paid equal portions of rent, and we all had a claim to that table. Whenever I was reading in the apartment, they used their earphones to play their music to avoid making noise for me. To reciprocate that gesture of considerateness, I opted to do most of my studies in the library at the college, and only came home to sleep.

After we had been living together for almost six months, my roommates vanished. It happened during the summer break. One day I came back from work and the men were gone. I mean that they did not come back home at night as they usually did, and they had not forewarned me. What gave me a fright was that all their belongings were still in the house. I called them, but they did not answer their phones. I told the landlady about their disappearance, and to my greatest relief, she knew their whereabouts. They had left the city to pursue their dreams elsewhere. She told me that someone would be coming to collect their belongings. After about a week, the student who had, in the first place, connected me with the Kenyans called me and told me that they had relocated to Chicago. The following morning, he stopped by to pick up their few belongings.

I still do not know why they had to leave without saying goodbye. It is not that they owed me any farewell, but they had become like brothers to me. I cared about their wellbeing as much as they cared about mine. If I were in their position, I would not have left without leaving a note. I tried to imagine the kind of emergency that could have compelled them to abandon me without a warning, but could not find any. I missed them. Perhaps they also missed me.

I was left alone in that back house. I was worried about how I would manage to pay the full rent alone. I tried to renegotiate the rent amount with the landlady—a very nice lady, but she insisted that she needed the full amount for the house. I do not count that against her, for she also needed the money to pay the mortgage for her main house. I was grateful to her for allowing me to stay a couple of months in the back house without signing an annual contract. I could have looked for other renting partners, but it was during summer break, and students were off campus. Even if it were during the semester, it would be difficult to find students willing to share the one-bedroomed backhouse with me. So, I was stuck with the house alone, without enough money to pay for the monthly rent. I also had other worries concerning how I was going to get the tuition for the next semester. I was glad that I did not owe the university any arears for the previous semester.

Everything looked gloomy. At some point, I felt that I needed to go back home to Zimbabwe. There was no way I could get enough money for both rent and tuition. The money that I earned from the library was barely enough for food and rent. Hopefully, I could get a scholarship, which would only cover about half the tuition. I thought that it would be a good idea to accept defeat, and purchase an air ticket to go back to Zimbabwe. The thought of going back home to Zimbabwe, empty-handed made me very sad. I thought about Mother's words. I should have listened to her.

At night, I sometimes cried, not because I did not want to go back home to Zimbabwe, but because of the shame of failure. What was I going to tell my friends and relatives back home? Would I tell them that my father had spent a fortune to send me to America to study, and I had come back home empty-handed? What would they say? They would laugh at me. My former teachers would use my story to warn other students who aspired to study abroad. I very much wanted to quit, for it was the easiest way out, but I could not. After all, things were more difficult in Zimbabwe than in America.

At some point, I was angry with myself. I should have listened to my mother. She did not want me to come to America. She warned me about the dangers of studying abroad. She knew that it was not easy. Yes, she warned me, but I did not listen. I tried to pray, but I could not quite gather my thoughts. Instead of praying, I kept repeating the same word as a mantra. I did not quite believe that prayers would help me, but I felt that it was one of the few options I still had. I knew that nothing short of a miracle could save me from my financial problems. Then an idea came to my mind just like a flicker of light. Maybe I needed to talk to someone, but who would listen to me? Who would understand my plight?

One morning, I gathered enough courage and emailed the dean of students' affairs of the university. I did not expect him to respond promptly, but he did. It was a compassionate email, which instructed me to visit the campus coordinator for international students. I scheduled a meeting with her, and the following day, I visited her office. The coordinator of international students listened to my story empathetically. She never interrupted me, except when she occasionally asked me questions for clarification. When I had said all I wanted to say, and shed all the tears I could, she gave me some advice that became the miracle I had been praying for. She told me of a small college to which I could transfer, and could get a full scholarship for my studies. That was the good news I had been waiting for.

That night I completed the online application and transfer process to that college. Within a week of my conversation with the coordinator, I sent in my application, to that other college. I was admitted into that college's financial administration program as a sophomore. They also sent me a link through which I could apply for scholarships, but they did not make any promises of financial aid. I did apply, and I was awarded three different scholarships that would give me enough money for tuition. I was so happy that I did not know what to do. I laughed, danced, and cried. Fortunately, I was alone in my backhouse, so, I could celebrate my miracle in any way I saw fit. I cannot recall if I remembered to thank God or not for the miracle, but I remember that the whole evening and night were spent in utter contemplation of the greatness of God. That evening, I had a one-man party, after which I slept soundly throughout the night.

The following day, I gave my notice to the landlady, who waived it to only a week since she had found someone to occupy the backhouse. About a week before the beginning of the semester, I took my few belongings and boarded the Greyhound bus on my way to my new college, which was situated in a small rural town, about three hours' drive from San Antonio. I got there in the morning, and registered for my classes. I also got a student job in the cafeteria, which became a big blessing for me. The cafeteria allowed us to eat the leftovers, and also to take a little bit of food home. After getting the cafeteria job, I signed a six-month contract for university shared accommodation, for I had saved enough money to last for four months. My roommates were all from Mexico, and were also on full ride scholarships. I was consoled that there were many of us facing financial challenges. At some point, I realized that their challenges were bigger than mine. At least, I had my papers. They did not. They were the dreamers, who had been brought to America by their parents as kids. Although our cultures were different, we were all immigrants, and we were pursuing our dreams. That common ground drew us closer.

The semester started, and everything went smoothly. For a month, I could hardly believe that my financial woes had come to an end. I could now send some money back home to my parents so that they could buy some cattle to replace the ones they had sold to finance my freshman studies. They were happy, and always reminded me to take good care of myself, and to study hard. I told my father that it was not about studying hard, but studying prudently, to which he agreed.

I also wrote back to the international students' coordinator at my previous college, thanking her for the valuable information, which led me to this new place, where I could realize my dreams. As I was proofreading the email, I cried. I think that they were tears of joy and relief. They were tears of realizing that human beings were kind, generous, and good. The coordinator responded and congratulated me for my new fortunes, and promised that she would keep in touch. In my subsequent emails, I felt the urge to call her "Mother," but I realized that I was not in Zimbabwe where I could endearingly and respectfully call every woman of my mother's age, "Mother."

Weeks became months, months became years, and before I even realized it, I graduated. I had no money to invite my parents from Zimbabwe to attend my graduation, but I now had friends who supported me. My friends held a small graduation party for me. Since, I had applied for an optional practical training year, and was granted, I started looking for a job. I got it in San Antonio, with one of the leading financial institutions there. Three years back, fate had driven me out of San Antonio, and now grace had decided to bring me back. It was a well-paying job with lots of benefits. Every morning, I pinched myself just to remind myself that it was real. After about six months of working hard for the company, they recommended me for a work permit. Eventually, I was granted a permanent resident permit.

Then something good happened to me that year. I met the woman who would become my spouse at a local hospital, where I had gone to get my annual flu shot. Getting an annual flu shot was a requirement at my workplace, and not something I would have volunteered to do. As I was walking out of the hospital, I saw her walking into the hallway from another wing of the hospital. We met at the sliding exit doors. We both exited the hospital at the same time, and I walked behind her into the public garage, just across the road. By the color of her scrubs, I could tell that she was a nurse. It looked like we were both heading for the same elevator, which would place us in an awkward situation in the elevator. Of course, I should not generalize, but I had heard that some women were not comfortable to be alone in an enclosed elevator with a man they did not know. Although I did not make lonely women feel uncomfortable in elevators, I sometimes found it difficult to be alone in an elevator with a woman that I did not know. My greatest concern was not about me, but about them. What would the woman be thinking about me? Is she afraid of me? What if the elevator breaks down and locks us inside? Will she panic and scream, thinking that I am going to attack her? So, to avoid causing unnecessary anxiety to other people, I usually skipped the elevator if I sensed that a woman and I were likely to ride it alone. It was a sacrifice that I was willing to make so that women could feel safe and comfortable in enclosed places.

As we waited for the elevator to come down, I decided to preempt the anxiety before getting into it, by greeting the nurse. She might have been thinking the same because she greeted me first.

"Hi," She said.

"Hi," I responded. "You look tired. Seems like it has been a long day."

"Indeed. I work a twelve-hour shift, four days per week."

"That's not easy. I don't think I would survive twelve hours of continuous work. You are very dedicated. Thank you for making such sacrifices for us."

"I am used to working long hours. Of course, there is an incentive for it."

"How do they incentivize you?"

"Good paycheck, and of course, long weekends."

"Lucky you."

"I am kidding. I can do with a pay rise."

"Maybe, you are not."

"I am. Do you also work for this hospital?"

"No. I had come for a flu shot. I work for a finance company in downtown San Antonio. Just graduated from college, you see."

"Where?"

I told her, and she shouted, "That's where my brother is studying."

"What program?"

"Business studies, majoring in accounting."

"Cool. I might have met him in one of the classes."

"True. Where are you from, originally?"

"Why?"

"You have an endearing accent, which is sweet to listen to."

"Thank you. I am from Zimbabwe," I responded while wondering how an accent could be endearing.

The elevator doors opened, and we jumped in.

"Where is Zimbabwe?"

"Africa. Southern Africa. North of South Africa. South of Zambia. And we have Mozambique and Botswana on our eastern and western borders, respectively."

"That's cool. Maybe one day I will visit Africa."

"Please, do come to Zimbabwe. We have the spectacular Victoria Falls, huge game reserves, and many other places of tourist attraction."

"That sounds exciting."

We exited the elevator on the same level of the garage.

"It was nice talking to you. It looks like we two have a lot to talk about. How about a cup of coffee together some day?"

"It's a great idea," she responded.

"Can I get your number?"

"Absolutely."

"By the way, what's your name? I am Peter."

"Maria."

I got Maria's number, and we went our different ways. The following weekend, we went out to eat together. That is how our relationship started. It did not take me long to decide that I wanted to marry Maria. She had everything that a decent man looks for in a wife. She was beautiful, kind, generous, openminded, hardworking, and forgiving. We both knew that there was a cultural barrier between us, but we were willing to compromise and to experience the discomfort of learning each other's culture. We were also aware that it would not be easy to rope in our families and relatives into our decision to marry. As a black man, I was concerned about how Maria's parents would feel about the union, but I did not think that they could stop us from getting married. I felt that Maria's parents would be shocked to hear the news, grieve over the "loss" of their daughter, but would recover. I did not expect my parents to object to our marriage because marrying a white woman would be considered a great achievement by our people.

Within a year of going out together, we engaged despite initial objections from Maria's father. Maria took advantage of her parents' goodness, and insisted that she would marry the man she loved, and that man was me. They gave in to her demands begrudgingly. It is not that Maria cared much about their approval of our engagement, but I felt that getting their approval was the right thing to do. After the engagement, we had a private party, which was attended by a few friends. From there, things moved faster. The following year, we wedded.

3

An Intercultural Encounter

Fortunately, or unfortunately, my parents got visas to attend my wedding. I think that it was a good thing that both got visas because Mother would have decided not to attend if Baba were not attending. When I asked him what had happened at the United States embassy, Baba said that only three questions were asked by the consular, or whoever the interviewer was.

"What's your purpose for visiting the United States?" asked the interviewer.

"We are going for a wedding. My son is marrying a white American woman. We are both excited and worried about it. It complicates things." Baba gave the interviewer unsolicited information. The consular is said to have ignored Baba's elaborate answer. That is what mother told me.

"How long are you planning to stay in the United States?" The consul continued.

"We don't know, my son. Maybe, three weeks. We cannot stay there for more than that because we have livestock at home. We cannot trust our younger son to take good care of the cows while we are away. And there are thieves too. We don't want to come back home, and find all our livestock gone," Baba explained.

"While in the United States, if you are offered employment, are you going to accept it?"

"My son, can't you see that we are old. We have had our hay days. We toiled for this country. Yes, we played our part, but that time is gone. They tell me that America is not a country for the old, and I believe them. We are going to attend our son's wedding, and after that, we will fly back home. We won't accept any kind of employment, my son."

"Congratulations! You have been granted visas to visit the United States. Enjoy your visit. One of you should come back to the embassy on Friday to pick up your passports."

Mother is said to have performed a thankful dance accompanied by some ululation. Baba is said to have clapped his hands, and wholeheartedly thanked the consular. I am told that a long conversation between Baba and Mother took place as soon as they got off the bus.

"You see, Mai Peter, what I was saying? I told you that we are going to get the visas."

"The winds of destruction were far away today," Mother responded.

"Tell me, when you were denied a visa twice, was it because of the evil spirits?" Baba wanted to know.

"Yes. Do you think that people were happy that I was going to America? And that I was going to board an airplane? Who in this village has ever boarded an airplane?"

"Please, spare me the evil spirits rhetoric. It is you who couldn't understand American English. Two times is not a joke. Maybe you answered what you were not asked. *Chinonzi chirungu,* sweetheart. When speaking to Americans, you should be precise and logical. They have no time to listen to rigmaroles. That is what I did today. Straight to the point."

"Get away. Do you speak good English as I do? Where were you educated? At Saint Nyoka?" Mother sarcastically asked.

"Education is education. It does not matter where you received it. Some of us were not as lucky as you were. Our parents could not afford to send us to boarding schools, but we still made it at those poor secondary schools."

Baba's feelings were hurt. We all knew that he had struggled financially to go through high school. My grandma, a widow at the time Baba went to high school, could not afford to send my father to a good school. He had to do menial jobs to pay for his education. He always talked of his high school teachers, most of whom were well meaning but not qualified to teach at a high school. But he made it. He indeed was a self-made man. Very intelligent and diligent. Full of purpose and ambition. Yes, he made it.

"It's you who started it. You said that I am not educated," Mother accused him.

"I didn't say that you are not educated. I said that you failed to comprehend the American English accent. Being uneducated, and failure to understand a particular English accent are two different things. I got you. In fact, we should be celebrating, not arguing."

"I didn't hear the word 'accent'. You are right, we should celebrate."

Baba was right. Getting a visa to visit the United States was not an easy feat. There were many stories of people being denied visas for no apparent reason. There were stories of students who were denied visas to come back to the United States to complete their studies. My parents were lucky.

I do not know how they celebrated their issuance of American visas if they celebrated at all. What I know for certain is that the preparations for the long trip started in all earnest that evening. The following day, my mother conveyed the good news to me over the phone. As soon as I put the phone down, I passed on the news to Maria, who jumped up and down in ecstasy. She was excited to meet my parents, even though the success of our wedding would not depend on their attendance in any way.

A couple of days after the visa interview, Baba went back to Harare to pick up the passports. It never rained but poured, for they were granted six months visiting visas. Of course, they did not expect to spend more than two months in the United States. They just wanted to attend the wedding, spend a few more weeks with us, and then return to Zimbabwe.

"Don't preach about it at church, Mai Peter. We know that some of you can't keep secrets." It was Baba.

"This is good news, and I should give a testimony about it in church this Sunday. Good news should be shared with others." Mother teased him. Perhaps, she intended to do it.

"Don't do that. We will be bewitched, Mai Peter. They will bewitch us. Not everyone is happy about our successes."

"Are you saying that there are witches at our church?" Mother asked.

"Why not? Witches are everywhere," Baba responded.

"Do you know their names, baba Peter?"

"Whose names?"

"The witches."

"No."

"So, how do you know that there are witches among our church members?"

"Am I in a court of law? Do I need to call my lawyer?"

"No, it's not a court, but I just wanted to remind you that it's not wise to accuse others of witchcraft without a shred of evidence."

"I understand it, but don't talk about our journey to people, please."

Mother did not respond.

My parents were afraid of witchcraft just like most other villagers were. The belief was pervasive in all of Zimbabwe, and Christian missionaries had failed to eradicate it. In fact, when I was growing up in Nyajena, there were two fears that relentlessly and mercilessly haunted our rural neighborhood. One of them was the fear of the Rhodesian Forces' helicopter machine gun. This fear was not a figment of our infantile or untamed rural imaginations, but real. On numerous occasions, we had witnessed the undisputed and invincible power of a helicopter machine gun. We had seen a helicopter gunner firing at a target until the target was torn to pieces. It was not in movies, *pero en vivo*. During those years, the sound of an approaching helicopter could send the whole village to the toilet with unstoppable diarrhea. It was the War of Liberation between African nationalists and the Rhodesian Front and its sympathizers. Like everything else in life, the War ended. Yes, it did. The killer helicopters became friendly again, and our traumatized spirits were consoled, and hopefully, healed.

The other fear, which contemptuously and tenaciously refused to be exorcized even by the attainment of Zimbabwe's independence from Britain—the fear of witches and their invisible and nefarious children, popularly known as *zvidhoma*, remained unfazed. For readers who are not privy to African cosmology, a witch is an evil person, who uses mysterious power to harm others, ordinarily in the dark. We grew up being told that witches, after causing someone's death, would devour the flesh of their victim in their nocturnal, ghoulish feasts. *Zvidhoma*, the invisible children of witches, could be sent on errands to beat up their targets. They were also known as *zvitupwani, zvikara,* or *zvevusiku*.

As kids, we feared *zvidhoma* more than we feared witches. I should be honest, we never saw any *chidhoma*, but we were pretty sure that they were ubiquitous. In our village, there was a place called Pamusheche, which was believed to be the august residence of *zvidhoma*. They had names, which I cannot remember, but I know for sure that their leader was called Bobo. Of course, Bobo was not related in any degree to the Bobo who later became the first black Prime Minister of the independent Zimbabwe. No one, except traditional ritual practitioners claimed to have seen *zvidhoma*. They were the African healthcare experts, and they had the means to identify *zvidhoma*.

Yes, there was amble evidence that their home was at Pamusheche. All villagers claimed to smell the saliva-inducing aromas from *zvidhoma's* never-ending deep frying of millet fat cookies, when passing through Pamusheche. I never smelt anything, but I ardently believed it. As if the ancestors were not merciful enough, our way to and from school passed through Pamusheche. I was always so afraid to pass through the place. Even though I never saw or smelt anything, I believed that Bobo and his insatiable crew were always watching me, and devising ways of entrapping me for fresh *fajitas*. On numerous occasions, while passing through Pamusheche, I had felt my hair standing on end, which was popularly believed to be a sign of the presence of evil spirits and *zvidhoma*. Sometimes, when I was alone, going to or from school, I always took a longer and unorthodox way home. The longer way took me through a swampy area, but I did not mind that as long as I was beyond the reach of Bobo and his brothers and sisters.

During those years, I unwaveringly believed that getting outside at night, alone, to respond to the call of nature was the surest way of becoming *zvidhoma's* next goulash. I knew that they were out there, patiently waiting for me outside. To be safe, everyone was supposed to stay indoors throughout the night. For many kids of my generation, it was better to wet one's blankets than to go outside where the wrath of Bobo was awaiting you. Of course, some nights, when the call of nature made it extremely difficult for me to enjoy my sleep, I would brave the winds by going out to help myself. Everywhere I looked, there were *zvidhoma*. I never saw them, but everything within me told me that Bobo and his WhatsApp group were always eagerly waiting in the dark, watching me, as I minded my business, as quickly as my outlet could allow me. In fact, darkness became the embodiment of *zvidhoma*. Where others saw darkness, I only saw *zvidhoma*. The objects that I knew were trees during the day became gigantic *zvidhoma* at night. My attempt to convince my mind that what I was seeing were, in fact, mere trees, was in vain. The fear was real and paralyzing. Any time, Bobo could pounce on me. Many times, I would run back into the house before I logically concluded the job for which I had gone outside. But I must admit, Bobo never grabbed me. Thanks to my mother's never-failing survival instinct and foresight.

Most villagers had to protect their families from the effects of *zvidhoma* and other deleterious spirits. My mother, a fervent and reliable fearer of *zvidhoma* and witches obtained for us some medicinal waistbands called *mutimwi* or *zango*, whose purpose was to chase off *zvidhoma* and witches. *Mutimwi* was made from a piece of cloth, which had some repulsive herbs sewed in it, in a lump. At that time, most boys had it, but as the years went by, some boys, whose parents had exorcized them of the fear of *zvidhoma* sooner, disposed of their sacred waistbands. Those were the boys who always laughed at me, whenever they saw my *mutimwi*. It was not easy to hide it because we had to take off our shirts whenever we were playing football, if we ever were wearing any shirts. To worsen the matter, *mutimwi* was not supposed be washed, so, you can imagine the number of lies that did find a dining room, and a constant fresh blood provider in it and me. I must have lost a few pints of blood to those broad daylight vampires. Eventually, the grip that fear had on me loosened. At some point, my shame of being laughed at outweighed my fear of *zvidhoma*. Then one day, I did the unthinkable. I threw my protective *mutimwi* into a termite hole to make sure that I could not retrieve it even if I changed my mind. Of course, I never changed my mind. I survived, not because *zvidhoma* had ceased to exist, but because I had gotten rid of the suffocating fear of them. I still believe that *zvidhoma* exist, but what has changed is the level of my fear of them.

So, Baba's fear of witchcraft was not baseless. For Mother, maybe, the joy of going to America outweighed the fear of being bewitched.

I was excited for my parents. They deserved that refreshing and rejuvenating trip to the United States. They had toiled all their lives on the farm, and had not quite visited any other country except South Africa. They had sacrificed everything to educate us. They deserved to experience how it felt to fly. Also, this trip would give me an opportunity to care for them. I would show them places, and cook American and Mexican dishes for them. I would also purchase nice clothes for both. My father had a penchant for suits and ties, and the ones he still possessed had seen better days. As soon as they arrive, I would take them to Burlington Store so that they can choose the attires they would wear at my wedding.

When Maria told her parents about my parents' visit, they were also excited. Whether their excitement was out of mere curiosity or respect for me, I could not tell. For me, their excitement was good enough. I did not expect Maria's family to like my parents because they had no obligation to do so. I was contented that they had not objected to me marrying their daughter. Not that their consent was particularly important to Maria, but it felt right to me. Maria was determined to marry me whether her parents liked me or not. She was an individual who had been empowered to make her own personal decisions. Her parents loved her, and she knew that her decisions, however strange, would be honored. I wish all kids were empowered in a similar way. Although she loved her family, Maria was an individual in her thought processes and decision making.

That is why I think that American individualism is as good as African communalism. They are different philosophies of life, but both have merits and weaknesses. American individualism makes an individual feel independent and free to pursue her own career and happiness. The individual has the power and right to choose the course of life that she wants to pursue. The individual knows that if she does the right things, and exerts the right amount of effort, she will achieve her dreams. Even though this pursuit of happiness happens with the assistance of the family, the family only plays a supportive role, and is bound to respect most of the choices made by the individual. These semi-autonomous individuals make up American communities. This philosophy of life allows individuals to own their victories and successes in life, and to learn from the mistakes they make. The philosophy can be summarized by the following phrase: "We are because I am." This phrase is a declaration that individuals are empowered to shape the community in which they live. They are free to make decisions about their own lives. The family and the community play a supportive role. They give the individual all the tools she needs to succeed in life, but may not compel the individual to follow a certain societal path.

On the other hand, African communalism is about a shared vision. Whatever decision that I want to make, I must think of the consequences that course of action has for my family and the community at large. Sometimes, I must sacrifice my own dreams and aspirations to appease the collective family and communal dreams. When choosing a career, one must check if it would bring food to the table, not only for oneself, but also for the extended family. One is free to choose a spouse, but the family must be consulted, and their blessings requested. After all, the bride belongs to the family, not just to an individual. African philosophy can be summed up by the phrase: "I am because we are." In other words, one's cultural identity and integrity come from one's unity with the family and community. Every decision must be evaluated against the collective needs and aspirations of the family and community. Although individual needs are respected, they should be compromised for communal needs if the two are opposed to each other. The community resembles the water, and the individual, the fish, swimming in the water. Without the water, the fish is nothing. Hence, without the community, the individual is nothing. The questions, which the individual asks are: "If I do this, what would my parents think? If I pursue this career, will my extended family have enough to eat?"

This philosophy does not mean that Africans do not respect individual choices or the private ownership of property. They do. For instance, a villager can purchase a bicycle, and everyone knows that it is privately owned by their fellow villager. However, that acknowledgement does not deprive other villagers of the use of the bicycle. They can borrow it for free whenever necessary. They may assist in its repair if need be. They know that although it belongs to their fellow villager, they are free to request for its use, and are not likely to be denied. Paradoxically, the bicycle belongs to both the individual and the community.

In an African community, one may be a hard worker who produces more agricultural produce than others, but that does not deprive others of enjoying the fruits of that villager's labors. A person who owns something that is scarce in the community cannot deprive others of its use provided they use it with care and respect. Our people understand and respect the significance of the private ownership of goods, but they still have the privilege of using such goods whenever necessary. Therefore, people must assess the benefits and setbacks of every decision that they make, against both individual and communal needs.

Maria and I came from individualistic and communalistic cultures, respectively. These cultural philosophies are different, and I knew that it would take some doing for both of us to avoid clashes caused by our different cultural identities and expectations. I should mention that neither of the above philosophies of life is better than the other. Neither is superior, nor more perfect than the other. Both have advantages and disadvantages. Later, I discovered that the combination of individualistic and communal worldviews brought a lot of blessings to our marriage.

In communal or collective cultures, families have a strong influence concerning one's marriage. For instance, in my Shona culture, a man or woman should choose who to marry, individually. However, once the partners agree to marry, the negotiations that follow are surrendered to the families of both the man and woman involved. The groom must pay bridewealth to the parents or guardians of the bride. The bridewealth negotiations that precede Shona customary marriages are carried out by the families of the bride and the bridegroom, which makes the involvement of one's family imperative. The amount of bridewealth paid depends on the social status of both the bride and the economic level of the bridegroom. If the bride is educated, or the bridegroom is wealthy, the bride's relatives may charge more bridewealth. However, the practice of bridewealth can be open to abuse by greedy parents, who may take advantage of the leverage they have to fleece the son-in-law.

Although the Shona people have no consensus concerning the origins and definition of bridewealth, there is a general agreement that in its original form, it was some kind of compensation given to the kin of the bride for the loss of the services of their daughter. In the past, some of this bridewealth would be used to pay bridewealth for the wives of the bride's brothers. It is one of the few Shona cultural practices that have defied the test of time and the influence of colonialism. Among the Shona, no marriage is considered a marriage unless bridewealth has been paid in part, and the rest promised to be paid in installments. The payment includes money, clothes, food and drink, and cattle. The payment of bridewealth ratifies a Shona marriage, which is consummated by the birth of a sufficient number of children.

No Shona person can imagine a marriage where bridewealth is not paid. It is not a marriage, for it is not recognized by the people as such. The bridegroom and his relatives pay bridewealth to acquire certain marital rights. The payment of *rugaba* gives exclusive conjugal rights to the husband. *Rugaba* is paid at the beginning of the bridewealth negotiations. The payment of *danga* (cattle) gives the man entitlement to children and the productive capacity of the woman. So, in Shona culture, the payment of bridewealth is crucial to the legality of a marriage.

I knew that Baba would have a hard time in accepting a marriage where bridewealth was not paid. I did not blame him for that because that was how he was raised. That was his worldview. I was different because I shared two different worldviews—Western and African. Both were good in their different ways. It took me a long time to realize that neither of them was perfect.

I knew that it would be exceedingly difficult, if not impossible to convince Baba to drop his bridewealth idea. I knew him. Once an idea germinated in his mind, he would nourish it to maturity, until it flowered and bore seeds. At this point in my life, I understood things differently. I had allowed some of my cultural values to give way to foreign ones, and I saw nothing wrong with that. Sometimes, ideas and convictions should be allowed to die prematurely, no matter how important they may be. Cemeteries are full of aborted and dead ideas. It is in allowing unachievable dreams to die, that new and realistic aspirations are born. In life, I have learnt that, at times, tenacity is an impediment to positive transformation. It is the flexible that adapt quickly to the changing environment, and are more likely to bring positive changes to the community.

It is not that I did not understand or appreciate the meaning of bridewealth in the Shona culture. I did, but this was a different context that called for a new way of doing things. I was afraid that the Webers would misinterpret the meaning of bridewealth to be the purchase of their daughter, which, if they did, would be extremely scandalous and embarrassing, to imagine the least. It would be degrading to Maria as well. The mention of the word "purchase" would drive her insane. Only other animals have a purchase value, not human beings. Humans are so valuable that you cannot put a price tag on them unless you first dehumanize them like slave traders did to Africans.

To avoid being overrun by Baba in the bridewealth argument, I decided that I would look for another elderly Zimbabwean to knock some sense into his head. I felt that Mother JK would be able to do that. Mother JK was the only elderly Zimbabwean who could be relied on to come over to my place to talk some sense into Baba because she had already promised to explain the American perspective of marriage to my parents. She said that she would also educate my parents on other American cultural practices. Knowing Mother JK as I did, I sensed that Maria would not be spared such intercultural competency lessons.

Mother JK was one of the few Zimbabweans who lived in Corpus Christi, which is about two hours' drive from San Antonio. In fact, I only knew about three Zimbabwean families living in Corpus Christi, at that time. In San Antonio, where I lived, there were about seven Zimbabwean families. It is not that there were not many Zimbabweans living in San Antonio, but those were the only ones that attended our birthday and graduation gatherings. There could have been many more Zimbabweans living in the same city, but I had not met them. I heard friends talking about some other Zimbabweans in San Antonio, who opted out of the gatherings, citing such gatherings as stressful.

Even though Mother JK lived in Corpus Christi, she always attended our gatherings, in San Antonio. She had become our informal village head. She was an incredibly good woman in her 60s. At that age, she was not very old according to American standards. She lived alone in a neat apartment in Corpus Christi. I am not sure if she was a Christian or not, for she never discussed her religious affiliation with anyone, and I never asked. In fact, there was no need to ask. However, in a sense, she was a very spiritual lady. I do not know how I knew that, but I just sensed it. She never started a gathering or meal with a prayer, but I always felt that she silently prayed.

She was hospitable too. She made it her own business to invite African newcomers from San Antonio to her home in Corpus Christi. She would come over to San Antonio, hunt them down, and invite them to her Corpus Christi apartment for traditional food and entertainment. Maybe she was lonely although she did not look like a lonely lady.

I met her at my first college a couple of weeks after my arrival in San Antonio. I do not know what she was doing at my college on that day. I never got to know her mission on that day because I never asked her. Maybe it was one of her hunting grounds for newly-arrived Zimbabweans. Perhaps, she visited all the universities in Texas in search of lonely Zimbabweans.

The day I met her, she came looking for me just before my statistics class started. The moment I saw her, I knew it was her. I had heard about her from a friend. She greeted me in Shona. I froze for a moment, and then gave her a hug. She had a motherly smile and warmth. She was the first motherly Shona person I had ever met since my arrival in San Antonio. She knew everyone from Zimbabwe, who lived in San Antonio. She also knew a few other Zimbabweans in Dallas and San Marcos. One of the weekends, she invited me to Corpus Christi. I went there on a Saturday, and when I arrived, there were several other Zimbabweans already gathered. We talked, laughed, and danced. And we ate *sadza* and braaied steak and chicken. In fact, she had all the Zimbabwean traditional foods that one could ever imagine—*mufushwa, madora, ishwa, nzungu,* and many others.

I visited her at her home in Corpus Christi on several other occasions after that. She also visited me at my home in San Antonio a couple of times. She became like a mother, not only to me, but to other Zimbabweans living in San Antonio. She had a genuine concern and love for people. She was an avid storyteller who had a rare skill of keeping her stories going both backward and forward. All her stories had the dramatic ending like that of a suspense movie.

What amazed me most about Mother JK was that she knew all the juicy secrets about other residents in her apartment block. She had mountains of information about them. It still boggles my mind as to how she gathered all that sensitive information from people as secretive as Americans. Perhaps people trusted her so much that they shared their stories with her in reckless abandon. Maybe her listening skills were so powerful that her neighbors threw down all their personal defensive walls when talking with her. She knew things about her neighbors that many people did not know. She knew those who were into drugs. She knew the men who were abusive to their wives and kids. She knew married couples who were starving each other of conjugal rights, and were about to divorce. She knew the families that were struggling financially. She knew the women who were unfaithful to their husbands. She knew those who always paid their rent last. She knew almost everything about her neighbors, which I do not think gave her any peace of mind. If you take to the habit of minding other people's businesses, you are likely to share the burdens brought about by those businesses. She also knew a lot about American political and racial issues, which I thought was a possible cause of necessary stress for her.

Just like all of us, Mother JK had her demons. She had a penchant for interfering in other people's personal affairs. Of course, she did not tell me that. I got this valuable piece of information from a lady who claimed to have nicknamed her, Mother JK. I still do not know why she was given that name. I also do not know what JK stood for. I just felt that it was a cool name. I knew that it was not her real name, but that is what all Zimbabweans in San Antonio called her. We never used her full name when she was around. We just called her, "Mother," and omitted JK. Perhaps J and K were her initials.

Some people told me that she was a matchmaker. She was always on the lookout for possible matches to bring them together. There were testimonies from couples she had brought into marital unions. Her talent did not end there, for she also assisted mismatched couples to divorce. I do not know how she did it, but I know that she could do it. Her hunt for matches was not limited to the United States, but spanned across the oceans to Zimbabwe. She matched some of us who were single with women in Zimbabwe, who we had never met.

She loved welcoming visitors from Zimbabwe and other African countries. Anyone in our group, whose relative was visiting San Antonio from Zimbabwe, would be certain to alert Mother JK. She would always make herself available to drive all the way from Corpus Christi, pick up the visitor from the airport, and entertain him or her while the host was at work. No visitor would go back to Africa without visiting her apartment in Corpus Christi for some traditional nourishment. I came to realize that it was in entertaining visitors where she got all the juiciest and latest news.

I was told that she never got married, and she was not looking for a match herself. Although she bragged about being the epitome of beauty, she was not looking for a husband. I also do not think that she was honest to herself about her looks. Of course, I cannot say that she was ugly, but I do not think that she was exceptionally beautiful as she claimed. Maybe, she used to be very beautiful when she was young, but the approaching old age had altered her looks. However, my less generous comments about her looks should not take anything away from her beautiful and kind heart. She had an infectious smile too. I think that she had come to a point where she realized that she was not going to get married, and had accepted her state of perpetual spinsterhood. I also do not think that she was jealous of the married couples in our group, for she wanted everyone to be happy. Moreover, she expected everybody who could, to get a marital partner. Perhaps she was married before, but she never shared that information, and I never asked her.

I came to realize that she was a gossiper too, so, I kept my secrets to myself. I never told her that things were difficult for me when I left San Antonio. I knew that if I had told her about it, she would spread the news until my parents got to know about my financial challenges. She would even exaggerate my woes, and lie to people that I was living on the street. So, I decided not to share my tribulations with her until I was settled in my new college. I also never told her about my relationship with Maria lest she spread the news prematurely. Of course, it would be folly on my part to hide the news of my impending wedding from her longer than was necessary because she was a natural event organizer, but I wanted her to learn about it a few days before the wedding day. I knew that she would be handy in explaining American culture to my parents. Also, if given a chance, she would give the Webers an unsolicited lecture on the Shona philosophy of *hunhu*. I also knew that she could only do that if she supported my marriage to a white woman.

When I finally notified her, she did not betray her feelings. She neither smiled nor frowned. She was as expressionless as a windowpane. She neither condemned nor praised me. Probably she was in state of shock. Perhaps, she was grieving the loss of her matchmaking role. I did not care much about what she would say, for she was not my mother. Of course, I respected her as I would respect my mother, but I would not allow her to make decisions for me, and she knew that very well.

My parents arrived in San Antonio about a week before the wedding. I went to pick them up from George Bush International Airport in Houston. We then drove for almost four hours from Houston to San Antonio. All the way, my father mused on the unparalleled beauty of America.

"This is what we call a country. Look at that tall building. Look at how wide the roads are. *Vakomana,* six lanes. Look at how big the vehicles are. Oh my God, Americans are really advanced!"

Everything American was impressive to my father. The roads, buildings, cars, birds, people, and trees were all out of this world for him.

"Look at that woman, driving that pick-up truck. American women are no pushovers. Mai Peter, do you see her?" Mother ignored him. "Oh, another one, driving that blue haulage truck. My God, my God. I love America."

My mother, who was sitting in the front passenger seat was not worried about the outside world, and she was not amused by Baba's loud admiration of the American panorama. Her main concern was the inside of the vehicle.

"This is a spectacular car, my son. It is clean. It's big. Is it yours?" She wanted to know.

"Yes. I just finished paying for it."

"It's too big for one person. Do you sometimes pick up hikers when going to work? You can make a lot of money with a car this size."

"No. In America, it's illegal to pick up hikers on the road. Most people have cars. Those who don't own cars can use public transportation. We have buses. In San Antonio, they are called Via buses."

"What happens if you pick up hikers?"

"It's breaking the law, Mother."

"Don't tell me that. Are you saying that one can be arrested for assisting people who need a ride to work?"

"Yes. This is America, Mother. It's also for drivers' safety. You never know if the people you are picking up are good or bad. Some may end up hijacking you."

"I see. Reduce your speed, my son. We don't want to die in America."

I apologized. "America is as good a place to die as any other, Mother."

"Peter, reduce your speed. I am getting scared."

"We are ok, Mhai. Look at all other cars on this highway. Do you see how they are overtaking us?"

"I see them, but let them go. Maybe they are driving under the influence."

"No, they are not."

"So, why do they overtake us like that?"

"It means that we are driving too slow, and we can get a ticket for that," I explained.

"*Babangu Moyo*. A ticket for not over speeding? Do they want people to die on the road?" She was shocked.

"No. For obstructing other traffic. If you drive too slow or too fast, you can get a ticket."

"A ticket for over speeding is understandable."

"If you over speed, you get a ticket, or they can send you to jail."

"Jail for over speeding?"

"Yes."

As we were having this conversation with Mother, Baba was busy musing on the buildings, trees, and anything that he saw outside.

On our way to San Antonio, nobody talked about the wedding. No one asked about Maria, which upset me a little bit. I knew they cared about her, but just did not know how to talk about her. They did not know what to call her—my girlfriend, wife, or small house? Ordinarily, Shona parents do not enquire about their children's girlfriends or boy friends' wellbeing. A girlfriend is not considered an official member of the family. I knew that they were curious to know if the wedding was still on. I knew that they cared. They had flown all the way from Zimbabwe, not just to see America, but to attend the wedding. I did not want to make it easier for them by starting a conversation about the wedding. We just talked about other things, particularly the political climate of Zimbabwe. Soon, we had to abandon the politics of Zimbabwe because we all disagreed about the best presidential candidate to take Zimbabwe forward. We also disagreed about the cause of Zimbabwe's economic collapse that had started in the year 2000, when the government compulsorily acquired white commercial farmers' land to resettle the landless Zimbabweans.

When we finally arrived home, Maria opened the door for us and hugged me. She also hugged my mother, who never exhibited any signs of resistance at such a welcoming gesture. When she moved to Baba, with her arms outstretched, Baba swiftly moved out of the way. Maria was not offended because I had forewarned her. She was just testing the waters. She knew very well that Baba's refusal of her embrace was not out of malice or any other evil intention, but he was just being respectful to her from a Shona cultural perspective. Baba then stretched out his hand to greet Maria, a favor which she returned with a smile. Even though Mother and I witnessed the drama, we said nothing. Mother just smiled. I think she had anticipated the drama. Maybe the reaction had been rehearsed during their layover in London.

Maria had already finished cooking. Food was served, and it was delicious, of course, according to my own standards. Maria had prepared rice, chicken, and dried *nyavhe* vegetable with peanut butter. For my readers who are not privy to Zimbabwe's traditional dishes, *nyevhe* is one of the Zimbabwean indigenous vegetables that have survived the test of time. It grows naturally, and is a favorite for many indigenous Zimbabweans.

I think that my parents enjoyed the food. Even if they had not enjoyed it, they would not admit it because complaining about food does not show *hunhu*. As per the dictates of the Shona culture, my father clapped his hands several times after eating. Clapping hands is a gesture of gratitude. Mother also clapped her hands, and said a few words about how delicious the food was. Whether she meant it or not, it was difficult to tell, but Maria was glad to receive such favorable comments concerning her food.

After supper, we talked a little, and then I showed my parents where their bedroom was, and they seemed a little bit embarrassed about it. However, I think that both were relieved that their bedroom had its own bathroom and a television set, which gave them some privacy. Baba tried to argue that it was still too early to go to bed, but I knew that he did not mean it. They were jetlagged, and they needed to rest. In fact, Baba was already dozing off on the sofa on which he was sitting. When he insisted that he was not yet ready for bed, Mother convinced him to accompany her to bed. She won. We all knew she would win because he looked exhausted.

The following morning was Saturday. Both Maria and I were off-duty, and there was no hurry to wake up early in the morning. By the time we woke up, around 9 :00 am, both Baba and Mother were already watching the television in the sitting room. They had a television set in their bedroom, but they felt it more sensible to watch the one in the sitting room. There was nothing wrong about it except that they might have expected us to wake up and join them. Baba seemed extremely captivated and amused by the news on the BBC news channel. Mother looked like she did not like the news because she kept browsing her phone. In fact, she looked agitated. I could not tell whether she was annoyed by the news or something else.

"Is this the time, *muroora* wakes up to cook breakfast for Baba?" Mother wanted to know.

"Is it too early?" I answered sarcastically.

"A woman should wake up early in the morning before sunrise. That's what we do at home. A woman should clean the house and plates before anybody else wakes up. That's what we were taught by our mothers."

"It's America, Mhayi. This is not Zimbabwe. Maria works as a nurse. She works long hours, and she needs to rest like all of us. And we have no kids in the house. So, we don't need to wake up early. Usually, we wake up late during weekends. In fact, we have wakened up too early today because you are here. Normally, during the weekend, we wake up when we are hungry. We can sleep all day long if we want. Nothing to fear. It's America," I told Mother.

Baba remained silent, pretending to be concentrating on the news. Maybe he was.

Maria came out from the bedroom, and greeted my parents. She then went straight to the kitchen where she started preparing breakfast.

"Mother, I will show you where we keep kitchen utensils so that tomorrow, you don't have to wait for me to make breakfast. This kitchen is yours. Please, don't starve. Feel free to cook anything that is available in the refrigerator or pantry. If you need something that is not in the fridge, please, don't hesitate to let us know. We will get it for you," said Maria.

"Thank you." That is what Mother only said. There was no enthusiasm in her voice.

"I will also teach Baba how to make coffee and bread toast," Maria said.

"I can't do that, my daughter," Baba responded without looking at Maria.

"You can, Baba. It's easy," Maria insisted.

"No, he can't do that." It was Mother.

"He can. Can't you do it, Baba?" Maria insisted.

"Baba, as a man, has no business in the kitchen. It is a sacred place for us, women, not men," Mother explained.

"What if he wants some quick coffee while you are not around? Say, you are taking a shower. Can't he fix himself a quick cup of coffee?" Maria asked.

"No, my daughter. Baba must wait for me to prepare it for him. It's not appropriate for men to cook when women are present. In fact, it's an insult to the women of the house."

"But Peter cooks. He is a very good cook."

"He cooks for you, but not for us. If he cooks for us, we will not eat the food." It was Mother.

Maria laughed, and went on with her cooking.

Baba moved closer to Mother, and whispered into her ears. "Mai Peter, tell him about his wife's dressing."

"Why the rush, Baba Peter? Why don't you just tell him yourself?"

"The sooner, the better, Mai Peter. Don't you see that it's inappropriate?"

"Peter, your father is talking about your wife's dressing. Don't you think that it is not the proper way to dress when we are here?"

"What's wrong with her dressing, Mother?"

"My son, I mean those tight pants, and the revealing blouse. A man's wife doesn't dress like that when visitors are present. That is embarrassing, my son. Your father is not used to that. She is our daughter-in-law, and she should dress in a dignified manner."

Mother pleaded with me. Baba looked aside, pretending not to be part of the conversation.

"That's her culture. That is how white women dress in America. Didn't you see them on the plane and at the airport?" I asked.

"We saw them, but this is different. They were not related to us, but Maria is our daughter-in-law, and she should follow our culture, particularly during our stay here. Those pants are not appropriate, my son. It's not proper for a daughter-in-law to have her back or breasts revealing like that. How can I look at her? It lacks *hunhu,* my son." Mother complained.

I looked at Maria and said nothing, but she realized that we were talking about her. Mother stood up and walked into their bedroom. She came out with a colorful piece of cloth called zambia in her hand. A zambia cloth is used by Zimbabwean women to wrap over their dresses or skirts to show their good manners. Normally, all daughters-in-law are supposed to use zambias when at home, in the presence of respectable people. Mother went straight to Maria who was busy preparing breakfast and whispered into her ear.

"Daughter-in-law, here is the zambia that we brought for you from Zimbabwe. You should use it to wrap around your waist when Baba and I are here. When you come to Zimbabwe, you should use it all the time. In our culture, you can't dress like that when you have respectable visitors like us. We are your *vanyarikani.* Both your pants and blouse are too tight. Only your husband should see your body curves. I hope I am not offending you, my daughter. This is your house, and you should dress the way you like, when we are gone. But while we are here, you must make some compromises for us, just like we do for you. It's a give and take, my daughter. Try it, my daughter. Please, put it on before you give Baba a heart attack." We all laughed.

Mother handed Maria the cloth, and she smiled, and accepted it. Mother looked appeased.

"Thank you, Mrs. Masika. Can you teach me how to wear it?"

"Oh, no, my daughter-in-law. You don't call me, 'Mrs.' I am your mother. You call me Mother, just like Peter does," She corrected her. "When you receive a gift or serve some food to me or Baba, or even your husband, you should kneel like this." Mother knelt to demonstrate what she was talking about. "Before you receive any gift or food, you kneel down, and clap your hands like this." She demonstrated how to do it.

"Why?"

"That's our culture."

Maria looked at her in utter amazement. She tried to imitate what mother had taught her. Mother smiled as a sign of satisfaction.

"That's good, daughter-in-law. You are a fast learner."

Mother helped Maria wrap herself, from waist to legs with the zambia. She then whispered into Maria's ears again. Maria disappeared into the bedroom, and came back wearing a t-shirt instead of her revealing blouse. I could tell that Baba's old-fashioned soul was appeased. He looked at Maria and nodded his head to show his satisfaction.

I did not say anything.

"I will teach her about our culture. She will be alright. She is a good learner." It was Mother.

"Teaching her Shona culture is okay, but don't try to make her a Shona woman because she is not. She, too, has her own cultural values, which you should respect. This is her house. She does whatever she wants. You can teach her the rest of the Shona culture when she comes to Zimbabwe. Not here." I intervened. I was a little bit irritated.

Father jumped into the conversation without warning.

"No. No. No, my son. Good manners are good manners. It doesn't matter whether they are Shona or American. She is your wife, and she should dress in a dignified manner. I should not see her breasts. I should not look at her ill-dressed bottom. She is my daughter. She should learn to dress appropriately. Even our ancestors want *varoora* to dress properly."

"Please, leave your ancestors out of this," I said.

"Why? If she is to become our daughter-in-law, she must be acceptable to the ancestors as well. Every wife belongs to the whole family, and ancestors are the invisible members of every family. In fact, every wife comes from the ancestors. Maria should prove that she has been given to us by the ancestors. As of now, we don't know. It starts with small things like the way she dresses, and greets elders."

"So, she is being evaluated?" I asked.

"I didn't say that. Please, don't put words into my mouth. She is under no examination."

"So, leave her alone."

Breakfast was ready. Maria invited all of us to come over to the dining table. Baba flatly refused to come over to the table where breakfast had been served.

"Baba, we are waiting for you," I invited him.

"I don't eat at the same table with my daughter-in-law. It doesn't show *hunhu,* my son. Let her bring my breakfast here, where I am sitting."

I took his breakfast and placed it on the coffee table. He was appeased.

"Why is Baba not joining us here?" Maria asked.

"Your Baba is shy, my daughter,*"* Mother responded. "In our Shona culture, a daughter-in-law and father-in-law don't eat at the same table. It's out of the respect they have for each other."

"I don't bite, Baba. Please, come and join us," Maria joked with him.

"Come and sit with your daughter-in-law, Baba," I said.

"It's not about biting, Maria. It's about good behavior, my daughter. It's about *hunhu.*" Mother corrected her. "Let him be. Let him enjoy his food. Tomorrow I will join him too."

"What's *hunhu,* Mother?" Maria asked.

"There is no clear-cut definition of *hunhu,* my daughter. It is the acceptable behavior, which includes, good manners, upright morality, gratitude, generosity, patience, humility, and all other virtues."

"Thank you."

We had breakfast. We survived each other that day, then the next, and the next. On the third day of my parents' arrival, we were invited for dinner by Maria's parents. I had been expecting it. We all looked forward to it except Baba, who seemed anxious about the invitation. He had too many questions about how he was expected to behave. He feared making mistakes. He also feared that he would be judged.

"Are they expecting us?" Baba asked.

"Yes, Baba. They invited us," I assured him.

"What should I wear? A suit?"

"No, Baba. Just casual clothes."

"Will we be sitting in our own room?"

"No, Baba, we will sit together. Maria will show you where to sit?"

"How about the food? Are we going to eat together?"

"Yes."

"I don't think it is proper for us to sit at the same table with our in-laws. It is tabooed in our culture. We should have our own sitting room, where we can be free."

"I understand, Baba, but they have a different culture. We sit in the same dining room, and eat at the same table. It's a sign of equality and acceptance."

"What kind of food will be provided?"

"Don't worry about that Baba, we will see when we arrive there."

I knew that he was worried about *sadza*. Without *sadza*, the dinner would be no dinner at all. We decided to take some food, including *sadza,* with us. That way, Baba's demons would be consoled. When Maria told him that Mother was cooking *sadza* to take to the Webers, Baba pretended not to like the idea, but we all knew that he was rejoicing deep within himself.

When we arrived, the Webers came out to welcome us. Like we had anticipated, we all hugged except Baba who extended his hand for a handshake. It seemed nobody took offence at that. However, I noticed that Baba was scandalized when my mother-in-law hugged me. He took a deep breath, and looked at me with wide open eyes. I just ignored him.

Maria and I did the introductions. Food and drinks were served. Maria introduced *sadza* to her family, which they tried without making a single comment. I guessed that it was not their first time to try it. Baba was gracious enough to try other foods that were served. Another surprise was that he used fork and knife, even when eating his *sadza*. I think that it was his first time to use fork and knife for eating *sadza*. Maybe not. During dinner, there was no talk of substance. Mr. Weber asked questions about Africa, and showed great interest in visiting Zimbabwe in the future. Baba and Mother told him that he and his family would be most welcome to their home in Zimbabwe.

After the meal, we had to talk about the wedding, a topic, which everyone had avoided until then. It was during this talk that Baba dropped a bombshell.

"Mr. Weber, are you happy about my son and your daughter's marriage?" Baba asked. The tone of his voice was sincere and concerned.

My mother-in-law, Andrea answered, "Absolutely. Peter and Maria love each other very much. We are very happy for them, and we are looking forward to their wedding."

"Why shouldn't we be happy?" Mr. Weber asked.

"We have heard stories about racial tensions here in the United States. We have heard that there is racism against blacks. We have heard that blacks are treated unfairly by the law enforcement agents. We have heard that white people don't like or trust blacks. There are so many disturbing stories out there. Our greatest fear is that our son would be excluded or mistrusted by your white friends. We don't want him to feel like is he is unwanted." It was Baba.

For a moment, everybody froze. Mother recovered sooner than anyone else.

"Baba Peter, we didn't come here to discuss that. Those are sensitive issues."

"It's ok. Let us talk about these issues," Mr. Weber responded. "This is the only time we might have. Yes, the issues make us uncomfortable, but we must talk about them."

"I don't think this is the right time. Let us not spoil the wedding," Maria's mother, Andrea, interjected.

"I think this is the right moment to talk about such issues. We cannot pretend that everything is okay. No, things are not okay. Let us talk about it." Mr. Weber was eager. "You are right David, in saying that there is racism in the United States. It's not a secret. Some white people don't like or trust blacks just like you have put it. But the resentment is mutual. There are also black people who don't like white people. They call it reverse racism." He paused. "Racism is a reality here, David, but the good thing is that, not every white person is a racist. And not every black person is a racist. As you can see, I am not a racist. My wife is not a racist. My children are not racists. That is why we support our daughter and your son's marriage. In fact, when I look at Peter, I don't see color. I don't see that he is black. I see a person created in the image of God." He was now preaching.

"Thank you, Mr. Weber, for accepting our son into your family. However, I should correct you a little bit. Maybe I am wrong. If I am wrong, I stand to be corrected. I understand that you like Peter very much. I am glad that you do and have allowed him to marry your daughter. I am also a Christian, and I believe that all people were created by God, in God's own image. However, I know that God gave us different colors. It's a fact that we cannot run away from. When I look at you, I see that you are white. There is no question about it. You are white, period. Mr. Weber, you should look at Peter again. Look at him. He is black. You cannot honestly say that you don't see his blackness. He is different. You cannot pretend that he is white because we both know that he is not. I think that our starting point should be to acknowledge and affirm that we are different. However, that difference does not make either of us better than the other."

Mr. Weber did not respond, but he was listening. He heard everything that Baba said.

Baba continued.

"When I look at your beautiful daughter, I think I like her. I respect that she chose my son. But I see that she is different. She is white, but I love her, all the same. I know that our culture will be hard for her to learn, but I know she will learn as much as she can. I know that some of our cultural practices will be very strange to her. I would like her to know that she can reject the cultural practices that are incompatible with hers, and observe what she can. I think we should start from the beginning, which is the reaffirmation of our different cultures and skin colors. Denying the existence of our differences doesn't make us better persons, but hypocrites, and we are not hypocrites. Let us accept that although Peter and Maria love each other, and that we support them, they are different. They are equal but different, not only in terms of their gender, but their race and culture."

There was silence.

"What do you want Mr. and Mrs. Weber to do?" Mother asked.

"To accept that we are different, and that Maria and Peter are equal but different."

"Thank you, David. Yes, Maria and Peter are different. Maria is white, and Peter is black, but I want everyone to be clear about one thing—we are not racist. We support this marriage. We respect the choice that our daughter has made because we love her. Yes, I should be honest with you. I don't want anyone to judge me." Andrea paused, crossed her legs, and looked at her husband as if asking for the assurance that she would be forgiven for what she was about to share.

She continued. "When Maria told us about her relationship with Peter, and we got to know that he was black, we were disappointed. I cried all day long. I tried to persuade her to find another boyfriend. She refused. She said, she loved Peter."

Mother interjected, "Why?"

"It's obvious, Tendai. They are different. There are many handsome white boys here in San Antonio, who Maria could fall for. Maria is beautiful, and she can easily find a white husband anywhere, any time. I was worried about my daughter's future happiness. I was not worried about money because I know that both Maria and Peter make incredibly good money. But I know that money cannot buy happiness. I was worried about my friends and neighbors. What would they say? That my daughter married a black man?" Andrea started crying. "I was worried about my grandchildren. I know that they would be segregated against because their father is black, and here in America, they would be considered black. Yes, I was concerned. You can judge me if you want. I have told you the truth. I hope you can handle it."

Her husband handed her some paper napkins, and started patting her on her shoulders.

"Then, I realized that I was wrong. I realized that it was Maria's life, not mine. It was her responsibility to choose a husband, not mine. I realized that black people are human beings too. I became aware that there are many black men who are more loving and caring than some white guys that I know. I realized that love is not about the color of one's skin, but one's heart. When I looked at Peter, I only saw his skin color, but I realized that Maria had seen his heart. That is what love does. It enables the beloved and lover to see each other's heart. I knew that it would take time for me to fully accept Peter as I would accept a white son-in-law. It surely did take some time, but I am now at peace with myself. I no longer care about what the neighbors say or will say. What I want is happiness for my daughter. And she is happy with Peter, and so be it. So be it."

Andrea, stood up, and walked to where I was sitting, and hugged me. It was a long motherly hug.

"I love you, Peter," She said.

"I love you, too," I responded.

"I mean it, Peter."

"I know you do."

Maria came over to join us in that embrace of love and acceptance. Then Mother, Mr. Weber, and Roland, Maria's bother, also came to join us. Baba did not. I knew he would not.

I was so touched by what Andrea had shared. I had not anticipated the confession. I knew that she did not like me in the beginning, but I felt that it was normal. Many mothers, if put in the same situation, would have felt the same.

She was right that she had changed her attitude toward me. I had noticed it, but I had never discussed it with anyone.

Now, hearing Andrea speaking about her initial prejudices and biases completely overwhelmed me. I cried. It started inside, for I tried not to shed a tear in the presence of Baba. Shona men should not cry, for it is considered a sign of weakness, but I still cried. I mean that I shed some tears. He saw me. Yes, Baba saw me, and then looked aside, pretending that he had not seen me. I did not care. I knew that he would talk about it later, or even use it against me as a sign of my weakness, but I did not care. All I wanted was to live in the present, and to know that I had been accepted by Maria's family, and that there was no hypocrisy in the Webers' attitude towards me.

We disentangled from the therapeutic embrace, and moved back to our chairs. I felt healed. I felt whole and alive. Perhaps, everyone felt the same.

Our meal had been disrupted for good reasons.

"Thank you." Baba still had the energy to talk.

"You are welcome," Andrea responded.

"We must confess, we also felt the same when Peter told us about Maria." It was Baba.

"Please, speak for yourself. I did not feel the same. I loved her right from the beginning," said Mother.

Mr. Weber asked, "How do you feel about it now, David?"

"I grew up during apartheid in Zimbabwe. Our white colonial masters made it abundantly clear that, we as blacks, were inferior to them in everything. It was impressed upon our consciences that we were unintelligent, ugly, lazy, and everything bad. When I was growing up, there were suburbs where a black person could not go without a pass. Blacks were not allowed to walk along certain streets in Harare, the capital city of the then Rhodesia. Blacks were not allowed to drink European beer unless they were licensed to do so. Interracial marriages were not allowed. In fact, it was a criminal offense for a black man to look suggestively at a white woman. Whatever the adjective, "suggestively" meant, only the whites knew."

"Are you talking about South Africa? We never heard about apartheid in Zimbabwe," Mr. Weber interjected.

"Oh yes, Zimbabwe. It was called Rhodesia at that time. Harare was still Salisbury."

"I am learning," said Mr. Weber.

"Now, you see where I am coming from? I could not imagine, Peter marrying a white woman. I had many questions. I was worried that one day she would wake up and report that she had been raped by a black man. Or that he would be considered an inferior by you. You may try to stand in my shoes, if you want to understand what I am saying. You don't want to make sacrifices, and send your son to study in America, for him to end up in jail because of falling in love with the wrong person. You want your son to be loved. Of course, not by everyone. You want him to be treated with dignity and respect as a human being." He paused. "I was worried, but now I have seen you, and listened to what you said. I am relieved. I now know that although it is difficult for you to accept him as you would a white son-in-law, at least, you will try to love him like a human being. That is fair enough. I shouldn't ask for anything more."

Baba was sad. I felt that it was good for him to empty what was in his chest. This was the moment of truth.

"Mother, would you like to say something?" I invited her.

"No. I am good."

Eventually, the topic shifted to cultural differences. This gave Baba an opportunity to offer bridewealth to Mr. Weber, who surprisingly, seemed not annoyed by the idea. Instead, he laughed. Andrea also joined him in the laughter, which became contagious. We all joined them in laughter except Baba.

"We have agreed that we come from different cultures, each with its own cultural imperatives and perspectives. We respect and celebrate our differences. For us, a marriage can only be a marriage after bridewealth has been negotiated and is partially paid. You should accept a little bit of bridewealth to make our ancestors happy. We will not give you the price of a person because she is not up for sale. It will be just a token of our appreciation for giving my family a provider, caregiver, and mother. A token with which to notify your and our ancestors about the marriage so that our children can receive the necessary blessings from our invisible family members."

"Just a point of correction, Mr. Masika. We don't worship ancestors here," Mr. Weber interjected.

"You do have ancestors, Mr. Weber. Yes, I agree that "worship" is not an appropriate word in reference to our relationship to ancestors. As a matter of fact, Africans don't worship ancestors."

"What do they call it?" Mr. Weber asked.

"We venerate or honor them," Baba replied.

"I still don't think that we, white people, have ancestors." It was Mr. Weber.

"You have ancestors, and you also honor them, just like Africans do. We only honor them differently."

"We don't honor ancestors, Mr. Masika." It was Andrea.

"You do," Baba insisted. "A couple of days ago, we passed by Sam Houston cemetery. There were white people there, gathered at different graves. Some were sitting by the graves. Others were standing around a grave. Some were placing flowers on some graves. I asked myself, why they were doing that if they didn't believe that their deceased family members could hear them, see them, and even appreciate the gifts of flowers, which they were offering. You see what I mean?" Baba paused.

"Certainly, you would not waste your money on flowers if you didn't think that the deceased would appreciate them. You wouldn't waste your time going to the cemetery if you didn't believe that the departed were still conscious. You wouldn't talk to the graves, if you didn't believe that the dead could hear you. You go to the cemetery because you believe that the departed family members still have some form of life and relationship with you. We Africans also believe the same. We both believe in ancestors, but honor them differently. We give them beer and tobacco, and you give them flowers and prayers.

Both are sacrifices that we offer our ancestors." Baba looked at Mr. Weber to observe the effect of his argument.

The logic was amazing. I had never thought about it in that way. I think that Baba got himself disciples that day.

"I think you have a point there, David." It was Andrea.

"Thank you for seeing my logic."

"Okay. What do you offer as bride price, David?" Andrea asked.

"That's wrong terminology, if I may correct you. It's bridewealth, not bride price," Mother corrected.

"What's the difference?"

"Bride price has the connotation of buying and selling. The moment you talk of price, you are likely to misrepresent the phenomenon of bridewealth. No price tag can be placed on a human being. Women are priceless, and are not up for sale."

"I see. What do you offer, David?"

"Five head of cattle," Baba responded.

"No. That's too much. We are not selling a commodity. We read a few books concerning the centrality of bridewealth in most African cultures. One of them was *Shona Women in Zimbabwe—A Purchased People?,* written by John Chitakure. I can't remember the title of the other one. We will accept just a beast for bridewealth," said Mr. Weber.

"The other book is by the same author. Its title is *African Traditional Religion Encounters Christianity.* I do have both books at our home," Maria intervened.

"We will accept a beast as a compromise; a sign that our reluctance to accept bridewealth is not out of malice or disrespect for your culture. We will accept it as a symbol of our willingness to accompany our children on their intercultural journey. I know that there are many things from your culture that you must forego temporarily because of this marriage. You have already started. Look at David; he used a fork and knife instead of his hands for his *sadza* today. It's a big compromise. Get me right, I am not saying that there is anything wrong with eating with one's own fingers. Or that fork and knife are better than one's own fingers. At least, one's own fingers have never been into another person's mouth." We laughed. "David has shown us how to live interculturally. We, too, need to make compromises. So, give us a beast, and our ancestors and yours will be appeased."

"We will give you two. One for you and the other for Mrs. Weber. Mrs. Weber's beast is called the beast of motherhood. Its purpose is to notify the maternal ancestors that their grandchild is married, and that they should intercede for her new family."

"That is very symbolic. We will accept two," said Mr. Weber.

"How do we get them to you? Can we use Western Union?"

Everyone laughed.

"You don't need to bring them over to the United States. Please, keep them in Zimbabwe on our behalf. If they bear calves, we would distribute them among our future grandchildren. When we finally visit Zimbabwe, God willing, you may slaughter one for us and our ancestors." There was a pause. "Do we need to sign any papers?" Mr. Weber asked.

"No. Your word and ours are as good as a written contract," Baba responded.

"What if you renege on your agreement? What would we show as evidence for this agreement?" Andrea asked, jokingly.

"Nobody reneges on what is agreed in bridewealth negotiations. It is a sacred agreement that is scribbled on negotiators' hearts, and that no one tries to change. Our ancestors are our witnesses." It was Mother.

So, the bridewealth contract was sealed. Baba was excited. I was glad that things had reached this stage without causing us much stress. I knew that Baba had not expected this level of understanding from the Webers. Yes, the deal was sealed. Bridewealth of two beasts for a wife from the ancestors was a fair deal. We all knew that it was a huge compromise on the part of the Webers. It was a good sign that came as a surprise to me.

A toast to the wife from the ancestors was proposed by Mr. Weber. Everybody complied. Baba crowned it all by standing up and offering a hug to Mr. Weber, and before we could realize what was happening, everyone was hugging everyone else. It was a win-win situation.

It was a great day. Baba, who had refused to sip any alcoholic beverages accepted a glass of wine on one condition—that he would pour a little wine on the ground as a share for the invisible members of the two families—the ancestors. I accompanied him outside, where he poured a little wine into the flower bed without saying a word.

That day, we left the Webers' place around eight o'clock at night. When we arrived at my house, we gathered in the sitting room for a little while, and then retired to bed. It had been a good day, indeed.

4

The Winds of Destruction

The winds of destruction arose and mercilessly descended upon us, as they sometimes did during those years, and perhaps, still do presently. It was only four days before the wedding when we had a visit from hell. Apart from the usual nuts and bolts issues that sometimes bedevil wedding planning, most things had so far gone according to plan. Everything had been prepared and planned to minute details. Of course, I do not take the credit for this meticulous planning for the wedding, for I was almost a spectator. All the credit should go to Andrea, my insightful mother-in-law, who had tirelessly toiled to smoothen the logistics of the wedding.

Mr. Weber had done his stint too, though he did not brag about it as much as Andrea did. He was that kind of a man who found gratification in praising and thanking others for his own achievements. I thought that it was out of his humility and generosity. It takes humility and generosity to thank others for the little that one would have benefitted from them. But Maria interpreted her father's virtues, differently. She believed that it was a result of her father's lack of self-esteem and confidence that compelled him to credit others for his own achievements. I am not saying that Maria was wrong. I guess, she knew him better than I did, since he was her father.

Maria's brother, Roland, who until now had not betrayed his feelings about our intercultural marriage, assisted his mother in his own small ways. He had just graduated from the same college as I, where he had majored in accounting. At that time, he was discerning whether to pursue further studies at a college in Chicago or to join the marines. His mother was for the former option, while his father resolutely supported the latter. His mother's main argument against Roland joining the marines was that he was not physically strong enough to withstand the rigorous training demanded from those who enlist as marines. She vehemently believed that even if he were to withstand the rigorous marine training, he was unlikely to make it in the battle front, for he lacked the ability to pay attention to minute details. As a mother, she did not want to worry about whether her son would come back home from overseas deployment in one piece or not.

Mr. Weber begged to differ. For him, Roland was strong enough to undergo any military training just like any other young person of his age. He had the necessary stamina to perform any military duty. To add icing on the cake, he argued that Roland was unfalteringly patriotic, which was one of the necessary virtues for those who dedicated their lives to defending their country's territorial integrity, international interests, and national sovereignty. As if that was not good enough, Roland was determinedly resilient. In the ensuing conversations to decide the path he would take, Roland never said anything, as if he had surrendered the determination of his ambitions to his mother and father. I guess, he did not want to appear as if siding with one parent at the expense of the other, which I thought was very smart of him.

Even though my input in this debate was not solicited for, to a certain extent, I sided with Andrea, for Roland was this tallish and thinnish guy, who looked almost fragile. He had a gentle and kind smile, which always ended as a grin. He talked a little, and rarely laughed, which I thought were great attributes of a military man. He was very intelligent, which is another attribute of a good soldier. Generally, he was a fine young man, who could, with the right kind of effort, be whatever he wanted in life.

Whenever Maria and I visited the Webers, Roland would greet us friendly, and then disappear into his bedroom until we left. Occasionally, he would come out of his bedroom at the end of our visit to bid us farewell. I interpreted that as a gesture of goodwill. Basically, he was a likeable young man. Maria loved her brother very much, and invited him to our home on numerous occasions, to no avail. Of course, he turned down the invites kindly. Maria was concerned about it, but I saw nothing wrong with that. In my Shona culture, a man does not visit his married sister's new home until bridewealth negotiations have been concluded, and some of it paid. He was doing the right thing. I mean if he were Shona.

Maria and I had just completed our prenuptial preparations conducted by the deacon of Maria's parish, Saint Teresa, situated along Highway 87 South, just before the small town of China Grove. Both Maria and I did not care much about getting married in church, not because we were bad Catholics, but because we did not quite understand and appreciate the efficacy of such a ritual. For us, a marriage was a marriage regardless of the rituals surrounding the signing of the marital contract. Even though both of us were baptized Catholics, like many other American Catholics, we barely practiced our faith. We went to church whenever we wanted, or during big obligatory days such as Ash Wednesday, Easter, and Christmas. I do not know why Maria found the church so boring because I never asked her. As for me, two issues had driven me away from the church—music and liturgy. I found the American church music extremely uninspiring, and the liturgy too cold for my comfort. Apart from not being regular church goers, we were not bad people at all. We were good people, but of course, not perfect.

Given a choice, I would have chosen to wed elsewhere, and not in the church. Why? Because wedding in the church involved a prolonged and complicated process. Maria and I had to take prenuptial classes for several weeks. Both of us did not want to do it. We did not have a convincing reason for subjecting ourselves to weeks of instructions on the Catholic Church's understanding of Holy Matrimony. We were busy. But Maria's parents insisted that we should be married in the Catholic Church as per their family's tradition. I found that insistence a little hypocritical, for they too were not practicing Catholics, but steadfastly supported and believed what the Catholic Church stood for. They also argued that apart from it being their family tradition to marry in the Catholic Church, it was also an honorable thing to do. Maria and I were reminded, on numerous occasions, to do the honorable thing. Maria was repeatedly told that every married female in her family had wedded in the Catholic Church, and she was not going to break that tradition.

"I don't care whether you are going to enjoy it or not, the tradition has to be followed," Maria's mother insisted.

"You can't force us to be religious, Mother," Maria responded.

"I am not forcing anyone to be religious or even to go to church. All I am asking you is to follow our family tradition. Only this time. We marry in the Catholic Church. That's what we do. Period."

"Even if we don't believe in Holy Matrimony?"

"That's beside the point. You don't need to believe in it, but I do. My faith is sufficient for you to get the blessings that should be derived from a church wedding," said Andrea.

"Who said we needed church blessings?"

"Your dad and I."

"And you expect me to just do what you want?"

"Absolutely."

"What if I say, no?"

"You won't say no."

"Suppose I say so?"

"You will do what I say. I am your mother."

"Do I need to be reminded of that?"

"I think so."

"Okay. We will wed in church. Are you happy?"

"Thank you, Maria. I am relieved."

Both Maria and I opened our mouths without uttering a word, in complete disbelief. I never knew that Andrea could be so pushy and unreasonable. She did not seem to care much about what we wanted. Her word was final. We both knew that any further arguing would be futile.

Begrudgingly, we attended the first session of our prenuptial instructions. After just a couple of classes with Deacon Savious, we were extremely glad that we had agreed to wed in the Catholic Church. Deacon Savious was the epitome of marital life wisdom. He knew every aspect of the Catholic faith, which he logically explained to us with much passion and zeal. His basket of knowledge was replete with examples and illustrations of what could possibly go wrong or right in a marriage. I guess he was speaking from experience. Maybe not. He also explained how we were supposed to effectively deal with tensions in a marriage when they arise.

"Tensions always arise," he forewarned us.

We did not dispute it. He was not revealing a secret to us.

Interestingly, he had a recipe for dealing with a nagging and interfering mother-in-law. I do not think he was referring to Andrea, for he did not know her. Maria and I looked at each other when he said that. I am not saying that my mother-in-law was bothersome, but I felt that a recipe of that kind would be handy in the future. I put it in the bag. Unfortunately, he did not have a recipe for dealing with a bad father-in-law. Perhaps, there were no bad fathers-in-law in America at that time. Certainly, in my country of origin, Zimbabwe, I had heard of the never-ending feud between daughters-in-law and mothers-in-law, but I had not heard of a similar rivalry between sons-in-law and fathers-in-law.

Deacon Savious also had an idea about the specific challenges that were likely to rock our intercultural marriage. I wondered how he could be so certain about some of the advice he gave us since he and his wife were both white. Of course, I did not ask him that question, for I did not want to spoil the relationship that was already beginning to blossom between him and us. After all, he was an educated man. The Catholic Church would not have entrusted him with the care of cynical people like us if he did not know what he was doing.

Deacon Savious did not only have a fair share of wisdom and practical examples, but he also had a kind and loving heart. He had empathy too. He could easily stand in another person's shoes, and try to experience how it felt to be in those shoes. I think that there is no student too incorrigible for a teacher who is wise, intelligent, loving, passionate, and empathetic. Sometimes, what is needed for a successful encounter between teacher and learner is not tons of reading material and homework, but a little love, a little respect, and a little empathy. Deacon Savious had all of them. As if that was not gracious enough, he had an infectious smile and a likeable attitude. Maria and I felt really connected with him. There was no doubt that he had become part of our future family.

Yes, all that happened in those few weeks of mandatory instruction. The man of God transformed our faith. On our last day of instructions, we whole-heartedly thanked him, and invited him and his wife for a dinner at the Texas de Brazil restaurant in downtown San Antonio. He accepted the invite. It was in the Texas de Brazil where we promised him that we were going back to the church. That does not mean that we had ever left the church, for we had not. We had just stopped attending church services as regular as we were supposed to do.

The deacon convinced us that the church loved and cared for us. We were glad that we allowed ourselves to be convinced. Sometimes, miracles happen in such mundane places, and it may be hard to accept them. Perhaps, the man of the cloth thought that we were under the influence of the tasty meats and amazing salads, incessantly served therein. But we truly meant it. I realized that sometimes people deviate from their religious practices because they have not met the right person to convince them to come back. We were lucky to have met the right person, who used his deeds and words to renew and transform our faith.

As the wedding day drew closer, we were a bit unnerved when we were told that the pastor of the parish, not Deacon Savious, would be the official witness of the church during our wedding. It is not that we did not like the pastor, but we did not quite know him. We had met him briefly in one of our rare attendances at the parish, but had never talked with him. Andrea said that he was a holy man, but we felt that the wedding could be more meaningful and inspiring if Deacon Savious had officiated. From my little understanding of the canon law, I knew that Deacon Savious could be authorized to be the official witness of the church if delegated by the archbishop via the pastor. We could have requested that favor from the pastor earlier, but we did not because Andrea stopped us from making such a request. She told us that it would put a wedge between the pastor and his deacon if we opted for the deacon. We all agreed with her. Maria and I strongly believed that a wedding was supposed to bring people together, not to divide them. So, we did not want to divide the pastor and the deacon. Later, we discovered that there was more to that than the fear of dividing the men of God. Andrea wanted the marriage to be contracted within the celebration of the Holy Mass, over which deacon Savious was not authorized to preside. Andrea also insisted that we were supposed to confess our sins before receiving the sacrament of Holy Matrimony, and Deacon Savious was not authorized to hear confessions. So, there were numerous impediments that prevented us from requesting the service of Deacon Savious.

When I shared our discussion with Deacon Savious, he said that we had done the right thing by opting for the pastor. I could tell that he was a man used to his position, as the pastor's assistant, faithfully and diligently doing the job assigned to him. Later, I was told that he did not receive any salary for all his services. They said that he was a volunteer. It shocked and inspired me at the same time. No one would have guessed that such a wise and knowledgeable man was offering his services free of charge. I realized that sometimes, money is not the only motivator in what people do. Later, we were told that the deacon could accept a small gift if offered. We offered him a generous gift, and he humbly accepted it. However, we were later told that he shared it with the pastor, who some people told us was on the parish's pay roster already. What a humble man! I mean Deacon Savious. I am not saying that the pastor was mean. I think he was just following the regulations of the church. As a matter of fact, he too deserved a generous gift for the part he played.

The wedding preparations were at an advanced stage. Some selected parishioners of Saint Teresa had been invited. Of course, we did not expect all the invited guests to attend the wedding for they barely knew us. Those that would attend would do that for the sake of Andrea. They knew her, not us.

The church hall had been booked. Food and drinks suppliers had been hired. The cameraman was ready. The pastor was ready. Most of the invited guests were ready.

As the wedding planning stress was about to ease, something that we had not anticipated happened. The winds of destruction arose as they sometimes do in life. This time, they had found a willing host in Mother JK, and a reluctantly curious disciple in Mother.

Mother JK, who until now had not visited my parents or invited them to her apartment in Corpus Christi, as was characteristic of her, came to our home. There was nothing special about her visit because it was not her first time to pay me a visit. The only difference between this visit and the previous ones was the presence of my parents at this visit. As I had expected, she brought an assortment of raw Zimbabwean food. There was nothing surprising about that too. She also had done her homework about my parents' cultural identity. She greeted them using their totems. She was smart. Among the Shona of Zimbabwe, greeting someone using his or her totem or sub-totem is the greatest sign of honor. The greeting is not only intended for the visible recipient, but also the invisible members of the family—the ancestors. Such a greeting warms the heart of the one being greeted.

Ordinarily, Mother JK knelt on the carpet like a good-mannered Shona woman, as she greeted my parents. When I was growing up, it was the norm for Shona women to kneel and clap their hands when serving food or greeting seniors. The kneeling cultural practice is almost gone now. For people of my parents' generation, kneeling and clapping hands when greeting elders are some of the indispensable characteristics of acceptable behavior or *hunhu*.

"How are you, Shumba, Sigauke?" She said that while kneeling and clapping her hands rhythmically.

"We are very well, and how are you, Mother?" Baba responded, while clapping his hands.

"We are doing very well," responded Mother JK.

"How are you, VaMamoyo?" This was directed at Mother.

"We are very well, and how are you, Mother?" Mother dutifully returned her greetings.

"How were they in Zimbabwe, when you left?"

"Everyone was well. We have not heard anything bad yet. Baba talked with our son who is in Zimbabwe yesterday, and he said that they were doing very well," Mother responded.

"We thank God and our ancestors for that," replied Mother JK.

When the greetings were over, Mother and Mother JK started preparing lunch. Maria could not help them because she had gone to work. As the two were cooking the traditional concoctions that Mother JK had brought, I could tell that they had already connected very well. Mother JK was busy narrating her life story to my parents. She told them where she was born and educated, in Zimbabwe, and how she had come to America, and how she had already become a United States citizen. She told them about her generous heart, and how she took care of many Africans who came to San Antonio and Corpus Christi, regardless of their country of origin. She also narrated how she took care of her relatives and some orphans in her rural neighborhood, in Zimbabwe.

In addition to that, she told them of how white kids came to her apartment for food and other treats, which I thought was a very dangerous thing for an African person to do in America. She could be sued if any of those white kids got sick because of the food. One of the things she said about herself that almost made me laugh was about the rich men who were attracted to her when she was young. She said she rejected them because she wanted to pursue her education.

"My sister, I was gorgeous. You can still see it now. Men chased after me like I was gold," Mother JK said.

"I see it. You are still beautiful, my sister," Mother affirmed her claim.

Mother JK blushed a little bit like a teenage girl.

"What happened? You didn't get married?" Mother asked.

"That's a good question, my sister. I think that I was too beautiful that men feared asking for my hand in marriage. Moreover, I was too busy with my education, and planned to wed after attaining my doctorate. My doctoral studies took more time than I had anticipated. By the time I graduated, I was too old for marriage, if there is anything like that. I also think that I had become too complicated and too careful to get a steady and reasonable suitor."

"You have a doctorate, Mother JK?" Mother asked.

"Yes, I am Doctor Mother JK, but it does not get into my head. I am still humble. I relate with every person equally. Most of all, I respect my Shona culture, and try to observe it, wherever I go."

"You are a learned woman, my sister. Congratulations!" Mother was impressed.

Mother JK was right. She respected and observed the Shona culture, particularly food.

"My sister, our culture is very important. Our children should be encouraged to observe it. That's why I am a little bit sad about Peter's impending wedding to Maria. It breaks my heart." It was Mother JK.

Although I was eavesdropping from my own bedroom, I could tell that Mother was petrified. She paused for a moment before she responded.

"What makes you sad about my son's wedding?"

"There is something I want to tell you about the white American culture. Perhaps I should say, white American cultures, because white Americans are not a homogenous ethnicity. We have Italians, Germans, Greeks, Irish, English, Dutch, Polish, and many others. But for the sake of this conversation, I will generalize a little bit. White women don't care about being faithful in marriage. They may have extramarital affairs."

"Isn't that true about women from other cultures as well. Marital infidelity happens a lot in Zimbabwe these days," Mother responded.

"I know, but it's not as widespread as it is here. Here, it's almost the norm."

"I can't defend American women because I don't know them. You know them better than I do, my sister. If it is true, then it's very sad, indeed. I just wanted you to know that marital infidelity also happens in Zimbabwe," said Mother.

"For them, marriage is not a lifetime commitment," Mother JK added.

"What is it?"

"It's just temporary. They wed today, and tomorrow; they divorce. The divorce rate is very high, here."

"That's very sad. Marriage should be for life. Unfortunately, the divorce rate in Zimbabwe is rising too. The devil is everywhere."

"You can't compare the divorce in Zimbabwe to that in America. It's far much worse here, my sister."

"You may be right."

"Some of the white women don't like to have children. If Peter marries Maria, you will end up with a daughter-in-law who doesn't have children. No grandkids for you, my sister."

Mother asked, "Is it common, or it's just some of them who are like that?"

"The majority of them, my sister." Mother JK paused. "Please, don't tell Maria what we are discussing," Mother JK implored. "I don't want to be put to task for gossiping."

"I am not a kid. I won't tell anybody," Mother promised.

"Would you want a daughter-in-law who can't cook your traditional meals? A daughter-in-law who can't cook *sadza*? Who can't speak your language? Who can't fetch firewood, or water from the well? A daughter-in-law who has no totem?"

Mother remained silent.

Mother JK continued. "Zimbabwe is full of beautiful women, who are looking for husbands. Women who know and respect our culture. Women who value marriage and can do anything to beget children. Women who treat their husbands and in-laws with respect. Women who dress appropriately."

"I think you are right, my sister," Mother interjected.

"I am not saying that white women are bad. You know what I mean? There are many white women who are good." It was Mother JK.

"Thank you for letting me know. Some of us have never lived with white people. We don't know them the way you do. We just see them from afar."

"I know them through and through, my sister," Mother JK bragged.

"Tell me about racism? Is it true that some whites don't like blacks, and consider them inferior?"

"It's true, my sister. Here, in America, whites don't like blacks. They accuse them of being lazy, thieves, rapists, murderers, and so on. Everyone knows about it. That's why I can't understand the reason a beautiful white girl like Maria would want to marry a black man like Peter. I am not saying Peter is not a handsome and good man. He is very handsome and kind. Your son has a beautiful heart, my sister, but he is black. Being handsome doesn't change the race of a person. It doesn't change the color of one's skin. Does it?"

"I don't know," Mother responded.

"You should know. White women are unpredictable and vindictive. A white woman can just wake up one day and claim to have been raped by her husband? If the husband is black, the probability of him being accused of marital rape by his wife is even higher."

"Is that a fact?" Mother was mesmerized.

"It's for real."

"It's unbelievable. I have never heard of anything as absurd as that. How can a man rape his own wife? What does it mean to be one's wife? What is the meaning of saying, "I do" when contracting a marriage?"

"Yes, it happens here."

"How does the judge decide if the woman is saying the truth? We all know that a husband and wife sleep on the same bed, under the same blankets. How then can either of them wake up and report that he or she was raped by the other?" Mother was genuinely confused.

"For your own information, here in the United States, a husband and wife may not share the same bed or blankets or even bedroom."

"That's very strange. I think you are right about my son's marriage. When a man is married to a woman, he must feel loved, safe, cared for, and respected. How can a man feel loved if his own wife can wake up one day and report him for rape? How can a man feel respected when his own wife or her people, suspect and accuse him of laziness and thievery?" Mother was getting excited.

"You are right. They don't even trust blacks. They don't give them jobs and loans to buy houses. If they do, they raise the interest rates. Life is never easy for a black man in America." Mother JK added salt to the wound.

"But you said you have a house of your own, Mother JK?"

"Yes, I do, but it was not easy to find a bank to finance my mortgage."

"So, what do you want here in America? Why don't you come back to Zimbabwe, where there is no racism?" Mother asked.

"Coming back? Where? Zimbabwe? Are you serious, *vakoma*?"

"Yes, come back home if you are not happy here."

"No. We would rather die of dehumanization than coming back to Zimbabwe. What will we eat in Zimbabwe?"

"You are right. There are no jobs back home," Mother agreed.

"Do you know that when white people divorce, the woman gets almost everything?"

"What do you mean by everything?"

"I mean everything—children, houses, cars, and money."

"What about the husband?"

"The man will have to start life again from scratch."

"Don't they share some of their wealth like they do in Zimbabwe?"

"Yes, they do, but the courts always favor the woman."

"They also do the same in Zimbabwe?"

"Really?"

"Yes."

"Why?"

"Maybe because the courts know that women are sometimes taken advantage of by men."

"That's very interesting. But here, women take advantage of men, my sister."

"That's different. Zimbabwean men are sometimes very oppressive to women."

"Do you know that white women are selfish too? Maria may stop your son from assisting you financially, in any way. Americans are individualistic. They think about themselves, not about the extended family. If you were living here, you would need her permission to visit your own son. You don't just show up at the door like you do in Zimbabwe."

"Why not just show up? What's wrong with that?"

"It's wrong. They must know when you are arriving, as well as the time you would leave. They say it helps them to make plans about welcoming and caring for the visitors."

"Maybe it's their culture."

"It is. But do you think it's a good cultural practice?"

"I don't know. I don't want to judge them."

"We are alone, my sister. We can say whatever we want about them."

"That's enough *vasikana*. I am confused. I think that VaMasika was right." Mother was convinced. "What shall I do?"

"He was right about what?" Mother JK asked.

"He didn't quite want Peter to marry a white woman."

"You should have supported him. Even now, it's not too late. You can still stop the wedding, my sister. You can't just allow your first born to get into a trap in broad daylight." She paused. "Do you know that most white women don't breastfeed their babies?" Mother JK asked.

"No. What do they give them?"

"Cow milk, and sometimes, breast milk, which they buy from other women."

"What do you mean by breast milk from other women?"

"People can sell, buy or donate their breast milk through stores or agents. The mothers, who don't want to breastfeed their babies can buy it from them to feed their babies."

"As for cow milk, there is nothing wrong with it, but I can't wrap my mind around human breast milk. It's appalling. I can't do or even allow it. Yes, it is understandable in cases of the death of a mother who leaves an infant. I don't think it's morally right to force babies to drink another person's breast milk when the mother can naturally breast feed her baby. It makes me very upset."

"I agree with you, my sister. That baby can be your grandchild. How do you feel about it? Your grandchild drinking another woman's breast milk?"

"I would feel upset," Mother responded.

"That's not all, my sister. White women don't carry their babies on their backs like Africans do. They carry them in baskets, or push them in baby strollers. You can imagine in this cold wind, a baby being pushed in a stroller. In fact, we are lucky here because Texas is warmer. In some other American states, there is snow and wind, but the poor baby remains in the freezing stroller."

"What's wrong with carrying babies on the mother's back? Don't they have baby slings?"

"Maybe they don't know that it keeps the baby warm and comfortable. Perhaps, they don't care enough."

"Why doesn't somebody teach them? Why don't you educate them? You are the doctor."

"My sister, you can't teach Americans anything. They believe that they know everything. They see themselves as the smartest people in the whole world. They don't listen to anyone but themselves."

"This surprises me. That's not good for the babies. Babies should be kept warm at all the time."

"You are right, my sister. Does Maria have a dog?" Mother JK asked.

"No. I haven't seen one ever since we arrived. Why should a woman need a dog? Do American women hunt alongside their husbands?"

"The dogs are not for hunting. They are their pets. They play with them as if they were children. The dogs live in the house. They sit on the sofas. They ride with them in cars. They carry them on their laps. They sometimes kiss them."

"Please, don't lie to me. I may be a visitor here, but I don't think they kiss their dogs."

"They do, my sister."

"Please, don't tell me about that. I don't want to lose my appetite. Why do they do that?" Mother was scandalized.

"It's their culture. Some even sleep with their dogs on the same bed, under the same blankets."

"Really? Have you ever seen them doing those things?"

"Like sleeping in the same bed with their dogs?

"Yes."

"No. But I have seen them kissing their dogs on numerous occasions."

"And after that they kiss other human beings?"

"Absolutely."

"Please, stop. Don't tell me any more of those things. What can I do?"

"Stop the wedding, my sister. Your son is in serious trouble."

"How can I stop it? It's too late, girl. People would think that I am crazy. No one will listen to me."

"Talk to Peter and his father. I can also assist Peter to get a good wife from Zimbabwe. My young sister has a beautiful and well-behaved daughter, who has just finished high school. Let me show you her pictures." Mother JK went to the coffee table and grabbed her phone. She started showing Mother the pictures of her niece, and Mother seemed impressed, to the greatest excitement of Mother JK.

"Talk to your son about my nieces. Show him the pictures that I have sent to your WhatsApp account, and let me know what he thinks. I can arrange for my niece's air ticket to come over so that the two can meet. We cannot waste a handsome and intelligent man like Peter. He deserves the best, and the best is in Zimbabwe, not here. Some white women marry black men for money, and not for love."

"But it's also true about some Zimbabwean women. They marry for money, and not for love," Mother said.

"It's different, my sister. At least, they are both black."

"I don't see any differences."

"Yes, blacks for blacks, my sister, whatever the motive might be."

"Okay. I will show him the photos. I will let you know what he would have said tomorrow. I am very worried about what you have told me. As a mother, I wish my children to be happy in life."

"It's normal for mothers to want the happiness of their kids. If I were in your shoes, I would feel the same. No one bears a son for him to be disrespected or mistrusted. A man needs to be loved. Not just any kind of love, but proper love." Mother JK wiped her glasses. "I suspect that Maria wants to marry Peter for his money. Do you know how much your son earns?"

"I don't know. I never asked him."

"You should ask him, and let me know the next time I come over to see you."

"I don't think I can do that. It's his money, not mine."

"No problem. I will ask him myself."

"Thank you, for the conversation, Dr. Mother JK. I now understand why they awarded you a doctorate. It's time for lunch. Let's call Baba to come in."

Mother went outside into the backyard to call Baba who was drinking his beer while basking in the sun. I also came out of my bedroom pretending that I had not heard the appalling conversation between Mother and Mother JK. Mother JK attempted a smile at me, which I returned with a grin. She might have sensed that I had heard the malicious conversation between her and Mother. Of course, she was that type of a person who did not care about other people's feelings. In fact, her intention was for me to hear the conversation. Later, I discovered that Baba, had also heard the conversation because he was sitting on the porch, just by the dining room door.

Lunch was served, and it was delicious. Everyone commented on how good the food was, and Mother JK was thrilled. She bragged about her unprecedented cooking prowess and her impeccable traditional recipes. She also boasted about how Shona traditional food was good for health. At first, I did not see where her comments were leading, but I did, eventually. Even if I had sensed where her conversation was leading to, there was nothing I could have done to stop her. She was on a mission, and was unstoppable.

"Our Zimbabwean food is wholesome. Here, in the United States, their food is over-processed, and sometimes, genetically modified. That's why I bring all my food from Zimbabwe," she boasted.

"I think you are right," Baba responded. "Your food tastes so different and delicious from what we have been eating ever since we arrived here."

"You also need a good cook to prepare the food," Mother jumped in.

"I agree. Without a good cook even the best of food would be put to waste. That's why we should educate our children about our Shona marital ethics," said Mother JK.

"Peter, are you listening?" Mother asked.

"Why me, in particular? I thought this was a conversation for all of us at this table."

"You are the one who is getting married soon."

"I am not marrying a Shona woman, Mother."

"That makes what Mother JK is saying more pertinent to you. From what I have heard, I think that you shouldn't marry a white woman, my son."

"Why not?"

"White people don't like black people. They just pretend to like them, but they don't. Their culture is disturbing. They don't care about having children. They don't take care of their parents. They may accuse you of sexual assault . . . .." I jumped in before Mother finished talking.

"Who told you that?" I asked.

"Mother JK."

"I think that you are wrong, Mother JK. You know better not to stereotype people. America is full of white people. If they don't like kids, where do they come from? If you go to our schools and colleges, you will find lots of white kids there. Where do you think they come from? Heaven?"

"You are a kid, Peter. I have been living in America for over twenty years now. I know white people. I can read them like a book. They don't like blacks. Many of them don't like having babies."

"You should say, some of them. It is equally true of some black people. Some black people don't want to have kids. Some don't like white people. You can't go around saying that all black people don't like white people. It's a fallacy of generalization. As a holder of a PhD, you should know better."

"Peter. Peter. You don't talk like that to your elders. Mother JK is your mother, just like I am. You should respect her, the way you respect me." Mother was embarrassed.

"Thank you, Mother, for the reminder. But I respect elders who also respect young people. Respect should be reciprocal."

"You are angry, Peter. I want to help you. You can't marry that woman." Mother JK was enjoying this.

"She has a name," I responded.

"I don't care. She is white. I can find you a beautiful woman. My sister in Zimbabwe has three daughters. Very beautiful."

I laughed. And laughed again.

"Why are you laughing. I can give you their phone numbers. I also have their photos on my phone. You can choose the one that you love."

"Mother JK, you are too late. I am getting married very soon. To Maria. It's Maria or no one else. It's unstoppable."

"My son, why don't you listen to her for a moment?" It was Mother.

"Why should I listen to her?"

"I think she is right. Maria is not a wife from the ancestors. No white wife for a black man can be said to have come from the ancestors. We want a daughter-in-law, who can cook our own food. A daughter-in-law, who can sing our songs. A daughter-in-law, who can dance to our own music. A daughter-in-law, who cares for the extended family, not only herself. A daughter-in-law, who can laugh like us. A daughter-in-law, who can dress like us. A daughter-in-law, who practices our culture." It sounded like a rehearsed sermon.

"I am sorry, Mother. You will get that kind of a daughter-in-law from my brother, Ben. From me, you will have Maria—a white angel."

Baba, who had been quiet until then joined the conversation. "Ladies. Ladies. We have heard you. You started this conversation a long time ago when I was outside. That's not good at all." He paused. "Mother JK, thank you for the food. With all due respect, we can't have this conversation. Peter is marrying Maria. They love each other. There is no discussion about it."

"What? Didn't you hear what white people are capable of doing?" Mother shouted.

"I don't care," Baba responded.

"You want my son to go to jail? You want him to be accused of sexual assault? You want him to marry a woman who can't cook *sadza*?"

"I didn't say that. Don't put words into my mouth, Mai Peter."

"What did you say?"

"I said that I want my son to marry the woman who he loves. End of story."

"Sigauke, you should give guidance to Peter. I think you are misleading him." That was Mother JK.

"Who are you to tell me what to teach my son? You can't just walk into my son's house, cook your "good" food, and then try to persuade my son to divorce his girlfriend. That's a serious lack of good manners. I will not have it. If you are that kind of a person, then you are not welcome here. I don't want to see you at my son's wedding. *Voertsek*!"

"I am sorry *babamukuru* if I interfered in your son's affairs. I thought that I was helping. I will leave in a moment. I will not attend your wedding. I don't want to be part of it."

"I said, *voertsek*! You should learn your manners." Baba was angry.

"I won't attend the wedding," Mother JK repeated.

"Suit yourself, Madam. I can't just sit here and watch you abuse my son. Peter is old enough to choose a wife for himself. He can marry whoever he loves. He can marry a Chinese, Japanese, Indian, Irish, Mexican, Greek, or whoever he loves."

"If Mother JK is not attending the wedding, I will also not attend. I can't allow my son to be used by white people. They only want his money." Mother looked like she meant it.

"Who cares?" Baba responded.

"I am leaving." It was Mother JK.

"Mother JK, I am not chasing you away. You have every right to say what you want. However, issues of love should be left to those directly involved. I was also against Peter's marriage, initially, but I was enlightened. So, the wedding will go on. If you want to attend, it's up to Peter and his wife. It's not my decision to make. I will be a mere guest just like everyone else." Baba tried to appease Mother JK, but she was beyond appeasement.

Mother JK left unceremoniously. She was upset because she could not have her way. She looked like someone who was not accustomed to being defeated or humiliated. She just grabbed her purse and walked out. We all ran after her to see her pull out of the driveway. The speed with which she backed up her car showed that she was mad. I silently laughed. For me, it was good riddance. I had heard similar stories about her. One of the boys from Zimbabwe, who was married to a foreign woman had told me about how Mother JK had tried to influence him to divorce his wife. She also is said to have tried to influence the young man's parents about divorcing his wife. I was told that she almost convinced his father, but not his mother. Thanks to Baba, my impending marriage was saved. Of course, I was going to marry Maria even if my parents were against it.

In another case, Mother JK is said to have tried to persuade a Zimbabwean woman married to a Zambian man to divorce her husband because he did not make as much money as she did. She almost succeeded, until the husband got to know about the Zimbabwean man, who Mother JK wanted to replace him. Things are said to have gotten bad. What was surprising was that, in all these instances, she already had substitutes. All the substitutes were her relatives in Zimbabwe.

Although she claimed to be the custodian of the African culture, she seemed not to care about upholding the principles of the Zimbabwean culture. There is no *hunhu* in trying to cause divorce. In fact, the Shona people are against divorce unless it is inevitable. Whenever there is a dispute between a husband and wife, the first instinct of Shona elders is to save the marriage. Divorce comes as the last resort.

Mother JK was different. She encouraged divorce, and she seemed to be against foreigners married to Zimbabweans. She accused the whites of racism, yet she was a tribalist herself. It was surprising because I had always thought of Shona people as racially tolerant, but Mother JK had proved me wrong. It seemed that the only Shona traits, which she evidently espoused were the language and her insatiable appetite for Shona traditional foods. Of course, she was also a storyteller, who could tell a story that went forward and backward at the same time. I think that her ability to tell stories was the charm that she used to make people trust her, and even believe her.

Yes, that day she drove away angrily. She revved her car as if she were in a drag race. It was mission unaccomplished. I felt sad for her, but happy for myself. I guess she arrived in Corpus Christi in an hour, or got herself a fat traffic ticket for over speeding or 'driving while angry.'

When we got back into the house, Mother was hysterical, but Baba was up to the game.

"Mai Peter, you don't know that woman. You just met her today, and she convinced you about white people. She is a scam." Baba tried to reason with Mother.

"I don't care whether I met her today or ten years ago. She knew what she was talking about. You disrespected her. You insulted her. You embarrassed me in front of my guest."

"She deserved it, Mai Peter. She can't just walk in here, and give us an unsolicited lecture on white people's shortcomings, biases, and prejudices. There are good and bad women in every culture, and we all know that. She can't generalize about white women just like that, and expect everyone to believe her. If her doctorate is real, she should know how to talk about other people objectively."

"Are you saying she was lying?"

"I didn't say that. She might have been telling the truth, but she is biased. She has her own prejudices, and what she said should be taken with a pinch of salt. She is also guilty of the racism that she accuses others of practicing."

"She is also a con woman," I added. "She was marketing her own nieces as if they were pieces of merchandise."

"Very shameful, *maningi stereki*," Baba shouted.

"Mother, did you mean it when you said that if Mother JK doesn't attend the wedding, you also won't attend?" I wanted to know.

"You embarrassed me in the presence of my guest, my son."

"Mai Peter, you even don't know that woman. Just ignore her. Just imagine nothing happened. After all, you may never see her again."

"That's why you insulted her?"

"I didn't insult her. I corrected her."

"You insulted her."

"I didn't."

"You did."

"Suit yourself. Are you going to boycott the wedding? Boycotting your own son's wedding because of a woman you just met today?"

"She is not just a woman. She has a name."

"I know she has a bogus name. If you boycott the wedding, there will be dire consequences."

"What do you mean?" Mother looked surprised.

"We came here for the wedding. We both knew that Maria was white. Now, if you decide not to attend the wedding, then you must go back to Zimbabwe. Today or tomorrow."

"Are you trying to chase me away from my son's house? Who are you, to try to deport me from America? Who are you? The president of America?"

"I am David. I will tell Peter to change the return dates on your air ticket. If you are not attending the wedding, you can leave tomorrow."

"No. We go back home together. You and me. Why do you want to stay here? Do you also want to get a white woman? We came here together, and we will go back home together."

"Yes, provided you stop being swept away by the evil winds brought by that woman. If you will attend the wedding, yes, we will go back home together. If you are not attending, we will ask the United States home affairs department to deport you."

"Are you crazy? You want to have me deported?"

"Yes."

"Why?"

"We came here for a purpose. If you change it, then you should leave." Baba seemed serious.

"It's okay, Baba. Mother didn't mean it. I know she is upset, but she will be alright." I intervened. "I am sorry, Mother. You know that I love you very much. We can't allow Mother JK to alienate us. We need each other more than ever before."

Mother was silent.

"Did you hear what your son said?" Baba asked.

Mother nodded her head.

"So, why don't you say something?"

"What can a dunderhead like me say?"

"Who said you are a dunderhead, Mai Peter?"

"Both of you."

Father gave up.

By the evening of that day, we had forgotten about the visit from hell. Maria came back from work, and we all pretended to be okay. I never shared with her what Mother JK had said, and how she had tried to influence Mother against us. I did not share that not because I was not honest with Maria—no, but it was out of my love and respect for her. I wanted to protect her from the winds of destruction that Mother JK had invoked. In addition to that, she had not met Mother JK yet, and she did not know what sort of person she was. I did not want to upset her unnecessarily.

I was also concerned about my own mother, who had quickly become a disciple of Mother JK. How can you tell your fiancée that your own mother does not like her? It was not easy. Of course, I vowed to tell her after the wedding. Not now. Now was not the time for sad stories.

I did tell her after the wedding, but it did not bother her. Maybe it did. She never told me that it did. She never changed her attitude towards Mother.

5

The Wedding

The wedding took place on a Saturday, on December 10. We were lucky because it was not as cold as the local meteorologists had forecast. It is not that I dreaded the cold weather much, but because ever since their arrival, Baba had always complained about the cold weather in San Antonio. Initially, we advised him to stay in indoors, but he wanted to step outside occasionally, to enjoy some fresh air. He argued that the first human beings were created in a garden, not indoors, and for him, that signified their interconnectedness with nature, and their right to a creator-given freedom to breathe fresh air all the time. He said that staying inside the house all day long was like being in a prison. It was just his imagination because he had never been inside a prison, and did not know how it felt to be inside one.

He was right in saying that there was fresh air outside, but it was at times, very chilly. Ironically, Baba complained that his body did not like inhaling cold air. There are certain things in life, which cannot be selected without risking courting other undesired elements, which cannot be separated from the option made. If he wanted fresh air, he had to brave the chilly air outside because there was no way he could be outside, and not breathe the chilly air. Of course, he had come to America expecting snow, and was a little disappointed to learn that there was no snow in San Antonio. As a matter of fact, it occasionally snows in Texas. Since I started living in San Antonio, it had only snowed once.

Maria and I were ready for the wedding. Of course, I cannot speak for my mother-in-law, who sometimes seemed more anxious about the wedding than us. Every time we met her or talked on the phone, she always had a new suggestion about something extra that was needed. There was always another thing that we needed to learn or remember. Sometimes, she would call us early in the morning to share with us her ideas about the envisioned wedding decorations, and I felt that she was overdoing it. Perhaps, Maria felt the same, but she never complained about it. Many times, I reminded Andrea to relax a little bit, and she always took offense. She did not want to be told what to do because she knew what she was doing. She accused me of being too naive and a little unorganized. I was not offended by the remark, for I thought that she was right, to some extent. I was naive. My idea of a wedding was that of exchanging consents in the presence of witnesses, offering food and drinks to our guests, receiving gifts, and maybe, a honeymoon.

It was different for Andrea. She was anxious about many things, some of which were way beyond her own control. She was concerned about the size and quality of the wedding cake. For me, a cake was a cake, if it served its symbolic purpose. She was worried about the food caterers. Would they bring food and drinks on time? Would the food be sufficient and delicious? She was concerned about the DJ. Would his speakers be loud enough? Would he play the right kind of music? She was worried about the priest, who was going to officiate at our wedding. Would he be on time? Would his homily be up to scratch? She was worried about my parents, and other black guests. Would they behave and dress appropriately? Would my father give a good speech? Would he give it in English or Shona? She was worried about Maria. Would she be in sound health on the day of the wedding? What would she do if she had diarrhea or just wanted to visit the bathroom? Would she be careful enough to avoid tripping over her wedding gown?

The more frequently she talked about these possible mishaps, the more likely we believed they could happen to us. Whenever I noticed that I was becoming Andrea's unwilling disciple in pessimism, I reminded her that, in life, sometimes, we needed to take a leap of faith. There were so many things that could possibly go wrong, but we needed to be positive. We should pretend that things will be alright. It is true that we should be prepared for mishaps, but we should not allow such thoughts to incapacitate us. Andrea would listen to my sermon on optimism while pretending to agree with me all the way, and then, would go back to her pessimism. I gave up. I let her be, but after warning her not to drag us into her unhealthy negativity.

My father-in-law did not talk much about the wedding, but whenever he did, he assured us that everything would be alright. He hinted that mistakes were likely to be made at our wedding, as what happens at any other wedding function. For instance, some guests would run short of food and drinks. Some guests would complain about loud music. Some guests would criticize the wedding gown. Some guests would jeer and laugh at the groom. Some would demand gluten-free food, which may not be available. Some would complain that the wedding kiss was not passionate or decent enough. So many dissatisfactions, but the wedding goes on. The bride and groom should do the best they can, to meet the needs of their guests, while knowing that the day belongs to them, and not to the guests.

For Mr. Weber, there were a few things, which were important for a wedding to be successful. First, the wedding had to start on time. Second, the bride and groom should be able to recite the marriage vows and sign the marriage contract. Third, the groom should be able to kiss the bride, and to slide the wedding ring into the left ring finger of the bride. That was all. All other things were secondary, according to him. That was the kind of talk that I wanted to hear, not a litany of possible challenges that we could encounter, and the mistakes, which we were likely to make.

Mother, as we had expected, quietly rescinded her threat to boycott the wedding. I knew that she did not mean it, but you never take chances with Shona mothers. If you do, they may surprise you. She might have uttered the threat just to save face. I think it was a little embarrassing not to have her way. Or it could be that Baba's threats to send her back to Zimbabwe, prematurely, had affected a change of mind in her. I do not think that Baba intended or had the mental stamina to do it, or even to talk me into it, but he just wanted to whip her into shape. I felt that it was his method of pushing her into a tight corner. Also, it could be that Mother had, upon reflection, changed her mind like mature people do. Sometimes, one needs to change her mind. Most of the time, changing one's mind is a sign of maturity and the ability to learn from others and our experiences. The inability to change some of our decisions, dreams, and views may be a sign of our incorrigibility and insecurity. After all, Mother knew that we all loved her and respected her. In fact, she was a good mother, and no amount of disagreement could change that. She might have realized that her demand was ridiculous. Perhaps, she realized that she was out of bounds because Shona mothers do not choose wives for their sons. In addition to that, Mother was a victim of Mother JK's shenanigans and unwarranted racist attacks on the white people.

I never took offense with what Mother had tried to persuade me to do, for I knew that all she wished for was my happiness. I was still her baby, and she wanted to protect me from the friendless world out there. If I were in her position, I would have felt the same, and perhaps, acted in the same manner. To worsen the matter, she had never witnessed an intercultural marriage of this nature before. This experience was new to all of us. Mother JK had taken advantage of her ignorance of the American cultures to plant seeds of doubt in her. Mother was gullible, not because she was not an intelligent woman, but because of the history of Zimbabwe. Zimbabwe was a colony of Britain for almost a century. In all that time, the Rhodesian whites preached their superiority over the black race. They made it abundantly clear that everything about blacks was bad. They said that blacks' hair was kinky and ugly. They said that blacks were lazy and evil. They condemned African names as ungodly. They demonized African food and vegetables as unnourishing. Africans were seen as a people without a religion or philosophy.

Many Africans accepted this harmful and dehumanizing narrative, and indeed, internalized it. Many tried hard to run away from their African culture in order to assimilate into the European culture. They dressed like them, built houses like theirs, ate their food, drank their liquor, and spoke their language. Some women resented their kinky hair, and tried to tame or straighten it using chemicals and many other artificial means. Some extended their kinky hair using human and synthetic hair imported from abroad. Hence, self-hate was created for Africans. Yes, they started to hate themselves, and to wish that they were white.

However, some blacks refused to be mentally subjugated, and rejected some aspects of the colonial culture. They knew how imprisoning it was to live a life that was not theirs. They refused to use artificial hair or wigs, and then pretended that their hair was straight and soft. Some accepted certain Western cultural practices, and rejected those that violated their cultural identity and integrity. They refused to live another people's culture. They believed that there was nothing wrong with being black. I guess, Mother was in this category. I felt that, for her, marrying a white woman was a public rejection and betrayal of black women, and an attempt to become white. It was also a betrayal of our traditions and cultural practices. In other words, it was an admission that black women were inferior to white women.

I did not see it that way. My marriage to Maria was out of love, not racial superiority, or inferiority. I saw her, and fell head over heels in love with her. I asked her out, and she accepted. I told her that I loved her, and she said she also loved me. I proposed a marriage, and she accepted. For me, that is called love. I do not want to pretend that I did not notice that she was white. I do not want to lie that I did not observe that her culture was different from mine. I did, and I still do, but I was not attracted to her because of her skin color, but because she is a human being. She is a woman, full of love, compassion, kindness, caring, generosity, respect, forgiveness, and gratitude. What else can a man look for in a woman he wants to marry? I do not want to deceive anybody by saying that I did not see her beauty. I did, and I still do. Every day, I look at her face, and thank the creator for a job well accomplished. However, it was not her beauty that stole my heart, but her inner person. It was not her skin color or hair texture that attracted me, for that was secondary to me. I fell in love with Maria's heart, and all hearts have the same color. If one day, she were to wake up black, blind, disabled, wrinkled, or ugly, but still having the same heart, my love for her would not change.

The long-awaited day, as it always does, arrived. Surprisingly, Mother JK attended the wedding. Yes, she did. I had not seen it coming. I had not heard from her since the kerfuffle at my home. I had sent her a text message twice, apologizing, and she had not responded. Here, she was, dressed to kill. Throughout the ceremony, she seemed to be enjoying herself. Maybe she just pretended to enjoy. Whether she truly enjoyed the wedding or just pretended to be, it did not quite bother me. I was glad that she had managed to put her ego aside, and found it necessary to let bygones be bygones.

Our unpleasant exchange of words at my home, and Mother JK's unceremonious departure, made her attendance a pleasant surprise. In fact, I respected her for her ability to transcend personal differences. Very few people are capable of forgiving in such a short period of time. If I were in her position, I would not have managed to attend the wedding, and to dance and speak with other guests with such grace as she did. Of course, she did not come to the wedding alone. She brought some Zimbabweans who I had not met before our wedding day, and had not been invited to the wedding. She had broken one of the Western wedding protocols—you do not attend a wedding unless you are invited. There are reasons for that protocol, but as an African, I did not care about wedding protocols. Most of the uninvited guests were from Dallas, and I was glad to see them. I thanked Mother JK for inviting those good Dallas people. In fact, it taught me a big lesson about people; no one is completely bad.

The wedding started with the celebration of the Holy Mass in English, though most of the hymns were in Shona. To spice up the liturgy, most of the Dallas Catholic guests had thoughtfully brought their drums and jingles. It was a lively Mass, which half of our guests had never experienced before. There was dancing and ululating too. I had attended many Masses in San Antonio, but I had never felt what I felt on our wedding day. At those other Masses, I was just there for the sake of being there. The music was boring. The homilies were too abstract and spiritual that I had no use for them in real life. The parishioners were so unwelcoming that I always felt out of place in God's house. Most parishioners were more concerned with their families than newcomers. In fact, I realized that during the sign of peace, the families on my right-hand side would form a small circle to embrace each other. The family on my left-hand side would do the same. I always found myself deserted, standing in the middle of families, with no one to offer me or accept the sign of peace from poor me.

Sometimes, at the end of the *Agnus Dei* prayer, one or a couple of the people on the same pew with me would offer me a belated sign of peace. I always resented it because they did that as an afterthought, and I felt that I was getting some leftover signs of peace, which I felt was more out of sympathy than of grace. However, I did not judge the people who denied me the sign of peace because it was not their fault. If I were in their position, I would have done the same. Now, that I had a wife, I would make sure that I offered her the sign of peace first before I thought of any other parishioner. I should make it clear that I had stopped going to church not because of the deprivation of the sign of peace, or listening to uninspiring homilies, but because I was going through a period of spiritual aridity. It could be that I mistook my spiritual dryness for the dryness of the liturgy and homilies.

I felt that the wedding Mass was different. I could feel the echoes of the music, jingles, and drums deep down in my heart. Every word that was sung was meaningful to me. The celebration reminded me of the Catholic liturgy at home, where my friends and I used to sing and play ritual drums at St. Theresa's Guwa. In those days, we were young, energetic, and faithful. Our virgin faith had not yet been tested by real life experiences. It was a crude faith that inspired us to believe that everything was possible to those who believed. We accepted everything that we were taught by our catechist and parish priest, without a doubt. Now, my faith was different. Life had taken me to places where I encountered questions for which religion had no satisfactory answers. Also, I was scandalized to know that there were some hypocrites in the church, some of whom had caused the church so much pain and shame. I could not separate the sin of a single Christian from that of the Church until I met Deacon Savious, who enlightened me. He taught me that the holiness of the Church cannot be tainted by the transgressions of its members. Hence, the Church remains holy despite the sinfulness of some of its members.

Coming back to the wedding, as we had expected, there were two groups of guests—mine, and Maria's. Maria's group was large, and occupied the left-hand side of the church. Their sitting arrangement was different from that of the other group—my group. Each family sat closely together. Before Mass, everyone was whispering to the persons sitting next to him or her. Throughout the Holy Mass, some couples occasionally patted each other's back or even hugged each other, to the greatest scandalization of my parents. I imagined them wondering how some people could behave so "indecently" in God's house. For most Shona people, kissing and hugging belong to the bedroom, not in the house of God. Mother and Mother JK kept giving such couples disapproving glances, and would then make some facial signals to each other. Some of the white guests might have noticed it, but may not have understood the significance of such facial signals. Perhaps, they thought that the two women were admiring each other's looks, or were under the influence of the Holy Spirit.

My black guests occupied the right-hand side of the church. It was not that there was an usher telling people where to sit as they entered the church, but it just happened unconsciously. A guest would just enter the church, and if white, she would walk straight to the left, and if black, she would go to the right.

The group on the right comprised my friends from Zimbabwe who lived in San Antonio, and about twenty Zimbabweans that I had not met before. Most of these had come all the way from Dallas, courtesy of Mother JK. They had come to give me support on my wedding day. Of course, they were not officially invited to the wedding, but they were welcome since they were part of the Zimbabwean family. The credit for inviting them should go to Mother JK, as I have said above. Most of these Dallas Zimbabweans acted as if they knew me before the wedding. Just before we entered the church, they greeted and hugged us. They laughed and giggled, heartily. Some of them called me brother, nephew, or uncle. Others called me, "my son." Maria was everyone's daughter-in-law. They called her *maiguru,* or *muroora.* We were all like members of the same family. They were so friendly that even Maria quickly warmed up to them. Both of us stopped worrying about them being uninvited guests, and appreciated the joy that their presence had inspired.

These guests—my guests, on the right-hand side of the church sat on their pews differently. Men sat on their own pews, behind the women. The kids sat alone in front of the women. As soon as they entered the church, they never whispered to each other. Even the kids behaved like adults—no noise, no playing, and no running around. They reverently sat, when it was time to sit down, and stood up, when it was time to stand. No one touched or embraced others during the solemn proceedings. During the sign of peace, they reverently shook each other's hand, and there were no embracing and kissing. They knelt on the kneelers when it was time to kneel. It was the very opposite of the fidgeting and whispering that were happening across the aisle, to my parents' greatest annoyance.

It seemed Maria's guests were astounded by the lively Shona hymns, accompanied by the rhythmic drums, which were punctuated by some reverent dancing. That type of active participation during Mass seemed strange to the white guests. At first, they just gazed at the black guests' graceful dancing and singing. It looked like they were witnessing some kind of active participation from another planet. After a couple of hymns, some of them started imitating the dancers on the right-hand side of the church. Initially, most of those who joined the dance were out of sync, but soon they got the rhythm. I do not think that they had planned to join the dance, but it just happened. There was something inspiring and compelling about those voices and drums. They could not just ignore them, for they were irresistible. Later, my sweetheart, Maria, told me that she could feel the rhythm of the seductive drums and jingles vibrating inside her heart.

Sooner than we expected, most of the white guests gave heed to the promptings of the Holy Spirit, and started dancing with reckless abandon. At first, it felt like they were doing it out of their respect for my culture, but later, it seemed like it was out of a sincere need to express their faith and prayers through dance and music. For me, it was a humbling experience. I was so touched and inspired to see the whole congregation in graceful motion. The liturgical presider, who at first looked dumbfounded by the sudden turn of the worship, eventually joined in the dancing from the sanctuary. It was a beautiful moment.

After Mass, Andrea pulled me aside and complained openly.

"Peter, who are all these people?" She asked.

"I don't know them, Andrea."

"What do you mean?"

"Well. I mean that I don't know their names."

"Did you invite them?" Andrea sounded upset.

"They are Zimbabweans from Dallas. They are our friends."

"Why didn't you notify me about them? You can't just invite people without letting me know. I oversee the provision of food for the guests, and I should know the number of the invited guests to provide sufficient food for them."

"I am sorry, Andrea. I didn't invite them. They are Zimbabweans. They heard that there was a wedding, and they felt that they had to support me by attending. They mean no harm or disrespect to your culture. For them, it's their brother's wedding, which makes it theirs as well. They need no invitation to attend a brother's wedding. Be that as it may, I understand your concerns."

"Who is going to feed them? There isn't enough food for them." I knew that she was worried about the food.

"Mother don't worry about that. If there is any need to pay for extra food, Peter and I will foot the bill. As of now, let us celebrate. We can't be seen arguing about food when our guests are celebrating." It was Maria who intervened.

Andrea was not convinced, but barely appeased. Of course, I had forewarned Andrea about the possibility of having uninvited guests. Maybe she had not taken it seriously. In Shona culture, there is nothing wrong with being an uninvited guest at a wedding. A wedding is so important that there is no time to worry about uninvited guests. All are welcome, and they should share the little food that is available.

As I reflected on the Mass later, I thought that it was interesting that the two ethnical groups unconsciously sat on the opposite sides of the church as if the aisle were an overflowing river, or a security fence that could not be crossed. It appeared like there was an invisible force directing people from different ethnicities to sit on a particular side, in church. It seemed like the aisle was responsible for dividing the guests, but it did nothing, and should not be blamed for the separation of whites and blacks in that church. The aisle was just there to assist people to get to either side of the church, and not to tell them where to sit. The guests were responsible for where they sat themselves. They were separated by the color of their skins—whites, sat on the left-hand side, and blacks, on the right. At first, it was not only a physical separation, but also a cultural and spiritual one. The whites laughed and whispered before the beginning of the Mass. They embraced each other and even kissed. Most of them were casually dressed. On my people's side, no one whispered as soon as they entered the sacred space. They either sat quietly on their pews, or were on the kneelers, in complete adoration of the divine. Most were formally dressed. Even kids behaved well, and sat still in their rightful places.

Most of the songs were in Shona, which further divided the guests. The black group seemed to enjoy every bit of the sacred celebration, while the other side seemed like they were there to fulfill an obligation. It also looked like the blacks could stay in church all day long, and the whites looked like they could walk out any time. It looked like the white group was waiting for God to arrive, but for the blacks, God had already arrived. Thank God, by the end of the celebration, the liturgy had brought almost everyone together spiritually, but of course, not physically.

When I looked at the aisle that divided the guests, I thought of one of Africa's greatest literary works, *The River Between*, published in 1965 by Ngũgĩ wa Thiong'o. The only difference was that Ngugi used the analogy of a river, but here, it was an aisle. The separation was not only physical, but also mental, social, cultural, racial, and unfortunately, spiritual. Although both groups responded to the same prayers, they were like two different parishes that had been forced to worship under one roof.

Initially, as we stood closer to the sanctuary with our backs to the people, it was clear that in that church, only Maria and I had transcended the racial divide, and crossed the dividing aisle to meet each other in the middle. I wondered what would have happened if the guests had sat together instead of keeping their cultural sides. Whites and blacks sitting together in church could have been a wonderful sight. Not on different sides of the church, but sitting with each other on both sides.

I imagined God's reaction to our sitting plan. I thought of heaven, and our everlasting stay there. Would God create different compartments for each ethnicity? What language would the angels speak? What kind of food would we eat in heaven? Tacos? *Sadza*? Pizza? Hot dogs? Rice? Potatoes? *Egusi* soup? Perhaps these planned and unplanned encounters between people of different ethnicities were intended to teach them about heaven.

I imagined what was going on in my parents' minds as they sat in that church. I also imagined what was going on in the minds of Maria's parents. What did they think concerning the black guests? What did they think about me?

I was sad and thrilled at the same time that Maria and I had crossed the aisle. We had crossed the racial boundary line. Our wedding had united people. It had forced them to worship under one roof. Our wedding had compelled both groups to tolerate each other, at least for a couple of hours. We had done something that encouraged people to think about our cultural differences and similarities. We had caused them to encounter each other. In learning intercultural respect, an encounter is one of the most important initial stages. You must encounter the other in order to begin to think about him or her. Of course, you can decide afterwards that you do not like the other, but at least, you would have encountered him or her. The encounter can be through movies, books, documentaries, or personal, like what had happened during Mass. Unless one is willing to encounter the cultural other, listen to her, trust her, give her a job, invite her to one's own home, and to share one's culture with her, all talk about intercultural sensitivities or living is just cheap talk.

The priest might have been disturbed by the ethnical separation just like I was, as reflected by the short but powerful homily that he gave.

The homily was on the need for ethnical unity, reconciliation, and love. He referred to Maria and me as cultural heroes who had shown that love transcends all ugly racial divisions and stereotypes. He said that the world would be different and a better home to live in, if more and more people would do what we had done. To put icing on the cake, he compared our love to that of God, who loves everyone unconditionally. It was a beautiful homily, which ended as follows:

"In every culture, religion, or society, it is always a blessing when two young people decide to respond to God's call to Holy Matrimony, just like Maria and Peter have graciously done. There is nothing that symbolizes God's love for God's people more than the sacrament of Holy Matrimony—the sacrament of love. Sacred scriptures tell us that God is love, and God wants us to actively participate in God's love by loving God, our neighbors, and our families.

"Love unites. Love forgives. Love compromises. Love sacrifices. Love cries. Love laughs. But most of all, love triumphs. Oh, yes, love conquers. Although we say that love is blind, paradoxically, love sees racial differences. Yes, it does. Love knows that people are different, but it does not give way to cultural or racial prejudices. Love sees our diverse skin colors, but love is not afraid to embrace them. Love sees the crocodile-infested river of the prejudice that divides the different races in our world today, but love is not afraid to cross it. Love yearns to experience what is on the other side of the ethnical divide. Yes, love sees and respects the aisle that divides our people even in the house of God, but it does not hesitate to cross it in search of God and the other. Love hears all the gossips about everything that is wrong concerning intercultural marriages, but love is not deterred to answer God's call to love across the racial divide. Love is beautiful.

"Maria and Peter, you have shown our community and church that love transcends all cultural stereotypes and hurdles put on our way by our own communities and our wounded past. The Church prays and hopes for a time when all God's people would look at all peoples from diverse races, cultures, religious affiliations, genders, sexual orientations, and only see the image of the loving God, not skin colors. We yearn for a time when people would not be judged by the color of their skin, but by what comes out of their minds and hearts, and of course, their human dignity that springs from God's likeness. A time when individuals can stand up to the racial mindsets that have always divided humanity.

"I say to you, this is not the end. This wedding shouldn't be the last time we gather here to celebrate a wedding like this one. It should be just the beginning. It shouldn't be the exception, but the norm. Maria and Peter, let me tell you something about marriage. Impediments will come your way. Temptations will visit you. When that happens, stand firm by your principles. Trust in our Lord Jesus Christ. Continue to love each other. Pray. Always ask for God's guidance and blessings, for God is the author of love.

"If God blesses you with children, please, bring them here, and we will baptize those lucky kids. Yes, I say 'lucky kids,' for they will have the best from two worlds, and will be a cut above other kids who are not blessed with parents from two different ethnicities. Some of you may ask me, 'Father, if you had children, would you approve of them marrying blacks?' I don't have the answer to that question. Truly, it would be difficult, but with wise friends like Mr. and Mrs. Weber, I would be educated. So, children, you should always remember that we are all here to support you on the journey that you have embarked on. God loves you. We also love you very much. Amen."

It was a beautiful homily. I shed a tear or two not because it made me sad, but because it vindicated our decision to cross the racial divide. It spoke to my heart. It addressed the issues we had been struggling with. I was happy that Mother JK and my mother had also listened to the same inspiring words of the man of God. It was after this homily when our white guests joined in the liturgical dancing. At first, they were hesitant, but eventually, they became more participative and rhythmical. The homily had transformed them. In fact, it transformed all of us, who had cared to listen to it.

Deacon Savious also cried. He was a good man. I did not see the reaction of every other guest, but I gathered later that many guests were deeply touched by the homily. Maybe some were offended. A couple is said to have called Andrea the following week to complain about the homily, which they said was biased, and was likely to influence their kids not to respect racial boundaries. I do not know how the Webers responded to that, for they did not tell me what they said to the complaining guests. If I were Andrea, I would have advised them to pray to God about it.

After the solemn vows had been exchanged, and the priest had pronounced us husband and wife, the people from both sides of the aisle came towards the sanctuary to congratulate us. Mother JK was among the first to come over. She ululated and joyfully danced as she approached the sanctuary. She seemed oblivious of our obnoxious conversation at my home a few days back. Or perhaps, the priest' inspiring words had redeemed her. Our parents and other guests followed behind her. I could see that my mother's eyes were moist, for she had been moved by the homily too. I did not know whether they were tears of joy or sadness.

It was interesting to see the different gestures used in congratulating us. All the guests from Maria's side hugged us. Some of them even kissed both of us. I could tell that my father was scandalized to watch all those kisses and hugs. He, like other Shona people of his age, was not accustomed to seeing the newlyweds being kissed in public. Most of the black guests just extended their hands to me for a firm handshake. However, most of the guests who offered me handshakes, changed the gesture when they came to Maria. They opened their arms and embraced her. So, even after the priest's inspiring homily, the cultural divide remained. I did not begrudge Maria for that because I knew how to celebrate unity in diversity. As a matter of fact, I did not see anything wrong with it. Whether it was a hug or a handshake, for me, the symbolic significance was the same. In fact, I praised the black guests for being contextual and sensitive, interculturally. Of course, Baba was not amused to see Zimbabwean men hugging Maria. Later, he pulled me aside and warned me that they were taking advantage of Maria.

"Those hugs, my son." That was Baba's statement. Perhaps, it was a question.

"What hugs, Baba?" I responded.

"The young men from Dallas, hugging my daughter-in-law. It's not appropriate, my son. They can't just embrace someone's wife life that. Never allow them closer to her again." He was jealous.

I smiled.

"Baba, are you a little jealous?"

"No. Why should I? She is not my wife."

"I thought you were a little jealous, Baba. You can also give her a little hug if you want. It's her wedding day, and what happens here stays here." I teased him.

"God, forbid! I will never do such a thing. I don't hug my daughter-in-law."

"You can."

"I told you, I can't."

"And I tell you that you can."

"I am not crazy, Peter."

"I was just kidding, Baba."

"Please, don't joke with me like that. Some things are sacred."

"I know, Baba. It's no big deal. A hug is just a form of greeting, and it shows people that you respect and care about them," I said.

"No. My son, I am old enough to tell the difference between an innocent hug and a passionate one. Some of those men held her too tight, while pressing their chests against hers. She is a woman. How do you embrace a woman without pressing against her bosom, inappropriately? It's not appropriate, my son. She is your wife, and they should respect her as a married woman."

"Thank you for the advice, Baba." I said that to make him happy.

"Be alert, my son. Protect your wife from those hyenas."

"I hear you, Baba."

"Don't say, I never warned you."

"Thank you, Baba."

After Mass, the wedding party left for photographs as the guests were walking to the church hall, where a catering company had already prepared lots of delicious food for them. We came back to the hall after about an hour. It was then, when we discovered that the Dallas group had brought its own food, which was enough to feed a rally. They had already brought it into the hall, and were warming it in the catering area. That was very thoughtful of them. My mother-in-law's concerns were appeased because there was not going to be any food shortages. My earlier talk of African hospitality and generosity had been vindicated.

Although the aroma coming from the African food was strong, perhaps overwhelming for some people not accustomed to it, it attracted consumers from both cultural groups. Some of the white guests who dared to try the African food seemed to like it, and they also invited their family members to take a bite. The pastor also tried and liked it. More and more people joined the line, after the pastor testified to the otherness and goodness of the African food. After the man of God had endorsed the food, every white guest wanted to taste it. For some, what started like a spoonful became a plateful of African goodies. In fact, most of the African food was the same American food, and its only uniqueness was in its preparation. There was fried chicken and fish, *sadza,* collard greens with peanut butter, beef, *nyevhe* with peanut butter, goat meat stew, peanut butter rice, and South African boerewors. Even though all the African food, which was served was delicious, *nyevhe* and boerewors were out of this world. Our white guests scrambled for more African food, and it made me very proud of my culture.

Some black guests were also served the American food that had been prepared by the catering company because they said that they preferred American food to African traditional dishes. Mexican food had willing takers from across the racial divide. There were *tamales, tacos, enchiladas*, and a little bit of *mole*. When Maria initially suggested that we also needed to prepare Mexican food, I did not quite think that there would be any takers, but I was surprised that almost everyone wanted a bite of the food.

Guests from diverse cultural groups started to mingle with each other while serving food. At long last, food, though at times one of the worst discriminators of races, had managed to break the cultural barriers, which had inhibited our guests from carrying out sincere intercultural conversations. The guests started talking to each other. The sharing of food brought guests together more than the worship had done. The river that had separated the people in the church had been breached. At that point, I realized the unifying power that resides in hospitality and food sharing.

Music also played its part in bringing the ethnically diverse guests together. Even though an experienced disc jockey (DJ) had been hired to play preselected music, such as *First Dance* by Justin Bieber, *All of Me* by John Legend, *Crazy in Love* by Beyonce featuring Jay-Z, and *I Wanna Dance with Somebody* by Whitney Houston, the Dallas group had brought its own sound system and music. At first, I feared that they would interfere with our official DJ and our preselected musical list, but to my greatest relief, they did not. They waited for an opportune time. After all the scheduled dances (Mr. Weber danced with Maria, while I was dancing with Andrea. Then Mr. Weber danced with his wife, while I was dancing with Mother) had been performed, Mother JK asked for permission to play a few African songs on the Dallas sound system. We all knew that the request was just a formality, and that no one would stand in the way. As soon as the Zimbabwean music started, all hell broke loose. Our black guests jumped into the dancing arena, and exhibited some spectacular dancing moves. A variety of African musical genres such as *ndombolo*, urban groves, dance hall, gospel, *jiti*, and rhumba, were played. The dancing was so intense that the guests from the other side came closer to the stage to watch. It seemed like they had never seen such dance moves before.

Of all the dancing moves exhibited by our black guests, our white guests liked the Borrowdale dance most. Some of them openly testified that they had never seen anything like that before. Sooner, some of the not-so-shy white guests joined the dancing arena. It was beautiful to see blacks and whites dancing together. Some of the white guests were out of sync most of the time, but their efforts were rewarded with some never-ending rounds of applause. Again, I realized that music had the power to encourage people to get involved, interculturally. Most times, people do not learn about other cultures not because they resist it, but because there has not been an opportunity to encounter the other. I was proud that our wedding had helped our guests to encounter and experience the other in such a profound way. The intercultural encounter, which had started during Mass with the African drums and American guitars, had ignited the process of intercultural respect. The sharing of food had deepened the encounter. And now, it was the dancing arena that took the intercultural learning to a new level. I had never realized that music could bring people together like that before.

Our parents also joined others on the stage. I had seen Baba dancing on numerous occasions, when I was young, and I knew that he was not gifted in that area. He tried his best, and most of the time, spectators loved it. He was the kind of a dancer who dances to enjoy himself or express his feelings, rather than to entertain others.

My mother also joined the stage rather reluctantly, after having been coaxed by Mother JK. Mother was the shy type, and would hardly volunteer to dance unless it was extremely necessary. I cannot remember having seen her dance before. I held my breath as she entered the dancing arena, and to my greatest amazement, her dancing moves were graceful. Indeed, she was talented. Although she still looked sad, she managed to smile. I was glad, and hoped that healing and reconciliation in the family had already begun, thanks to the therapeutic power of the dancing space.

Mother JK's dancing moves forced all the dancers out of the arena to watch from outside. She was a seasoned and refined dancer who could move her body with grace. I could see that she was trying to keep her movements under control lest some guests would be scandalized. Everybody cheered for her and rewarded her talent with some ululation and whistling.

Maria's parents tried their luck with the African music on the dance floor, and they did not disappoint. It was a show of great talent.

Then Roland got into the arena too, and what a talented dancer he was. It seemed so natural for him to dance to African rhythms. He was so good that some of us, the less gifted Africans were jealous. Suddenly, Roland was joined by one of our young guests, an African Queen from Dallas. The two danced together as smoothly as if they had rehearsed it. Although there were other dancers in the arena, Mr. Weber's eyes never left Roland, and they followed every bodily move that he made with the sharpness of an eagle's sight. I thought he was concerned that Roland's heart might be stolen by that African girl. I did not think that he would be happy to have another mixed marriage in the family. At some point, I saw him whispering to his wife, who immediately entered the arena and gently tapped her son on the shoulder. Initially, Roland ignored her, but Andrea tapped his shoulder again. This time, he stopped dancing, and followed his mother out of the arena. The African Queen was left alone in the middle of the dancing circle, and she looked disappointed. As she stood there, undecided about what to do next, another taker, this time, an African young man from San Antonio, who I think was becoming worried with the connection our African sister and Roland were making, invited her to dance with him. She accepted the invite, and the two did not waste time. They jumped into the dancing area, and before we recovered from the shock of seeing Roland exiting the stage unceremoniously, the black brother was all over the lady.

Baba was on the dance floor on and off, and he did not disappoint every time he danced. Every one of his dancing moves went well until Baba tried break dance, which was an unmitigated disaster. He looked like an amateur practicing *karate*. I had never seen any break dance like that one. Mother was offended, and she quickly walked into the dancing arena, grabbed him by the hand, and pulled him out. Baba did not resist. He walked out as natural as if he had expected it. Everyone gave him a round of applause. For the white guests, it was out of their genuine appreciation of his unprecedented dancing moves, but for the black guests, the applause was perhaps more out of the respect they had for the father of the bridegroom than for his dancing moves. They all knew that there was no break dance that looked like that. Baba did not have any regrets, for he had enjoyed himself. For him, dancing was about entertaining oneself, and not about impressing the spectators. Of course, it would be icing on the cake for him if spectators were entertained in the process.

The wedding reception ended with the offering and presentation of gifts. As a matter of fact, most of the white guests had already brought or sent their wedding gifts a day or two before the wedding day. I was alerted that some of our white guests would send their gifts later. As per American tradition, there was nothing wrong about it. I was told that in the past, invited guests had up to one year after the wedding, to send in their gifts. Nowadays, some American guests may send in their gifts within three months after the wedding. So, we did not panic.

Zimbabweans are different. Most guests bring their wedding gifts on the wedding day. The wedding gift remains a secret until it is announced by the master of ceremonies. Most of the invited guests on my side had brought some cash, checks, or some kitchen or household utensils. Baba and Mother stood up to the expectations of the guests when their turn came. Both congratulated us, but not before giving us a few words of encouragement and advice.

"We are so happy, my son, that you are now a man. Soon, you will be a father, and we will be proud grandparents. Be a responsible head of the house. Treat your wife with respect. Protect her from the many dangers of this world. Guard her jealously against disrespectful men. There are many dangers for married women in this American jungle. Protect your wife—the mother of your kids. But most of all, love her with all your heart. Look at me and your mother. We have come from afar, and we still have far to go. But whatever tribulation we will face, we will face it together, as a couple, and we will defeat it."

I could tell that Baba was happy. There was ululation, whistling, and dancing. Mother JK jumped into the dancing arena while chanting the popular Shona song of rejoicing.

"Chigutiro!" She shouted, repeatedly.

"Tamba wakaguta!" The crowd responded.

"Chigutiro!" She repeated.

"Tamba wakaguta!" The crowd shouted back.

"*Ukamai?*" It was Mother JK.

"*Hunenge usawhira!*" The crowd responded.

There was more ululation and whistling.

Then it was Mother's turn to give her small speech before the presentation of her wedding gift, which would be offered jointly with Baba.

"I am so happy, my son, you are married. *Wakura.* I am proud of you. Today, more *sadza* has come into the family. You, Maria, my daughter, we love you so much! God gave me only two boys. Today, to us is born a daughter. You have become, not only the mother of the family, but also the wife of the whole Masika clan. You are our special daughter-in-law, and we will treat you well. You are, indeed, a wife from the ancestors, and we welcome you with both hands."

Mother JK burst into another *chigutiro* chant amid piercing ululation, clapping of hands, and whistling. Our white guests were spellbound. It looked like they had never witnessed such a joyous people before. They did not complain that the African group was hijacking the wedding proceedings as I had anticipated. Maybe, they did not notice it. I did, or I just imagined it.

Mother continued. "Your father and I have a small gift for both of you. Two cows and three goats. They are in Zimbabwe. You can get them from Zimbabwe. They are waiting for you. We will keep them for you until you come to collect them. I guess we cannot send them through DHL."

There was another round of *chigutiro* chant. This time, our white guests joined in the ecstatic dance. After the presentation of gifts, there were toasts to the new bridegroom and the bride from the ancestors.

The following day, we had two separate meetings. The first one, concerned the need to have children. Mother started that conversation. "So, who will look after your kids, when they come, since both of you are working? Are you going to hire a maid?"

"Mother, it's too early to talk about kids. We will have to make plans first. Here in America, it's expensive to raise kids, Mother. There are no affordable maids, like you do have in Zimbabwe. It's too early to talk about kids right now. We need to plan, first. We will cross that river when we come to it," I told her.

"There is nothing wrong in talking about kids now. Marriage is all about bearing children. Isn't it?"

"Not in every culture, Mother. Marriage is about love. Kids may come as expected by-products of that love. If they don't come, love is not affected."

"Peter. You cannot teach me about love. With love or no love, kids are still needed in any marital union."

"I get it, Mother."

"So, who will look after the kids?" Mother insisted.

"One of us has to stop working for about a year or so, to take care of the kid," Maria joined the conversation.

"Don't they give you more time for maternity leave, here in America? Everything is big in America. In Zimbabwe, it's three months of maternity leave with a full salary."

"Not here, Mother. I am not sure, but it may be about three weeks without a salary for employees of private companies. I think the government offers its employees more time and benefits for maternity leave."

Mother was shocked. "Three weeks only? But this is America. We never knew that they treated their women like that."

"They do. Their argument is that one has to work to earn a salary," I explained.

"That's unfair. Will the companies go bankrupt because a pregnant woman is on a full salary for only three months while on national duty? How much profit do those companies make? Giving birth and taking care of babies is a national duty, which should be incentivized." Mother was a little irritated.

"It's different here, Mother."

"How can it be. Americans go everywhere preaching equal rights, yet they don't practice the same for their women. Why do they deny their women three months maternity leave with full benefits? America should do better. America should show us the way."

"You are right, Mother, but people out there have an overromanticized idea of America. Do you know that some companies here, give more pay to men than women even if they have the same qualifications, same experience, and work the same job?"

"Don't lie to me."

"True."

"Isn't that hypocrisy?"

"Who cares?"

Baba jumped in the conversation. "Mai Peter, women are oppressed everywhere in the world. It's only that when Westerners come to Zimbabwe, they want to portray our ways and culture as oppressive to women, yet they treat their women worse than we treat ours."

"Sir, why do you think we are worse off here?" Maria joined the conversation.

"I say worse because I have seen how you wake up early in the morning going to work, just like men do. I am sure it's not easy driving in these freeways of yours. If women work the same hours as men, they should be awarded equal salaries. On top of that, they don't offer them reasonable maternity leave here. Don't you know that giving birth to children is a national duty? Women should be paid for just doing that. Those children would become the soldiers that protect us, yet no one cares about the welfare of their mothers."

"Baba, American women work because they want to. It gives them financial freedom," Maria argued.

"Maybe, they gain financial freedom, but I think that American women work because their husbands don't earn enough money for the family's needs. I am told that some people have more than one job," Baba seemed concerned.

"Two jobs, yes," I responded.

"That's modern-day slavery. America should be able to pay employees enough salaries to enable the women to manage homes while looking after children. They shouldn't treat their women like that. Give people enough money, then, women may become mothers of our nations. As of now, they are too busy running around trying to make ends meet."

"Not only mothers should get the maternity leave, but also fathers. Dads should also look after their kids," said Maria.

"You are right there, my daughter. If a couple agrees that the mother should continue working, while the father looks after the baby, I see no problem with that," Mother said.

"Of course, there is nothing wrong with that, but it just doesn't feel right for me." It was Baba. "The man should toil for his family, so says the good book. It would be embarrassing for the man to stay at home and look after the baby, while his wife goes to work."

"Baba Peter, I think that there is nothing wrong with that as long as the couple agrees," said Mother.

"Maybe," Baba agreed, begrudgingly.

"Baba, please, don't drag us into politics," I said.

"This is not politics, Peter. It's about basic human rights and fairness," Baba responded.

"I now see how difficult it is for families here to raise children. It's expensive." Mother was upset. "You should come to Zimbabwe, and raise your children there. We can take care of them free of charge."

"There are no jobs in Zimbabwe, Mother," I responded.

"You are very educated. You can get jobs in Zimbabwe," said Mother.

"There are many educated people in Zimbabwe who don't have jobs. Many of them roam the streets selling vegetables, trying to earn a living. We will stay here. Yes, the salaries are pathetic, but at least, we have jobs. We will do whatever we can to care for our kids, here, not Zimbabwe. By the way, we do have daycare centers, where we can leave our children when we are at work," I explained.

"You are right, Peter. Please, don't make a mistake of coming back to Zimbabwe looking for a job. At least, not now. There isn't a future for children in Zimbabwe. Yes, you may come to Zimbabwe as your mother is saying, and you may get good jobs because you have good degrees. But your children will not be able to inherit your jobs. Yes, they can inherit your home, but what good comes from a home if the owner is not employed? You better stay put." It was Baba, and I think he was right. Most of the things we do, or the sacrifices that we make, we make them for our children. We want them to have better lives than ours.

Maria asked, "Why is Zimbabwe's economy so bad, Baba? Peter tells me that you do have land, minerals, and other natural resources. Where are they going?"

"Corruption is our greatest scourge, my daughter. There is a lot of corruption in Zimbabwe. Everyone is corrupt. You know what corruption does? It starts with the big fish—the politicians, who are immune to scrutiny, and it cascades to the grassroots. You don't get anything in Zimbabwe unless you have power, or you bribe someone. That's how bad it is."

"That's not the whole story, Baba Peter. When you talk about these issues, you should strike a balance. Tell the whole story." Mother was unamused by Baba's simplistic explanation.

"What else do you want me to say. Our suffering is a result of corruption that has been allowed to blossom by the politicians. If people know that they would be arrested if found wanting, they would be accountable. They are not arrested, so they don't care."

"Say something about sanctions," Mother intervened. "Maria, Zimbabwe has been on the United States and European sanctions since 2001. This is what happened. About that time, a new constitution was written, and a referendum was conducted. A new political party, the Movement for Democratic Change (MDC) that had just been formed campaigned against the constitution, and the people heeded. The Zimbabwe African National Union Patriotic Front (ZANU PF), which was the ruling party was agitated and forewarned about its possible defeat by the MDC in the forthcoming elections. To appease its landless supporters, ZANU PF incited the people to compulsorily acquire the land that belonged to white commercial farmers. Some farmers resisted eviction, and there was a little bloodshed. The European Union and the United Kingdom accused Zimbabwe of violating human rights. They imposed sanctions. The United States, not to be outdone by her allies, also imposed sanctions on Zimbabwe through the Zimbabwe Democracy and Economic Recovery Act (ZDERA) of 2001. Also, some targeted sanctions were imposed on certain individuals who were believed to prop up Mugabe's regime." Mother paused while drinking some water.

"What about the violations of human rights? Tell us the whole story?" Baba encouraged Mother to go on.

"That came later, Baba Peter. The issue was about the land. How can these black people get our land without paying for it? The British were infuriated."

"Where had the British gotten the land from?" Maria wanted to know.

"They came to Zimbabwe in 1890, and stole the land from the blacks. They drove them to infertile lands, which they called the reserves."

"So, the British didn't purchase the land?" Maria was curious.

"Some of the later generations might have purchased the land, but not from its original owners. They bought stolen property," Mother responded.

"What about the human rights violations?" I asked.

"They happened. ZANU PF harassed the members of the opposition party. In fact, some of them lost their lives. Some were raped, and others were maimed, but that was secondary. The human rights violations were blown out of proportion to justify the imposition of sanctions. The violation of human rights was not the reason the sanctions were imposed. The British used those human rights to disguise the actual reasons. They were not happy about the dispossession of their kith and kin."

"Mother, you sound like a politician. I am impressed."

"I am. Everyone in Zimbabwe is a politician. We know that sanctions have failed to affect a regime change in Zimbabwe. They have succeeded in making us, the poor, suffer. Politicians never lose sleep because of sanctions. They continue to build mansions. They drive big and expensive vehicles. They eat good and healthy food. When they are sick, they go abroad to receive first class healthcare. Sanctions, don't affect them in any way."

"If sanctions don't work, where is Mugabe?" Baba asked.

"President Mugabe wasn't overthrown by the sanctions, but by the army. It was a coup. ZANU PF sensed that Mugabe had become too old and a liability to the party, and they dethroned him to strengthen the party. That's why they never taunted or harassed him and his family. They never took a thing from him. We were disappointed because we were prepared to go to the Blue Roof to dance *kongonya* in Mugabe's sitting room."

"Why didn't you go?" Maria asked.

"Where?" Mother asked.

"To the Blue Roof," Maria responded.

"Blue Roof? There were soldiers guarding the house. President Mugabe's family was still there."

"So, is it corruption, or sanctions, or both?" Maria asked.

"I think both Mother and Baba are right. I think that both corruption and sanctions have contributed to Zimbabwe's economic quagmire. So, we won't come to work in Zimbabwe. We will only come there to visit." I wanted to end the political debate.

"It's complicated. I read a book that blamed the mismanagement of the economy by the leadership as one of the contributing factors," said Maria.

"You are right, sweetheart. There is a plethora of factors that have contributed to Zimbabwe's economic collapse. For instance, some people blame the MDC for having requested sanctions from America."

"They did that?" Maria asked.

"They may have done it, but Americans would not have sanctioned Zimbabwe just because the MDC asked for it. The MDC is just used as a front."

"I agree with you," said Baba.

"It's complicated, but we will not come to work in Zimbabwe," I said.

"It's up to you. Whatever you decide to do, please, don't forget to teach your kids the Shona language." Mother tried to change the topic. She was convinced that we had heard the message.

"The kids will be American. They don't need Shona," I responded.

"You are wrong." It was Baba. "You are very wrong. They need both English and Shona."

"They will be American, Baba."

"It doesn't matter. They still need to speak Shona. Why not teach them both languages? It will be to their advantage. Your kids will be Shona in terms of cultural identity, and a language is an integral part of one's culture. They will need it in life."

"How?" I asked.

"We are their grandparents. We will need to talk with them in Shona. They will come to Zimbabwe to visit, and they shall need to communicate and play with other kids. Many people in Zimbabwe don't understand English. We want your children to feel that they belong with us, but they can't have that feeling if they don't speak our language." Baba had some energy about this. "After all, it doesn't hurt to speak two different languages. You don't even teach them. You just speak it with them, and the kids shall learn."

"You are right, Baba. I think that there is nothing wrong in teaching the kids more than one language. I will make sure that they learn it. Don't worry, Baba," Maria intervened.

"Thank you, my daughter. You have a good heart," Baba said.

Baba was appeased. He smiled. He had lost the political debate, but he had won the cultural one. Mother, having won the political debate, decided to stay out of this one. Maria and I had learnt something from these debates. There is always something to learn if you engage others with an open mind. I am not talking about being taken advantage of, but accepting other people's opinions if they sound more reasonable than yours.

Long after the conversation had ended, Mother was still shocked to learn about the position of women in America. Maria and I were also shocked to learn about the politics of sanctions and corruption in Zimbabwe. The debate had been a double-edged sword because everyone got out of it with something.

Maria's parents arrived soon after our debate about the economy and politics of Zimbabwe, and it was time for our second discussion, which concerned our honeymoon. Right from the beginning of the wedding planning, we had talked about the possibility of having our honeymoon in Honolulu, Hawaii. Of course, it was my mother-in-law's suggestion. Maria and I also felt that Hawaii was a great place to go honeymooning. However, I did not quite commit myself because I felt that a honeymoon was not extremely necessary. Indeed, I valued it, though it was not part of my culture. Even though Maria' parents had footed most of the wedding bill, a honeymoon would further drain more money from our meager savings. I would have opted for a more affordable destination if I had been asked for my opinion. I would have suggested going to any of the fifty states of the United States. Perhaps, I could have mentioned Mexico.

We had avoided talking about it on the wedding day, which may have annoyed Andrea. She had not mentioned it when she called that morning to alert us that they would be stopping by our home later that day. I think that Andrea's main objective for the visit was to talk about the honeymoon. We tried to let them know how exhausted we were, but they were in no hurry to leave. She waited, but we did not talk about the honeymoon. When she felt that we were not going to talk about it, she brought up the issue.

"When are you two leaving for the honeymoon? Are you still for Honolulu?" Andrea wanted to know.

"That's a good question. We will postpone it until next year," I responded.

"Why?"

"We are tired. We just want to rest a little bit."

"That's the reason for the honeymoon. Wedding planning is so exhausting that you need a nice place to go and debrief. It's intended for resting."

"We can rest here, Andrea." Baba looked at me because I had called my mother-in-law by her name. I ignored him.

"Is money the issue?" Mr. Weber wanted to know. "I can lend you some money at no interest, if you need it."

"It's not about money, dad. We have enough money to go for a honeymoon. However, we decided to postpone it to July of next year," said Maria.

"Why not now?"

"Mother, thank you for your concern, but now is not the right time for the honeymoon. We do have guests in the house. We can't just leave them alone?"

"They are not kids. Are they? They can cook, right?" Andrea was visibly annoyed.

"Yes, they can cook, but they are new here, and you know that, Mother. They wouldn't know what to do if anything went wrong in the house. They don't even know how to call for an ambulance if either of them gets sick."

There was a pause.

Then Baba found an opportunity to join the conversation.

"May I ask a question?" No one answered, but he asked his question anyway.

"I think that a honeymoon is important, but not necessary. In our Shona culture, we don't have it. We didn't even know about it until recently. A newlywed couple only needs a bedroom. That's their sacred place, and that's good enough. With a house as spacious and nice as this one, why waste money in a hotel?"

Mr. Weber and Andrea were completely astonished. They froze for a moment. Andrea recovered first.

"With all due respect, Mr. David, you should always remember that Maria is not Shona. She doesn't understand some of your crazy practices. If you want this marriage to work, you should be willing to meet us midway. We can't be sacrificing our culture all the time in order to make you happy. It should be a give and take situation."

"Crazy? You just called my husband, crazy? Are you serious, Mrs. Weber? You call our ways, crazy? Isn't trying to waste money in Hawaii crazier than staying here in their home for free?" Mother was upset.

"Yes, I said it. Crazy! We have been putting up with you for too long. You should be ashamed of yourselves. You cannot just dictate everything to us and expect us to agree with you all the time." Andrea paused while rearranging her hair. "You Should understand that we are not Shona. We are American. In our culture, going for honeymoon is a must. It shouldn't be debated. We have been compromising many issues for your comfort. Please, return the favor. Now, it's your turn to compromise."

Mr. Weber joined the unpleasant conversation. "Ladies. Ladies. Let us be sensitive to each other's feelings." He turned to Andrea and patted her on her shoulder. "Sweetheart, I agree with everything you just said, but I don't think "crazy" is quite a nice word. Don't you think it's nice to apologize to David and Tendai? Surely, you didn't want to say, crazy."

"I think you are right, honey. I am sorry, Tendai and David. I didn't mean to disrespect you."

"No problem. I accept your apology," Mother said without looking at Andrea. I knew she did not mean it. She had not forgiven her.

"Maria and Peter can come to Zimbabwe for their honeymoon. We have wonderful places such as the Victoria Falls, Great Zimbabwe Ruins, Nyanga Mountains, and many game parks. You two can also join them so that you can see where your daughter is married."

"Good idea. What do you think, Maria?" Mr. Weber asked.

"It's a great idea, dad. Let us go to Zimbabwe in July."

"Are you in, Andrea?" Mr. Weber wanted to know.

"Let's not rush things. Let us cross that river when we come to it. It's only that they had planned to go to Hawaii. It seems they have changed their minds. Maria, you need to take your time."

I think that both Mr. Weber and Andrea were happy about the invitation to Zimbabwe. Mr. Weber's readiness to accommodate the suggestion looked like they had thought or talked about it before. Yes, the trip would not be without its fair share of challenges. Before embarking on such a journey, they would have to be vaccinated for Malaria and other tropical diseases. Alternatively, they could use mosquito nets and repellent substances strictly. There would be the danger of venomous snake bites. They had to be prepared for the culture shock, which is always a possibility for people visiting places of people with different cultures from their own. They had to be vigilant for pickpockets, which are ubiquitous in most African countries. In addition to all the above, they had to perceive things differently or at least, suspend their preconceived judgment of other cultures.

The meeting ended on that note. The honeymoon to Honolulu was called off. As a matter of fact, it never was on our schedule. Although it was an attractive option, we were thinking of other less expensive and closer places.

My parents stayed for four more weeks after the wedding. I learnt a great deal from them. Frankly, the learning was mutual. Their brief stay in the United States transformed them, to a certain extent. There is no way one can visit the United States for over six weeks, and go back to where one belongs without experiencing some kind of transformation. That is what intercultural interaction does to people. It is always a give and take process. For me, my parents' visit allowed me to have more intimate conversations with them that I would not have had if we were in Zimbabwe. Our circumstances in the United States forced us to spend more time together and to have more personal discussions. In Zimbabwe, young people and adults do not quite spend time together. They mostly talk to each other when necessary. I also learnt to respectfully agree or disagree with my parents, which is a recipe for a healthy parent-child relationship.

Most of my parents' myths about the United States were demythologized. They got to know that the United States was not a land flowing with honey and milk, a misconception they had when they arrived. It was a place just like any other, with its graces and blemishes. They discovered that the United States was a place with so much to offer, yet with so much to learn. A place rich in cultural diversity, but also in need of learning and deepening intercultural respect. They learnt that it was not only a place of joy and happiness, but also a place of suffering and inequalities. It was the same place where billionaires lived, and also where some people worked two jobs to make ends meet. They realized that the United States was a place of so much cultural diversity and ethnical divisions. That was the America they came to and experienced, and it was up to them to present to their friends back home, the story of America, objectively or subjectively.

Maria and I were both sad and relieved to see them go. On the one hand, we had grown accustomed to having Mother cooking our food, cleaning the house, and doing all our laundry. Initially, Maria offered to pay her a little stipend, but she flatly refused. She claimed that she was not working, but just performing some household chores for which she was ordinarily responsible as the mother of the family. She struggled to understand that Maria was the mother of the house, not her. Maria could not understand why my mother refused a stipend for her help in the house because she felt that she deserved it. But Mother claimed that trying to offer her a stipend would be an insult to her. We understood her concerns, and just let her be, and she was happy that she could assist us.

During their stay, Baba and I were not allowed in the kitchen much. It is not like somebody told us that we were completely banned from entering the kitchen area, but we just sensed it from the way Maria and Mother constantly hovered in there. Baba and I decided that the kitchen had become a no-go area for both of us during those few weeks. We were also not allowed to get anything from the refrigerator by ourselves, and we had to ask Mother or Maria to fetch for us whatever we needed. Mother said that she feared that if we frequented the refrigerator, we would not arrange the food in the refrigerator properly. Even though she did not complain directly when I helped Maria with some chores in the kitchen, I sensed that my duties were more appreciated outside in the garden or in the garage. There, nobody bothered us. This new arrangement felt good for me. However, I knew that I would have to relearn my good American husband behavior when Mother was gone.

"Men don't interfere in the kitchen, my son. It's offensive to women to see men near the stove or the refrigerator," Mother said.

"It's offensive to you, Mother, not to Maria. She is very happy to see me there, assisting with the cooking and wash-up."

"Maybe in the past. Now, she knows that the kitchen is a sacred place where women interact with ancestors. Men can only be there with permission, and only if they do not interfere with the cooking. It's our place, where we should be free to gossip, and experiment with our recipes and love potions. It's also a classroom where we teach our girls how to cook."

"That's not the American way of doing things, Mother. If I fail to assist Maria in the kitchen, I would be divorced within a week. Here, men and women help each other to do household chores."

"No woman can divorce a man for being respectful. The kitchen is the women's sacred space."

"What about the sitting room, Mother?" Maria asked her.

"Men are allowed in the sitting room, but they can't just sit in there all day long. Men should do the things that men do outside."

"Like what?"

"Taking a walk. Socializing with other men at the beerhall. Working in the garage. Playing soccer outside. It gives us, women, an opportunity to share our experiences without men eavesdropping."

"What experiences do women want to share in the absence of men?" I asked.

"About women things, and a little gossiping about our men."

I was disarmed, but Maria was not. I knew that she was just waiting for Mother to go back to Zimbabwe, so that we would begin to share the kitchen and laundry duties, like we had always done. I saw nothing wrong with that.

Father took Mother's advice seriously, and was always out in the garden. It was cold, and the vegetables were not growing much, but he would always find something to do. I was okay with that if he did not try to drag me into his plans. He sometimes did, and I refused to help him. He was annoyed, but there was nothing he could do about it. Sometimes, we went for a ride to La Vernia, and he loved it. He never drove a car in his life, but he was full of good defensive driving ideas.

"The way you drive, Sigauke, you won't be able to drive in Harare."

"Why not, Baba? Don't you like my driving?"

"Driving in Harare is not for the faint-hearted, my son. You must be alert all the time. The combi drivers can do whatever they want. As if that's not dangerous enough, the roads are full of potholes. You can't just hold the steering wheel with one hand, in Harare."

"I see. There are too many reckless drivers, in Harare. We do have them here, too. Here, some drivers are so impatient that they can just cut in front of you without a warning."

"Not like in Harare, my son."

"Father, you never drove a car. You can't be a good driving instructor."

"What's so special about driving a car, son? In America, you have wide tarred roads, and no potholes. You have functioning traffic lights. You have nice intelligent cars, which tell you when you are getting out of your lane, or when it's not safe to change lanes. Come to Harare, my son. You would abandon your vehicle in the middle of the road, and ask me to drive you home."

I laughed. Maybe he was right. I had never driven a vehicle in Harare, so, I could not dispute what he was saying. When I left Zimbabwe, there were not so many cars, and the roads were still in good condition.

We enjoyed those little conversations and humorous moments. He shared many stories that he had never shared with me before. I realized that there was a lot that I did not know about Baba. For instance, I did not know that he had worked as a temporary teacher when he was a young man. He shared with me his experiences at some of the schools where he had taught, and I found them really entertaining.

The first experience he shared with me was about his brief teaching assignment at a school called Jameson Secondary School, in Zaka, Masvingo. Below, is what he shared about his journey to the school, and his brief stay there:

"After we had walked for about two hours, and we hadn't even covered one third of the journey, I realized the mistake that I had made. I had overzealously, foolishly, and impetuously embarked on a journey without any slight knowledge of the distance to be traveled. Two things had impeded my judgment. First, I so much needed a job that all patience had run out of me. I didn't want to imagine a situation where I would not get to the school that same day to claim the position. Don't ever allow impatience to cloud your decision making, my son."

I nodded in agreement.

"Second, I had over trusted my past walking stamina. Having grown up and attended high school in the rural areas, I had walked long distances before, but this was 1998, not 1990 the year I completed my Ordinary level of education at Mudarikwa Secondary School. I hadn't realized that the five years I had spent at College in Harare had robbed me of my walking stamina. As if that were not bad enough, I had also lost my sound judgment concerning distances that I could possibly walk on foot. As I reflect on that journey now, I also discover that this habit of basing present decisions on past capabilities has become one of the vices I need to curb. A couple of years ago, I strained my thigh muscles while playing soccer with my friends. I erroneously thought that since I used to play soccer when I was in high school, I could still do it at that point. I was wrong, and my body punished me for that mistake. The strain reminded me that I wasn't young anymore."

"You are right, Baba. Things do change. What then happened?"

"Since I had made the decision to walk, I had to do it. Soon, I realized that I had just become a shadow of my rural days when my friends; Vitalis Mutinha, Herbert Machimbira, Innocent Mwise, and I would climb up and down Chitakai Mountain while running. This journey was beginning to wear me down both spiritually and physically. The untarred road that wound through the plains and hills of Zaka was wet, and seemed to be going on forever. There were no vehicles plying that route on that particular day. There were signs that it had rained incessantly in the past few days, and water springs were gushing out on the sides of the road. Even then, the skies were beginning to prepare another unappreciated gift for the earth. Black clouds could be seen gathering in the sky, and a distant rumbling of thunderstorms threatening from the East. Thank God, it didn't rain until later that night. The cyclone, whose name I can't recall had been pounding Masvingo for several weeks, and had destroyed crops, and taken away any hope of a decent harvest for the farmers. As if that was not bad enough, the dust roads had become impassable, except for the few daring bus drivers."

"You were brave, Baba."

"Brave? I was stupid. I should have waited for the bus that plied a different route."

"Did you arrive on the same day?"

"Wait. I was tired and hungry, but I wasn't going to give up. In life, there are certain irreversible decisions that one makes, and for me, this was one of them. The two men who had misled me into walking for almost a hundred kilometers seemed to enjoy the journey. They appeared to be jovial and happy, for they had saved some money. I could easily tell that they were hardened men, accustomed to the rough side of life. One of them had taken off his shoes, and was faring pretty well, barefooted. The other one had his jacket tied around his waist, and seemed unfazed by the long journey. I trailed them with my small bag in my hand. And we walked and walked, but the men told me that we hadn't done anything yet."

"Were you angry with the men?"

"Not with the men, but with myself. I had allowed myself to be misled."

"Very sad, Baba."

"The excitement of finding a job, at long last, had overshadowed my judgment. I had spent two consecutive nights on the road, and I was determined not to spend another one. Not that day, I had vowed. In Chinhoyi, I had slept by the side of the road, in the city center, in the company of not so trustworthy cross border travelers, who were waiting for trucks to carry their merchandise to Zambia. Every time a truck pulled up the Nyamapanda Highway, they would wake up and run for it to check if the driver could transport their commodities to Zambia. Someone told me that they were making a killing in Zambia by selling cigarettes. I didn't quite trust these guys, and I don't think they trusted me either. I slept on the cardboard boxes that I had spread on the veranda of a clothing shop, and used my handbag as a pillow. Throughout the night, I made sure that I kept one eye open, watching. Maybe they did the same. As I think of it now, I feel that they might have suspected me more, since I had no merchandise like they had. I was vigilant not because I had any commodities that could be stolen, but I had to jealously guard my hard-earned academic certificates. Of course, I also had my identity card, which I could not afford to lose."

"You slept on the street, baba?"

"I did, not only once, but on several nights. Of course, on different occasions, but that night was different. To add to my tribulations, the tenacious mosquitoes never ceased to harass me with their uninvited funeral tunes whenever I ignored their presence. It seemed like they had invited their extended family for a feast. Of course, I believe to have lost half a pint of blood to those insatiable blood sucking vampires that night. I don't think my companions suffered the same loss since they were always awake, waiting for the trucks. I know this because I never saw them waving their palms in the air or beating their butts in an attempt to appease or frighten the flying vampires. Or the mosquitoes were used to their blood that they wanted to try mine, which I believe might have tasted different and delicious for them. Anyway, I survived the mosquito bites."

"You are a hero, baba."

"The following night, I put up at Karoi Bus Terminus. There were many other people there. We had a roof above our heads, but no walls except for the security fence. Again, the mosquitoes tormented me, but it seemed they had fallen in love with other stranded travelers. I survived again."

"What about the long journey?"

"Now, back to that never-ending journey. After we had walked for about four hours, one of the men announced that he had arrived at his destination. The two of us continued, silently. We were tired, and there was nothing to talk about. A couple of kilometers from the first man's destination, the second man also reached his home. Before he departed, he gave me directions, and assured me that I was almost halfway to my destination. Instead of being encouraged with that news, I was disillusioned. Imagine, I had walked for almost four hours, and now I was being told that I hadn't covered half the distance to my destination. I was angry. Obviously, not with the man, but with myself. I shouldn't have trusted these men in the first place. I had graduated from college, but I wasn't any wiser."

"It wasn't your fault. They misled you."

"Maybe, but I should take some responsibility over my own mistakes. That's what honorable people do. About thirty minutes of walking by myself, I arrived at Svuvure Township. I got into a shop, bought half a loaf, and devoured all of it in no time, and I was still hungry. I talked to the shopkeeper, hoping to find accommodation for the night, for it was almost dusk, but he gave me some good news instead. He told me that there was a small pick-up truck that would leave for Chiredzi via Jameson Secondary School, and that's where I was going. If I say that I was relieved, it would be an understatement because I rejoiced. I wasn't going to spend another night on the road."

"You were lucky."

"I should have told you how it all started. I had graduated from the University of Zimbabwe with a diploma in religious studies, and that was at the beginning of 1997. The Ministry of Education, Sports, and Recreation had deployed me as a teacher to Mashonaland West Province. So, I went to Chinhoyi where the provincial education offices were. They deployed me to Karoi District. I went to Magunje District Education offices, where they attempted to deploy me to a very far away secondary school. That is why I had to spend a night in Chinhoyi and another one in Karoi. I had no relatives there, and didn't have money for a hotel room. I decided to go back to the provincial education offices in Chinhoyi to request redeployment to Masvingo, my home province. They agreed, and I took the bus to Masvingo, where they deployed me to Zaka/Jerera Education District."

"That was a good idea," I said.

"It was. I arrived at Zaka education offices around 1:00 pm. There were other prospective temporary teachers waiting there. Soon, I was posted to Jameson Secondary School to teach Commerce, but there was a challenge. The only bus that plied the route between Jerera and Jameson Secondary School was out of order. I was told that it hadn't been on the road for a couple of days. I later learned that the bus was just a small and fun-shaped creature, which they called, Big Dad. It had seen better days, and perhaps, better owners. It spent more days off the road than on it due to breakdowns. Even on the days when it was sound enough to ply the route, the bus driver and its conductor would spend a couple of hours under it, trying to fix some mechanical issues. At first, it worried me, but those who were used to traveling aboard Big Dad knew that it would eventually arrive at its destination. Big dad would never fail them, and they were right because it never did."

"So, what happened next?"

"I walked to the Masvingo–Chiredzi Highway, which was just a stone's throw from the offices. That is where I met the two men who had been waiting for some private vehicles at the junction. Since I didn't know where I was going, I asked them for the directions, which they enthusiastically offered. After a couple of hours waiting, they started talking about walking to their homes. I inquired if I could walk to Jameson, and they said that it was a walking distance. I joined them. I can't blame the two men because they were trying to help me. They never promised that it would be easy. They never said that there wasn't another route to the school as I later learned. It was my fault because I never asked, and I paid dearly for that sin of omission. In fact, I thanked them for having tried to help."

"You are very forgiving, Baba. They were not good men at all. They didn't have good intentions."

"Perhaps, they intentionally misled me, like you are saying. I should go back to the pick-up truck at Svuvure. There were three people—two elderly men and a small boy of about ten years of age, in the back of the white pickup truck. Although it was already dusk, the dark clouds had made it even darker. The two men in the back of the pickup truck were talking, but the little boy and I remained silent. The duo was concerned about the small boy in the truck, and were rehearsing what they would say when they arrived at their destination. Just by listening to the conversation, I learned that they were brothers, who worked in Bulawayo. Once upon a time, they had a sister who was impregnated by a certain local teacher, who refused to marry her. It seemed like he was paying maintenance for the boy. At some point, he had requested to take the boy into his custody, and the mother had refused. He later got married to another woman, and had two children of almost the same ages with his older son. At that time, the mother of the boy in transit had died, and her brothers decided to take the boy to his father."

"Very sad, indeed."

"It wasn't very sad. At least, he had a father who loved him. When I asked them to let me know when we arrived at my bus stop, I discovered that they were getting off at the same bus stop as I. As if that was not serendipitous enough, they told me that they were going to the same school where I was going. To add honey to my cake, they were visiting the headmaster of the school where I was going to teach. It was then that they realized that I had heard everything that they were discussing. From that experience, I learned never to talk about other people if I didn't know the strangers in my company. The men were relieved when I promised them that their secrets were safe with me."

"You never told anybody?"

"Never. I am telling you, now. We arrived at Jameson around 7:00 pm, and it was pitch dark. The headmaster and his wife welcomed us into their house, and we introduced ourselves. Supper was served with delicious fish. Soon after supper, the visitors told the headmaster the reason for their unannounced visit, and he thanked them, and told his wife what his former brothers-in-law had said. The wife told him that there was nothing wrong about them bringing the boy, and promised that she would take care of him, just like her own child. I thought that she was a good woman, for she sounded so natural and well-meaning in her acceptance. The uncles, then told Ray, the little boy, that they would leave him with his own father, and he nodded his head in agreement. I later learned that the little boy had his father's first name."

"Did he cry?"

"I don't know. It was dark, and I could hardly see his eyes. When I told the headmaster about my ordeal with the two sojourners, he was visibly agitated. He momentarily stopped eating, and looked at me. "Those men are evil. They misled you. There is another route to this school. You should have boarded one of the buses going to Chiredzi that use the highway. You would have then got off the bus at Chekenyere Shopping Center, just after Pelilendava. From that bus stop to here, it's only an hour's walk."

I thanked him for his sympathies, and explained to him that it wasn't entirely the men's fault, for I hadn't done my homework properly. I hadn't asked if there was any other way to reach Jameson. They may have withheld that information from me because they needed a companion for the long journey. I had learned my lesson."

"So, there was another bus route?"

"Yes. That night, the two uncles and I put up at another teacher's house who had a whole house to himself. The uncles refused to use the blankets that the headmaster had given to us, but requested for some blankets from the young teacher. I asked them why they didn't want to use the headmaster's blankets, and they told me that they were afraid that the blankets might have been used by their brother-in-law and his wife, and were not washed. I understood their concerns. That night, we slept very late because the two gentlemen kept asking questions. I can't recall what they were asking about, but it seems they were questions about some things that I knew very well, which they were very curious to know.

"The teacher, at whose house we put up for the night was probably a Mathematics teacher. Although I didn't stay at the school long enough to know him better, he seemed to be a very fine young man. He was Christian too, and his church gathered for worship every Sunday in one of the classrooms, which brought about some tension between him and the headmaster. I can't really recall what had happened, but I think that the worshipers were no longer welcome to use the classroom for their services. The headmaster must have communicated this reservation to the teacher who was an elder of some sort in that church. I think that the headmaster wanted the Mathematics teacher to break the sad news to his congregants, which he did. Later, it turned out that the headmaster was not happy with the way the teacher had conveyed the news. It seemed that the Mathematics teacher had presented the news in a manner that portrayed the headmaster as a bad person. Ordinarily, the word came back to the headmaster, who in one of the staff meetings lambasted the Mathematics teacher for having misrepresented his concerns to the congregants. He told the Mathematics teacher that what he had said to the congregants had portrayed him as a very bad person, and that he was not happy about it. Apart from that confrontation, it seemed that the two were not at loggerheads at all."

"That was too bad," I commented.

"The headmaster was a very educated man. During that time, he had just returned from the University of Zimbabwe, where he had graduated with a master's degree in education. He was very proud of his academic achievements, and claimed to be a self-made professional. He encouraged his teachers to also further their studies, which I thought was not wrong except that he said it in a forceful and patronizing way. The first to be confronted was one of the Agriculture teachers. She had a certificate in Agriculture, and the headmaster reminded her that she was not educated enough. She needed a certificate in education so that she would become a qualified teacher."

"The headmaster said to her, 'Madam, this school is not a farm. These children are not animals. This is not the right place for you unless you further your studies.' I don't know how the Agriculture teacher felt, but the comments should have been heartrending. Zimbabweans get so angry if you tell them that they are not educated. Almost everyone wants to be considered educated, and to present herself to people as such. I think she was really devasted. During such conversations, she never answered, but would just look on the floor, and blink a thousand times. The incessant blinking may have been her own tactic of preventing tears from flowing out of her eyes. I guess if she had cried, the insults might have appeared worse."

"He was rude. I mean the headmaster," I commented.

"Yes, he was. He continued. 'Madam, don't pretend to be educated because you are not. You just have a certificate in Agriculture, and for our purposes here, that is not being educated. Go back to college, and study pedagogics, then come back relevantly educated.' It was another piece of heart-piercing and unsolicited advice. I felt sad for her. I also felt sad for myself because I knew that the day of reckoning would come. Yes, it did. One day he just said, 'you Masika and Edson, you are temporary teachers.' Edson had a Bachelor of Arts and I had a Diploma in Religious Studies. 'Yes, you are temporary teachers though on indefinite employment contracts with the Ministry of Education.' He repeated it to make it sink in. He never told us to go back to school, but I sensed that he would do that behind our backs. However, the headmaster wasn't the type of man who would talk behind one's back, for he was arrogantly frank. Of course, we didn't need him to remind us of it barely two weeks after our graduation. We would go back to school, sooner or later, but we still had time, and we were still young. We already knew that we needed to obtain some diplomas in education, but not so fast."

"He belittled you, Baba. You were educated in your own way."

"The deputy headmaster too, was not spared from the harassment. That came at the time when the Mathematics teacher had been admitted to a Bachelor of Science program at Africa University to further his education. 'Sir, you also need to begin to think of going back to college. I have a master's degree, and I can't be seen to be deputized by a person who only possesses a certificate in education. I want to forewarn you that when the Mathematics teacher comes back with his new qualification, I will make him my deputy. He will be more educated than you, and you won't complain about it.' He forewarned him. I can't recall the deputy headmaster's response, but I think he was devasted."

"The headmaster was full of himself," I said.

"He was. Another Agriculture teacher, whose name I can't quite remember was also harassed. Whatever crime that teacher had committed, I didn't know, but the headmaster found it extremely hard to forgive him. I now realize that I should have asked him about that teacher's offence. Right from the day of my arrival, the headmaster, in no uncertain terms, warned me about the unprofessional machinations of that teacher. 'Masika, I want to warn you forthwith, not to befriend that man. He is a very bad influence on teachers. Please, don't talk with him. If you go to the shopping center, and you find him there, please, don't talk with him.' I was stunned by such advice. The teacher didn't seem to mind what the headmaster was saying behind his back. When we talked about it, he just laughed it off. I guess, he knew why the headmaster was saying that."

"The headmaster wanted teachers to be up to date with their work plans. At the beginning of that school term, he announced that he wanted every teacher to set all the tests her or his students would take throughout the term. The deadline for setting the tests was too close, and none of the teachers managed to complete the task on time. The term had just started, and teachers were busy preparing teaching schemes, and the ultimatum for tests became an unnecessary burden. Time moved. The deadline for setting the tests came, and no one cared. Then one day, without warning, the headmaster came into the staffroom, where about five teachers were busy preparing for classes and grading their students' work. He went straight for the English teacher, another new teacher who had just come from college."

"The headmaster said, 'Madam, may I have the tests for all your classes?' The English teacher, who seemed to have been prepared for an occasion like this remained silent. She never looked up, or did anything to acknowledge the headmaster's presence. She just pretended not to have heard him. The headmaster patiently waited for a response, which never came. I think he knew what was in store for him. The teacher started packing her books as if preparing to go for a class. When she stood up, and made for the door, the headmaster, who had remained calm until that time, lost his temper."

'You, Sarah, where are you going? I need the tests.' The English teacher momentarily froze, looked at the headmaster straight in the eyes, and gave an utterance that shocked me.

'Sir, I don't want supervisors who interfere with my work the way you do. I am not your kid. I know what I am doing. You don't tell me how to teach. For your own information, I just graduated from Gweru Teacher's College, and I passed all my examinations. I am qualified to teach, and I know what's good for my students.' She paused."

'I know why you are harassing me. I know you, Sir. I have been told everything about your improper tactics. You instill fear into female teachers so that when you propose love to them, they don't turn you down. Now, let me tell you this, right from the onset. I don't love you, and I am not afraid of you. You are a married man, and you should respect your wife.' She stopped and came back to sit on her chair. For a moment or two, the headmaster couldn't find the right words to respond. I guess, the English teacher had taken him by surprise. Eventually, he managed to open his mouth."

"He was done. What did he say?"

"He said, 'You Sarah, who told you such lies? Is it Joshua (the agriculture teacher)?' He looked at Mr. Joshua, who was as amused as all of us. Starting this week, no one is allowed to finish work at noon on Fridays. You have to work until 5:00 pm.'

'Why?' The English teacher responded as if the new rule was only intended for her. 'Don't you see that we are in the bush. There are no buses, and we have to walk all the way to the highway. We need time to reach there. You can't tell us to work until five, on Fridays.'

'You, Sarah. Which bush are you dreaming about? Is this how a bush looks like? Are you thinking about kwaMuroyi, the bush in which you grew up? A place where you saw a bus once in a year? You are a fool.' "The English teacher looked at the headmaster and smiled. I think that she guessed she had won the battle. She had managed to divert the headmaster's attention from professional to personal issues.

I pitied the headmaster because after this episode he could no longer ask for the tests from any other teacher. However, he didn't look defeated or humiliated. I didn't see anger and bitterness in his eyes. He was wise because he realized that he could no longer win this battle, and decided to let it go. Sarah had personalized it. After about five minutes, the headmaster put his tail between his legs and unceremoniously walked out. I don't know what was in his mind as he walked back to his office. I just imagined how he would report the issue to his wife, who was a teacher at a local primary school."

"You say he was wise? I don't think he was wise at all. He remained quiet because he was defeated."

"Maybe. The English teacher saved all of us on that particular day, but I am not sure if what she said was something that I would ever think of saying if I ever found myself in the same situation. Up to now, I don't know if her allegations against the headmaster had any substance at all. I never asked the English teacher. Probably the ubiquitous and malicious hand of Joshua was behind those allegations. Perhaps, the headmaster eventually found some way of retaliating, but until three months later, when I left the school, he had not avenged his humiliation."

"He learned a big lesson," I said.

"He did. He also had a penchant for wrestling. How do I know this? I shared a house with the deputy headmaster, who was obsessed with the music of Leonard Zhakata. Every morning, I woke up to the tune of Zhakata. The volume was always at full blast. It was a ritual that I had to endure every morning. I could have complained, but I was too junior, for he was the deputy headmaster. Even now, whenever I hear one of the songs from that album being played, memories of Jameson come back. Thinking of it now, I suspect that that's when the gentleman and his wife performed sacred rituals, and didn't want to scandalize other occupants of the house. During those days, I resented him for the noise, but as I look at it now, I have come to appreciate his considerateness in protecting us from the sounds coming from the sacred games."

"You should have complained," I said.

"Back to the headmaster's love of wrestling. The deputy head had a television set, which was powered by solar. Once or twice in a week, there was a wrestling show on the television. The headmaster never missed any of those programs. After super, he would come to the deputy head's house to watch wrestling. He always came with his other son, not the one who had just come to live with him. There was nothing wrong about him watching wrestling at his deputy's house because I also watched it on the same television. Television sets were expensive, and only few teachers could afford them. Initially, the headmaster would watch the wrestling in silence, but as the game progressed, he would lose it. He would shout and jump as if he were in his own house. At those moments, he seemed to be oblivious of our presence in the same room. He behaved like it was only him and his son, Jacob, in the room."

'Jackie, Jackie, do you see that? Oh. My God, Jackie, look! He is choking him. Yes, give him some more. Please, don't climb on the ropes. You will miss him. Jackie, look, look.' "He was so excited. Instead of watching the wrestling, I watched him. The deputy headmaster, his wife, and brothers, and I didn't seem to exist in the headmaster's world. During the wrestling program, the headmaster literally took over the house and the program. No one else talked except him and his little boy. After the wrestling, he and his boy would leave, and peace would come back to the house until at dawn, when Zhakata's songs would take over. The deputy head and his family seemed to understand and tolerate the head's enthusiasm. They never commented about his behavior after he had left."

"That was funny."

"It was not funny at all. Later, I got to know why wrestling excited him so much. He enjoyed watching people fighting. This is how I got to know it. It was at the end of the month, and we were coming from Jerera Growth Point, aboard our famous bus, Big Dad. The miserable bus was full of teachers from our and other schools. Mr. Tomson, our deputy headmaster, had an argument with a teacher from another school. I don't think that the misunderstanding warranted a fight, but due to the encouragement by the headmaster, the fracas degenerated into a fight. Soon the wrestling men were outside of the bus. The teacher from the other school was pinned to the ground, like in a typical wrestling contest, and the excited headmaster was beating the ground like professional wrestling referees do, until the teacher from the other school was defeated."

How long did you teach at that school?" I asked.

"For about three months. Soon, I received my acceptance letter to pursue further studies, and I left for the University of Zimbabwe."

These were amazing stories, and I was hearing them for the first time. I really appreciated Baba opening up to me like he did. We talked like friends, which we had never done before. When my parents returned to Zimbabwe, I missed the stories and other experiences, which I had shared with them.

On the other hand, the returning of my parents to Zimbabwe was good in that Maria and I could reclaim our space and privacy. I could now go back to my position as the father of the house, a position, which I could not claim when my father was around. Maria went back to dressing the way she liked, instead of dressing in a manner that appeased my parents. Furthermore, she went back to her position as the sole mother of the house.

On the day of my parents' departure, Maria and I drove them to George Bush International Airport from where they flew British Airways. They had a four-hour layover at Heathrow, London, and another two-hour layover in Johannesburg, South Africa. They arrived back home safely.

Later, we were told about how Baba bragged to his friends and relatives about his trip to and experiences in America. Some of his friends are said to have brought it upon themselves because they visited my parents just to ask them about their American experiences. Mother also told me that, Baba, most of the time, exaggerated a little bit when talking about America. One of the earliest persons to visit my parents for a dose of their American experiences was the village head's police officer, named Fatso. Fatso is my aunt's son, therefore, my *muzukuru*.

"So, tell me about flying, uncle. Were you not afraid?" Fatso asked him.

"It's easy, *muzukuru*. You don't even feel a thing. It's like you are sitting in your house. You only feel something when the plane is taking off or landing. During take offs and landing, you should sit as if preparing for death. The safety belt should be tightened, and the seat put in an upright position. Once you are airborne, you don't feel a thing, except a few moments of air turbulence."

"What about food, uncle?" Fatso wanted to know.

"The airplane hostesses and hosts bring you food and drinks. If you want some beer, or wine, they give it to you."

"Do they have our traditional beer like *chibuku*, in there?"

Baba laughed. "No. It's only European beer. They give you just a small bottle or can."

"I was told that passengers on an airplane eat cakes only. Is it true?" It was Fatso.

"Not true, *muzukuru*. I don't know the kind of food they serve. You get just a little that doesn't even fill half your stomach."

"You don't need to eat too much, uncle. You are gluttonous."

"Who is gluttonous? Are you referring to yourself? You know that I am a moderate eater, but still the food was not enough."

"Why didn't you ask for some more food, uncle?"

"That would be embarrassing. I was not alone on the plane. There were other passengers, who ate the same kind and quantity of food. Why would I ask for some more?"

"Tell us about America. Is it like paradise?"

"There are a lot of white people. Everywhere you look, you see white people. In fact, I saw very few black people on the plane, and in America."

"You are lucky, uncle. God loves you. You sat and ate with white people? They looked at you, and you looked at them. They saw you, and you saw them. They greeted you, and you greeted them. You should thank your ancestors. Some of us will never fly in an airplane."

"Yes, nephew. In America, I spoke only English. Good English, nephew. Occasionally, I would throw in a jawbreaker, and some of them would pip into my mouth to check if there was not a little white person sitting in there. I used words like, flabbergasted, serendipity, cantankerous, plethora, pugnacity, incorrigible, and many others. You know me, nephew. I taught them how to speak their own language."

"Did they clap hands for you?"

"No. Some didn't even understand some of the words that I used. I had to switch back to basic English."

"Come on, my uncle. You are impossible, uncle. I wish I were there with you, just to cheer you on. Don't they speak English, in America?"

"They speak very simple English. When they are speaking, you just hear words like, is, that, the, take, and many other simple words. They don't use big words like we do here. They don't know them."

"*Vakomana*! They speak grade one English. I think I am better than them. Why don't they use Shona if English is so difficult for them?"

Father laughed. "Shona? They don't know it. They only speak English."

"So, can some of us who are not very educated understand their English?"

"If you don't understand a little English, you won't survive in America. You need to ask for directions. You need to order food, and you should do it in English. If you speak some Spanish, you would be okay."

"Are commodities very cheap over there? I was told that bread is given for free."

"That's not true, nephew. Americans know the value of money. They don't give away anything for free. There are all kinds of bread for different prices. You buy the type that you can afford. I think the cheapest bread is about a dollar."

"But bread is bread, uncle. One dollar is nothing in America. My friend told me that every American is a millionaire. Everyone drives a car. Everyone has a house."

"Nephew be careful about what people tell you, and what you accept as reality about America. Indisputably, there are millionaires in America. Unfortunately, we never met any one of them. Take it from me, *muzukuru*, it's true that most people own vehicles, but some people have to borrow money from banks to purchase those vehicles and houses. In America, your worth can be measured according to your credit score."

"What's that, uncle?"

"I am not sure if I can clearly explain it to you. I shall tell you what your uncle, Peter, told me. It's about trustworthiness in borrowing and returning money from and back to lenders. The more money you have borrowed and retuned to lenders, the more trustworthy you are, and the better chances you have of getting more credit lines. If you borrow some money, and you default in your payments, you ruin your chances of getting more loans. You have to borrow and return some money to be allowed to borrow more."

"That's weird, *sekuru*. Borrowing money is not a good thing. A person should be able to live within his means."

"What you just said is true in Zimbabwe, but not in America. It's very difficult for people to live within their means because most people earn very little. They won't be able to afford college fees, cars, houses, and house furniture if they don't borrow some money from banks."

"But you said they pay back the money with interest?"

"Yes."

"Suppose most people could not afford to pay college fees, or purchase cars or houses, wouldn't the prices go down? Don't you think that institutions can charge any amount for fees or other things because there is a bank that is benefitting from lending money to the poor and charging interest for it? If there were no banks willing to loan money to people, goods and services would be cheaper because of less competition. Maybe I am wrong, uncle, and I stand to be corrected."

"That's impressive, *muzukuru*. You reasoned like a very educated man. It could be that the same lenders push up the prices of services and goods to force people to turn to them for loans so that they can get more interest. Also, institutions and businesses know that they can charge any amount they want because there are banks that have the money, which they may lend to the poor so that it's paid back with interest. That's the reality."

"Are Americans happy about that? Do they know that things can be affordable if they refuse to borrow money from the banks?"

"I don't think that they know it. Most Americans never doubt their processes and systems. Hence, they do not learn from other people. Of course, their systems are good. The cars are big. The roads are wide and smooth."

"Do they have spaghetti roads?"

"What are spaghetti roads?" Baba asked.

"Intertwined road traffic interchanges," Fatso responded.

"Many. Who told you about them?"

"I first heard about spaghetti roads from one of Zimbabwe's 2018 presidential candidates."

"I see."

"Tell me about their food, uncle."

"There is a lot of food. Chicken and pork are very affordable, but are not as tasty as our own. It's not good meat at all. Beef tastes better, but it is very expensive."

"Are you serious, uncle?"

"Serious about what?"

"Are you sure that chicken and pork can ever be not tasty? That's an insult to some of us who have never been to America. Meat, uncle? Are you talking about the meat that I know, uncle?"

"I don't know how I can explain it to you. The chickens are too big and fat. The meat doesn't taste like our chicken. The pork looks good, but the taste is not right. I just ate it a few times, and I gave up, nephew."

"But uncle, tell me about *mababes*. You know I am not married. Can uncle Peter find a woman for me in America?"

"What do you mean, Fatso, my nephew?"

"I mean a white lady who may want to marry me."

Baba laughed.

"Why are you laughing, uncle. Do you underrate me?"

"Nephew, why would a white lady, who has never seen you, fall in love with you? Don't we have women in our surrounding villages, nephew?"

"But uncle Peter got a white lady?"

"You and Peter are different people. Peter lives in America, and you have never been to Harare. Peter speaks good English, and you don't. So, how do you expect a white lady to fall in love with you? Why don't you try our own beautiful women, here?"

"It's about money, uncle. Money. If I marry a white woman, my poverty will disappear like fog. Perhaps she may take me to America and make me an American citizen. You would never see me again, uncle."

"If wishes were horses, beggars would ride."

"But uncle, tell me. Is uncle Peter's white woman, a real woman?"

"What do you mean?"

"Is she like our women. You know what I mean?"

"How would I know that? You will ask her husband when he comes to visit us."

There was a pause.

"Uncle, what about beer?"

"It's cheaper in supermarkets than in bars. I never went inside a bar, but I was told that beer that is sold there is prohibitively expensive. In supermarkets, it is much cheaper. You can buy a case of beer, and drink it at your home."

"Drinking beer alone, uncle? Beer tastes better when you share it with others. You can't enjoy beer alone."

"I agree with you, nephew, but that's the way things are done in America. People stay in their homes, and they spend lots of time with their families."

"Thank you, uncle. We can't finish all the stories today. I have one last question, did you like America?"

"I did, very much. Americans are very good people. They are kind and respectful to other people. They mind their own business. Of course, I wouldn't want to live in America permanently, but I would love to visit occasionally."

"Thank you, *sekuru*. I will come back tomorrow to listen to more stories about America."

"You are welcome. You can't leave now, because your *mbuya* is preparing food in the kitchen."

"Mbuya! What are you cooking?" Fatso shouted. "Are you making use of your American recipes?"

"Yes, *muzukuru*. Just wait and see," Mother responded.

Fatso sat down and waited for lunch.

6

A Trip to Zimbabwe

It took forever to prepare for our journey to Zimbabwe. For me, it was just another excursion to the land where I was born. A voyage to the soil where my umbilical cord was buried. A journey to the sacred place where I could reestablish my connection and relationship with my ancestors. A visit to the home where I could renew my allegiance to the ancestors, and reorient my fortunes. A long haul to a country where I would meet the community that helped my parents to raise me. A sojourn to the mountains where I would reaffirm my relationship to my so many mothers, fathers, sisters, and brothers. A trip to a home where I would experience genuine love, respect, and self-esteem. A trip to a place where I would offer and receive gifts. A long haul to the land where I could laugh heartily without the fear of being judged. A journey to the kitchen where I could eat the food I craved without the fear of offending others by the aroma from that food. A trip to a country where I would reassert my commitment to learning the wisdom of the elders. A journey to a place where I could look at or lift children without the fear of being suspected of being a pedophile. A trip to the land where I could be free to be myself.

For Maria and her family, it was a different kind of expedition altogether. It was going to be the longest trip Maria had ever embarked on. A long haul to the jungles of Africa where wild animals were believed to roam the streets like there was no tomorrow. A journey to the cradle of humankind as historians and anthropologists want us to believe. A travel to the mother of poverty and diseases. A journey to the home of political despots and violence. A travel to the residence of corruption and economic mismanagement. A journey to the mother of all black people. A journey full of uncertainties. An expedition riddled with unknown life-threatening dangers, insatiable sexual perverts who roam the streets while holding their manhood in their hands, looking for women to assault and violate in broad daylight. A journey to the audacious pickpockets that can snatch away food from one's belly. But still a trip of a lifetime.

One day, Andrea visited us at our home, and started questioning Maria about our scheduled trip to Zimbabwe.

"Maria, do you think this is the right time to go to Zimbabwe?" Andrea asked.

"Absolutely," responded Maria.

"Why don't you wait another year?" Andrea was concerned.

"Mom, why should I wait for a year?" Maria asked.

"There are diseases in Zimbabwe, Maria."

"I know. There are also diseases in the United States, Mom."

"There is Ebola in Africa. It's deadly."

"Not in Zimbabwe, Mother."

"What about Malaria?"

"It's now winter in Zimbabwe, and mosquitoes are in hibernation. We will use mosquito nets and repellants, and other preventive measures."

"What about other diseases, Maria?"

"What diseases, Mom?"

"Like cancer."

"Mother, are you saying that I can't get cancer, here?"

"No. But you never know the kind of cancer they have in Africa."

"I am a nurse, Mother, and I know how to take good care of myself."

"Graves are full of nurses, Maria. Nurses die too, for they are human."

"You are right, Mother. I understand your concerns, but please, allow me to make my own decisions. Allow me to live my own life. There are people in Zimbabwe, white people included, Mother. I won't be alone. If I become sick, they have doctors and hospitals."

"Do you know that there are poisonous snakes, in Zimbabwe?"

"Poisonous snakes are everywhere, Mother."

"What will we do if you die over there?"

"They have cemeteries too, Mother. They will bury me. After all, death is ubiquitous. One can die anywhere."

"What happened to your reasoning, Maria? You sound very arrogant and illogical."

"It's called maturity, Mother. I am no longer a baby. You cannot continue to make decisions for me any longer. You better get used to it."

"Okay. Suit yourself." Andrea accepted defeat after putting up a good fight. I perfectly understood her. If I were in her position, I would have felt the same. Many bad stories about Africans were being paddled daily by news reporters on televisions and on social media. Stories of starving children, women subjugation, killings, dictatorships, and corruption were on the news daily. That was the mindset Maria's mother was operating on. It was not her fault because she did not create the erroneous narratives about Africa and its people. Many whites have the same perception about Africa and Africans, and it takes a lot of trust and courage for someone to demystify such myths about Africa.

Andrea's misconceptions about Africa were understandable, and to some extent, forgivable. No one in her family had ever been to Africa. No one had ever studied African history or culture. No one had read a book or watched a positive documentary about Africa. No one had ever dreamt of visiting Africa. But unlike most of her family members and friends, Maria knew where Africa was located on the globe. Her knowledge had now been widened and deepened because she could pinpoint the position of Zimbabwe on the map of Africa. She was not only prepared to marry a Zimbabwean, but also to acquire a working knowledge of the geography and culture of Zimbabwe.

Maria had friends who knew nothing about Africa or Zimbabwe, although some of them knew a thing or two about Africa. Some of them had watched movies depicting Africa as the cradle of poverty. A place where aimless and barbaric wars were fought. They knew Africa, the home of virgin jungles where uncountable animals lived. Some of Maria's friends and relatives thought that there were only five countries in Africa, namely, Africa; every black person's country of origin, South Africa; Nelson Mandela's country, Kenya; President Barack Obama's country, and Nigeria; Kunta Kinte's birthplace. The fifth was a recent African country called Wakanda, the home of unparalleled economic prosperity and technological advancement, where vibranium was mined.

On many occasions, I heard Maria trying to educate them about the geography of Africa during introductions. She indeed had become an ambassador for Zimbabwe.

"This is my husband, Peter. He is originally from Zimbabwe," Maria would introduce me.

"Nice meeting you, Peter. I had a friend at college who was from Nigeria. You may know him. His name was Oduduwa, a very nice fellow," Maria's friend would innocently say.

"Oh, no. Zimbabwe is in Southern Africa, and Nigeria is in West Africa. The two countries are more than a thousand kilometers apart."

"I am sorry. I thought that Zimbabwe was not far from Nigeria."

One of Maria's friends would introduce me to her family as follows:

"This is Peter, Maria's husband. He comes from Africa."

Maria would quickly jump in to correct her.

"He is from Zimbabwe."

"Do you know Barack Obama's family that lives there?"

"No way. President Obama's family is from Kenya, not Zimbabwe," Maria would correct them.

Maria empathized with her friends. She knew that their lack of knowledge about Africa was not their fault. Their educational system did not allow them to learn much about Africa. There was nothing for them to learn about Africa because her story was pitiful. Maria always educated her friends about Africa with empathy and patience, and the majority of them appreciated her efforts, and promised to learn more about Africa. Perhaps, some of them might have made such a promise out of the respect that they had for Maria, but it was still consoling to me. It was always therapeutic to know that some people cared about me and my roots.

When the dates to visit Zimbabwe were scheduled, we started packing. The packing lasted three months. Time and time again, I would bring a new shirt, a jacket, or dress to our home, and Maria would ask, "Whose is this?"

"I bought this shirt for one of my uncles," I would respond.

"Whose is this dress?"

"For my aunt."

"What about the jacket?"

"The jacket is for my uncle's son."

"What about this other dress?"

"It's for my other aunt."

This kind of conversation continued for about three months. When I continued to bring different kinds of clothes home so that we would take them to Zimbabwe, Maria was a little bit upset.

"How many uncles, aunts, nephews, and nieces do you have? Certainly, you cannot buy clothes for the whole village. It's not like you are their father or a donor of some kind. Or you want to be a hero?"

I tried to explain why it was imperative for me to bring a little something for every relative that I was going to meet in Zimbabwe. She listened as I explained.

"In our Shona culture, one is everybody's son. When I think of my family, I can't exclude the villagers and our extended family. We belong to each other. They assisted my parents in raising me. We belong together. We assist each other as much as we can. That's how we were raised, to think of others and assist them as much as we can. Since I expect other villagers to assist my parents when I am not there, I should also be willing to make sacrifices for others. You will see how embarrassing it is, not to give people presents when we get there. Everyone will expect a small present from us, and this time, their expectations will be greater."

"Why?"

"Because I am married to you, and you will be with me."

"How will my presence increase their expectations?"

"You are white, Maria, and white people have lots of money."

"Who told them that?"

"I don't know. It's just a perception that our people have about white people, which originated from colonialism."

"I see. You will have to tell them that I don't have money."

"I will, but it won't lower their expectations."

Maria was quiet.

I continued. "It's not easy. It's a sacrifice that we are taught to make right from birth. That's what everybody does for the family and community."

"Give me a mental picture of your rural village. I know you have told me a dozen times, but I guess that one more time won't hurt."

"I can do it a thousand times," I told her.

"I know."

Maria knew that I loved telling my story. In fact, there were times when I overdid it, or even exaggerated a little.

"I was born by the foot of Chitakai mountain. Chitakai is part of a range of big mountains that pass through our village, and stretch for almost a hundred miles. Our rural home is at the foot of that mountain. There, we had round, grass-thatched huts in which we lived. They are still there. My parents and brother still live in them. There are about two dozen homesteads in the village, and each homestead has about five round huts. Of those five round huts, three are likely to be bedrooms for the parents, boys, and girls, and the fourth hut should be the kitchen, which is also used as a sitting room, dining room, and a sacred place for traditional rituals. The fifth, though the smallest, is the most important hut, for it is the granary, which sometimes is divided into numerous compartments, which are used to store different kinds of grains. The staple grain is maize or corn. Small grains such as sorghum, millet, finger millet, and others are also grown, and are used to brew beer or cook *sadza*."

"One round hut for all the boys?" Maria asked.

"Yes. And another round hut for all the girls. When I was growing up, most brothers would have a single reed mat and blanket, which they shared. It was the same with the girls. Now, things have changed because people can afford more blankets, and at times, beds. Moreover, some people now have bigger houses with many rooms instead of the traditional round huts."

"Where are the schools located?" Maria asked.

"The schools, churches, and the township are located beyond the Chitakai mountain. When I was in primary and high school, we would climb up and down the mountain going to and from school or church. We would climb the same mountain to play or to herd our cattle. I was not alone. I had friends. Most of them have died. Some of the deceased are buried by the foot of the same mountain. They left families. Children. And I should try to assist those families as much as I can. If I were one of the departed ones, I would wish that one of my friends, should take care of my kids. I am one of the few, who is still living. I am one of the fortunate ones. Perhaps, I was spared for a reason."

"It's a very sad and touching story. You sound like you miss the mountains," Maria said.

"I miss not only the mountains, but also my relatives. Our climbing of the mountain going to and from school reminds me of the ups and downs of life. Indeed, the mountain delayed us on our way to and from school. It made us sweat and dirty, but it also conditioned our health.

We were strong and in sound health. During those days, even tenacious diseases such as influenza could hardly infect us."

"Do you also miss your childhood friends? I miss a few of mine."

"I do, sometimes. I wish they would be at the village when we arrive there, so that we could talk and laugh about our childhood mischief. I must do something for their kids to honor my childhood friendship with their parents, and to thank the ancestors and God for taking me this far. Just small gifts will do. They make a great difference in their lives."

"You sound nostalgic, Peter."

"Absolutely, but also, sad. Maybe, more nostalgic than sad."

"It's the right kind of sadness, which propels you to be kinder and more generous. You are a good man, Peter, and I love you so much," Maria said this as she embraced me.

"Thank you, sweetheart. I love you too. You are very considerate. Very few people would understand and tolerate this kind of philosophy."

"You have to do what you need to do for your friends' kids," Maria said.

"Thank you," I replied.

"Thank you for doing what you can for your people. The world would be a better place if more people shared just a little of their wealth with the less fortunate members of our society."

"I appreciate your understanding and empathy, sweetheart."

The packing continued until we had six suitcases full of clothes and other small items. I also went to the bank to get a few bundles of five-dollar bills to take with us to Zimbabwe. The bills would make it convenient for us to offer monetary gifts to my relatives.

Andrea donated a suitcase of used clothes for us to take to Zimbabwe as gifts for my family and friends. She also promised that she would bring some more if their planned trip to Zimbabwe would be successful.

Since we had to depart on a weekday, we decided to use one of the public busses, which plied the route between San Antonio and George Bush International Airport, in Houston. It was a big mistake as we discovered later. We realized that we should have allowed Mr. Weber to drop us at the airport as he had offered to do. We arrived at the bus station in San Antonio about an hour before the take off. We weighed and paid for our excess baggage. There were many other people, sitting in the shelter, waiting for buses to different destinations. Some of the passengers had young children. Later, we realized that most of them were immigrants coming from the Mexican-American border, on their way to other American States.

When it was almost boarding time, we stood on the line inside the bus station. The bus was running late as we had feared. When it finally arrived, we all followed the line towards the bus. When we finally got into the bus, we were shocked that most of the seats were already taken, not by passengers, but by some small items, which had been placed on vacant seats. These items were intended to alert other passengers that the seats had already been taken. We later realized that the immigrants had been with each other for a long time. They knew each other and were now behaving like a family. So, the first few to get on the bus, reserved seats for their friends who were still outside, standing on the line behind us. In the end, even the passengers who were standing behind us on the line, chose their seats before we did. Consequently, we got the very back seat, which was leaning against the bathroom wall.

As soon as the bus left the San Antonio station for Houston, a line of kids and mothers quickly formed to use the bathroom. It was like the parents had not advised their children to make use of the bathrooms at the bus station, or they had given them too many drinks before takeoff. Maria and I had no problem with the kids lining to relieve themselves since the bathroom door was almost soundproof. As a matter of fact, I was not as comfortable with this seat as Maria was. Just sitting there, made me conscious of the people getting in and out of the bathroom. Of course, it was an African thing, which had nothing to do with the people's business in there. Some Africans consider a toilet to be the dirtiest of all places, and some of them would rather die of thirst than drink clean water from a water tap situated in a toilet.

A big challenge, which I had not thought about arose when we were halfway to Houston. One of the passengers, a disheveled black man in his early thirties got into the bathroom. I mention the man's ethnicity not because what he did was caused by it, but because it was significantly noticeable, since there were only two black persons on the bus. There was nothing strange about him getting into the bathroom, but what followed was not only queer, but also scary. There were two kids standing behind the disheveled man, waiting to get into the same bathroom, hoping that the scruffy man would spend some reasonable time in it. He did not. He just disappeared into the bathroom. The kids waited and waited until they returned to their seats. The man did not emerge from the bathroom, and sooner, I became concerned. He had been in the bathroom for almost thirty minutes, and there was no sign of him getting out.

Some frustrated women came to join the line, but the scruffy man did not come out. I could see from their faces that they were becoming impatient, perhaps, because of the urgency of the nature of the business they wanted to accomplish in the bathroom, but the bathroom door did not open.

At first, no one seemed eager, impatient, and courageous enough to knock on the bathroom door, but I felt that sooner or later someone would brave the winds, and pound on the door. I was right. We did not have to wait longer before one of the older women on the line walked to the door of the bathroom and knocked softly. At first, the scruffy man inside the bathroom did not respond, and I felt that he was not only inconsiderate, but also arrogant. The brave woman knocked again, a little bit louder, this time. There was no response from the bathroom. She knocked for a third time, while trying the door handle, and the man inside the bathroom screamed and shouted simultaneously. It was then that I realized that the bathroom was not soundproof at all, for I could hear every word that the man said.

"Go away! Go away! How dare you knock on the door? How dare you disrespect me? I am still in here! I am using the bathroom!" He shouted from inside.

The woman stopped knocking, and stepped back a few steps. She looked more embarrassed than upset. I was glad that she had knocked on the door because the man inside had got the message. If he thought that the bus bathroom was his private bedroom, now he knew that other passengers were also entitled to using it. I felt that any reasonable person would hurry up in consideration of other passengers who were waiting to use the same bathroom, but the man did not come out of the bathroom. His action or lack of it defied all logic.

All the passengers standing on the line to use the bathroom went back to their seats. Within ten minutes, another elderly woman, accompanied her kid back onto the line. The kid was making faces and pressing his legs together to express his urgent need to use the bathroom. It was obvious that he was seriously pressed by the call of nature. The woman standing with him could no longer take it in, and she hesitantly walked closer to the bathroom door, and knocked gently. The man inside did not respond. She knocked again, and this time the man went berserk.

"Go away, you stupid immigrants. What do you want here? You only think of using the toilet. You got to have some respect. You cannot be immigrants, and have no respect of other people, at the same time. If you keep knocking, I will get out there and kick your asses," the man shouted.

The woman and her kid reluctantly left for their seats. Suddenly, an idea crossed my mind. I needed to alert the bus driver because the man's actions were suspicious. What was he doing in there? No one would use the bathroom for so long unless something was very wrong. I thought that he could be making a bomb. Since Maria and I were siting against the bathroom wall, if the man were a terrorist, we would be the first to die. I did not want to die, for it was not a good day to die. Maybe, some other day would be good for dying, but not that day. Of course, my guess was wrong, but that is what came into my mind. I whispered to Maria, who until then had seemed oblivious of what was happening. We started whispering about it.

"I am going to report him to the driver," I told Maria.

"What are you going to tell him?"

"That there is a suspicious man who has been in the bathroom for over thirty minutes. And that there are some kids who would like to use the bathroom."

"Do you think that it is a good idea?"

"Yes."

"Maybe, he is doing drugs," Maria said.

"Maybe, but they say, 'if you see something, you should say something.' The kids want to use the bathroom, and he is not getting out. He should know that the bus bathroom is not only for his private use, but also for the use of other passengers. He should be considerate."

"Be careful, what you say to the driver. You don't want the FBI flooding the bus because of a false alarm."

"You are right, but I think that the man is up to something not good."

"Good luck!"

I stood up and started walking along the aisle towards the bus driver. One of the women, who might have been pressed hard to use the bathroom went ahead of me straight to the driver. I did not hear what she said, but immediately the bus got into the exit ramp and headed for a nearby restaurant, and I was relieved. I went back to my seat. The bus stopped at the restaurant, and several women and kids ran out of the bus for the restaurant to use the bathroom. The inconsiderate man was still inside the bathroom.

Then, I heard the bathroom door opening, and the thoughtless man emerged, still cursing at no one in particular. He was not looking at anyone, but he seemed like he was cursing at someone he knew. He walked with a slight limp. I gazed at him as he shamelessly walked along the aisle, without giving me the benefit of looking me in the eyes. Although he denied me the pleasure or displeasure of looking him in the eyes, I was relieved, not because I wanted to use the bathroom, but because I was afraid that he was up to something bad. I guess, my wife was right. He may have been doing his drugs therein. Maybe I am being too judgmental. Whatever he was doing in there, it was wrong to lock himself up in a public bathroom for more than thirty minutes like a person who was pooping barbed wire. Probably, he was not feeling well, but a sick man would not have cursed at people from inside the bathroom, the way that he did.

We arrived at the airport about three hours ahead of our boarding time, and it was not a surprise because we had planned it that way. When I am flying, I always arrive at the airport, at least two hours ahead of check-in time. When check-in for our flight started, we were among the first ten passengers to present ourselves to the counter for baggage check-in. We were glad that all our check-in bags were within the flight's weight limits, and then we hit a snag. They were also weighing the carry-on luggage, and it was a bad surprise because I had never had my carry-on luggage weighed before. At home, we had weighed the check-in suitcases, but not the carry-ons, and we were up for a high jump.

Both carry-on bags were well above the weight limit. We were then sent away to fix our carry-on bags. We tried to adjust the weight by offloading some of the items from our carry-ons into the check-in suitcases, but we could not come to the seven pounds that were the upper limit for each carry-on. We then decided to give away some of the items that were in one of the larger suitcases to offset the weight of the carry-on luggage. We were lucky because one of the women working as a cleaner at the airport accepted the gift. I was relieved that at least, we donated the items to someone who would use them, rather than just throwing them away. We also removed the heavy jackets, which we had packed in our carry-on luggage. I went to the nearby bathroom, and put on two more jeans on top of the one I was already wearing, and when I emerged, I was like a moving wardrobe, but it worked.

Maria was upset. She could not understand why they would make such a fuss about a few extra pounds above the weight limit. She became more irritated when she noticed that other passengers' carry-ons were not weighed like they had done to ours. She was puzzled, but I was not. I thought I knew what was happening, although I was not so certain about it. On the one hand, I felt that it was a racist thing because some of the white folks' carry-ons were not weighed. On the other hand, it might not have been racism because the persons manning the check-in counters were all black, unless if they were taking orders from racist supervisors sitting in some offices somewhere. Perhaps, at play, was just white privilege not racism. It could be that the attendants knew that white passengers tended to pack their carry-ons within the weight limits. You can never be sure of these things.

Soon, we were airborne to our first layover in Dubai. We spent about six hours in that beautiful airport. Next, we were on our way to board our flight to Harare via Zambia. To get to the airplane, we had to get on a bus, which seemed like it would never get to the terminal. It was extremely hot, but the bus kept going. When we finally got there, we had to walk from the bus to board the plane. We were sweating as we climbed the improvised steep steps into the gigantic metal bird. Just before the plane took off, one of the air hostesses sprayed the inside of cabin roof with a substance from two cans. She held the cans in either stretched hand, and walked gracefully along the aisle while simultaneously spraying the odorless substance. She did not explain to the passengers what it was she was spraying. She also did not feel the need to explain the reason for spraying. She did not care if some passengers were allergic to that kind of substance or not. I guessed she was just doing her job.

The sprayed substance was odorless and invisible but that did not make it harmless. In fact, Carbon Dioxide, one of the deadliest gases, is odorless and invisible. Immediately, I felt my sinuses beginning to congest. Perhaps, I just imagined my sinuses clogging up because I do not think that the airline would spray chemicals in the plane, that some passengers would be allergic to.

"Why are they spraying the cabins?" Maria asked.

"I think that's what they do," I responded.

"They didn't do it on the flight from Houston."

"You are right. Maybe, they do it only to flights going to Africa."

"What if someone is allergic to the substance?" Maria was concerned.

"I am, but I think they don't care."

"They can be sued."

"I guess not."

"Why not?

"Maybe they are authorized to do it. After all, the passengers are African."

"Don't Africans have rights?"

"They do, but suing anybody is the last thing they think of."

Yes, they had not sprayed the plane from Houston. I still do not know why they did not spray the plane from Houston to Dubai, while they did it to the one going to Africa. It is only now that I think that I should have asked the air hostess. In life, I have come to learn that sometimes, we save ourselves from unnecessary speculation by asking for clarification. I did not ask, and I am still wondering why they did it. It is so easy to play the race card, which may in some cases, prevent us from looking at other explanations. Clearly, I am not trying to exonerate the airline. They may have sprayed the plane to get rid of African insects that the passengers may have brought in there. You never know.

The flight to Harare was smooth, and I soon forgot about the spray. The plane made a brief stop in Lusaka, Zambia, where some passengers disembarked, and others boarded the plane. The taking off from Lusaka was uneventful. Soon, we were at Robert Mugabe International Airport, in Zimbabwe. Both of us were glad that we had arrived home safely. It was about 7:00 pm, and it was already dark outside. We stood in a long line that inched towards the single checkout point that was open. Eventually, another checkout point was opened. When the line began to move a little bit faster, disaster struck. There was a power blackout, and the whole airport was enveloped in darkness. We stood there in the darkness for a good ten minutes before the airport generators kicked off. Maria and other visitors who were not privy to the power cuts in Zimbabwe panicked. Some passengers screamed. I explained to Maria that power cuts were normal in Zimbabwe, and there was no need to worry. However, I had not anticipated power blackout at the only international airport in the country.

Even though it took about ten minutes for power to be restored at the airport, it took another twenty minutes for the tired old computers to reboot.

"Why is it taking so long to serve us?" Maria seemed impatient.

"Welcome to Zimbabwe, my darling," I ignored her question.

"Why are they not serving?" She changed the question.

"I think, they are waiting for the computers to reboot. They have old computers that take almost a day to reboot."

"Are you kidding me?"

"Nope."

"I thought the blackout was a terrorist attack." Maria shocked me.

"Seriously?"

"Yes."

"You shouldn't worry about terrorist attacks here because we don't have terrorists in Zimbabwe. You should worry about some different kind of terrorists called pick-pockets, and some vampires called mosquitoes. We are lucky, this is June, and it's cold."

"No pick-pockets in June?" Maria asked.

"No. I mean the little flying vampires. They retire in June."

"Not even a single one?"

"Maybe one or two hardcore vampires. The rest will be hibernating or dead."

"Are they as deadly as people say?"

"They are, but not everyone bitten by a mosquito gets malaria. Also, not every mosquito carries malaria."

"I see."

As we talked, the attendant started serving visitors. We stood on the line for almost another thirty minutes before we were served. When our turn came, I was served first. The attendant was very friendly, and smiled all the time. She stamped my passport while talking. She then handed back my passport and receipt for the visa. Then, it was Maria's turn to be served. The attendant looked at her passport and at Maria several times. Finally, she looked at me, and I knew it was coming.

"Is she our *muroora*, my brother?" The attendant asked.

"Yes."

"You are sophisticated, brother. Congratulations!"

"Thank you," I replied.

She started processing Maria's visa.

"Does she understand Shona?" The attendant asked without even looking at us.

"A little bit," I answered.

"*Ndichadzidza zvakawanda, Shona*," Maria responded.

The attendant looked at Maria admiringly.

"Welcome to Zimbabwe, *muroora*."

"*Tatenda zvakawanda,*" Maria responded.

I handed the attendant another thirty American dollars, and she stamped Maria's passport, and then handed it back to her. Maria slipped it into her handbag. It was not until after two days when we discovered that the attendant had not issued a receipt to Maria. The visa had been granted, but there was no receipt inserted into Maria's passport like she had done for my payment. Maria was very concerned, and wanted us to go back to the airport to collect the receipt. I laughed at her before I explained that the omission was deliberate.

"What do you mean?"

"It's called corruption, sweetheart. Your payment was for her personal use, and there is nothing you can do about it. There wasn't a receipt issued, in the first place. She knew that you would not check for it right away."

"We can go and report her to her supervisor. I guess she will lose her job."

"It doesn't work like that, here, Maria."

"Why not?"

"Because the supervisor might also be involved."

"So, what do we do? I have no receipt."

"We do nothing. You have your visa, and that's all what is needed."

"But if no one reports them, they may continue stealing from visitors, and giving a bad name to the country."

"You are right, they will, but what can you do? The whole system is rotten. This is only a tip of an iceberg. You will see more."

"If she does that in the United States, she would go to prison."

"I know, but she very well knows that this is Zimbabwe, and not the United States. She can get away with it without a pinprick."

We were now in the baggage collection area. From a distance, we could see that only our suitcases, and a few others were still there. All our bags were tapped with yellow tap. As we stood there wondering why, one of the airport caretakers quickly ran to us.

"How are you, *blazo*? Is this your wife?" It was the caretaker.

"Yes."

"How are you, *maiguru*?"

"We are very well, if you are also doing well," Maria responded.

The caretaker looked at me and whispered, "There is a very big problem, my brother. You see these yellow tapes? You know the meaning?"

"No."

"Well. Let me tell you. It means that your bags have been preselected for further inspection, and they will ask you to pay duty for everything that you are bringing into the country."

"These are personal clothes, my brother."

"Any new clothes? Phones? Watches? Computers?"

"Yes," I responded.

"Trouble, my brother, but I can help you?"

"How?"

"Easy, my brother. I will remove the yellow tapes from your luggage, and then load it into this cart, and you should push it. I will be walking behind you. You just keep walking. Look ahead. Nothing will happen."

"Is that a free service?" I asked.

"Don't shout, my brother. It is free, but I accept gifts. I have a family to feed, my brother."

"How much do you want?" I wanted to know before we were rendered the services.

"Ten US dollars, my boss."

I agreed to give him the money not because I was keen to encourage airport corrupt activities, but because I always knew when I was defeated. I knew when it was futile to fight a war. That was one of the wars in which I felt defeated even before the battle started. I could have refused to pay the money he was asking for, but then they could have kept us in the airport for all eternity. Or they would have made us pay exorbitant duty for the donations that we were bringing to Zimbabwe. That is what corruption does to a people. It corrupts everyone, some willingly and others, unwillingly. It gives good people no other option except to participate in it, though unwillingly. For ordinary citizens to be able to fight corruption, there should be some people with power who are willing to eradicate it by making corrupt officials accountable for their corrupt activities if reported. I do not think that many such incorruptible, powerful people can be found in Zimbabwe. I am not saying that all Zimbabweans are corrupt because there are many Zimbabweans who are not corrupt.

Guiltily, we followed the corrupt guy as I vigorously and guiltily pushed the trolley, full of our suitcases. From the way he walked and smiled, I could tell that he was carrying a dead conscience. Yes, he did not have a conscience at all. How could one smile while robbing people in broad daylight? We stopped momentarily at the last checkout. When we were asked if we had anything to declare, we said 'nothing,' which was true. We were then ushered out, still following the thieving caretaker.

In less than ten minutes, we were at the taxi loading area, outside the airport, and our villain was still with us. He called his friend on the phone, and immediately a taxi pulled up. He helped us pack our suitcases into the cab, and when we were done with the packing, and now we were sitting in the cab, he came to our window, and asked for the ten American dollars that we had agreed to pay. We did not argue with him. I just handed it to him, and he walked away briskly. He was celebrating, for he had made a fortune. We immediately got on the road, on our way to my aunt's place. I still do not know if he was not the one who had tapped our suitcases or not. I also do not know if he was indeed a *bona fide* airport caretaker or just a thief who had gained entrance into the baggage collection area. I am not sure of what could have happened if we had left the yellow taps on our suitcases.

It was almost 9:00 pm, and the flow of traffic was still slow. The cab driver used shortcut roads that I had never used before. He was a good driver, and seemed to be a good man as well. He sounded and behaved like a man who earned his living honestly. He asked about life in America, and showed a keen interest in whatever we said.

"*Blazo*, you are impossible. *Hamuite*. How did you get a white woman?"

Maria responded, "We fell in love."

"Just like that. We thought there was racism in America."

"You are right. We have that challenge in America, but love always overcomes every hurdle placed in its way. It triumphs over hate. That's what love does." Maria was philosophical.

"Very true, *maiguru*. I am so happy for you, guys. I wish I could also go to America."

"Please, don't," I said.

"Why not?" He wanted to know the reason.

"You will make a lot of money, but you won't buy anything with it. The cost of living is too high, my brother. Your monthly salary will not be enough to pay for your rent."

"Is that true? People tell us that life is so good and easy in America?"

"Yes, for some people, but not for everyone. You can't go to America at your age, and expect to live like a king. Of course, you may be able to get a bank loan to purchase a car or a house if you are lucky."

"What's wrong with that?"

"Nothing, except that the interest rates are very high, and you won't own the property until it's fully paid for. If you fail to pay, they are likely to repossess it, and you go back to square one."

"People say that America is like heaven."

"That's not entirely true. Maybe it is for some people, but not to the ordinary people."

"That's too bad. Here, in Zimbabwe, I don't make much money, but at least, I have my cabs and a house. They are all mine. I don't owe anybody anything."

"You are lucky, my brother."

"So, people lie to us about America?" He was shocked.

"Some people have a tendency to exaggerate," I said.

"Do you want to tell me that some people rent houses in America?"

"Many."

"You mean black people?"

"And whites, too."

"White people renting a house in America? I never dreamt about that." He was in disbelief. "I thought that all white people have lots of money, and can afford to buy whatever they want."

"Some of them have a lot of money, but there are also white people who struggle to make ends meet. Of course, whites have more advantages than blacks."

"Like what?"

"White skin color. It pays to be white in America. The white skin color carries certain privileges, which the black color does not have. For instance, if you are looking for a job, and you have your qualifications, experience, and the white skin, you are likely to get a job earlier than a black person who has the same qualifications and job experience."

"That's very disturbing. Isn't that apartheid?"

"Not exactly. They call it racism."

"Maybe if I go to America, I will get a white wife, and I would become as rich as you are, my brother."

I looked at him, and laughed. He seemed to mean it.

"Do I look like I am rich?" I asked.

"You should be grateful, my brother, you have a white wife."

"I am grateful, but we are not rich. We are just ordinary Americans who struggle to make ends meet."

"I thought you were married," Maria said.

"Yes, I am. I have four kids, but I will get a second wife if my life depends on it. A white woman this time." He looked serious.

Maria was surprised.

"My brother, polygamy is illegal in America. You would be arrested if you tried to get a second wife," I explained.

"Even if you try to do it secretly, no woman will fall for it," said Maria.

"Why not? Am I too ugly for a white woman? Look at me properly." The cab driver looked at Maria.

"No. No. I didn't mean that. I think you are very handsome, but it's against our values as Americans. You can't have more than one wife."

"So, American men don't have small-houses?" The cab driver asked.

"What are small-houses?" Maria wanted to know.

"Mistresses or side chicks," I told her.

"I think some men do have them," Maria admitted.

"So, you have polygamy. There is no difference. It's just a different name. I will get a very rich mistress," said the cab driver.

"What about your wife? What will she say?"

"I don't think she will be jealous at all. Who doesn't love a white woman? I would tell her that it's business. I will fill up all her cooking pots with American dollars. She won't complain."

"Yes, you can keep it a secret, but what about your conscience and integrity as a person?" Maria asked.

"Integrity is a good virtue, but you should understand that nobody eats integrity. Most businesses prosper by taking advantage of their employees and customers. If you look at European countries, they acquired their wealth from Africa and Asia by hook and by crook. Where was their integrity?"

We all laughed. We went quiet. And we laughed again.

"Don't worry, Maria, he will not get a visa to go to the United States. One of the questions they ask during visa interviews is about having no intention to engage in polygyny."

Maria did not respond.

When we arrived at my aunt's place, I handed the cab driver fifty American dollars, which he had told us was the fixed fare for the ride. For a moment, he held the money in his outstretched hand while gazing at me without blinking like an animal dazzled by the headlights of a car. He opened his mouth as if to say something, but no word came out. After a moment, he managed to thank us, and drove off. When I told my aunt about the cab driver's reaction, she claimed to know what had happened. He was shocked that we had given him fifty American dollars when he expected fifty Zimbabwean dollars, popularly known as bond dollars. At that time, fifty American dollars were equivalent to over five hundred bond dollars.

My aunt was upset because the cab driver had robbed us.

"He robbed you. He is a thief. He should have given you back your money," my aunt complained.

"It wasn't his fault. I handed him the money. It was my mistake, not his."

"He is a bad man. Do you have his phone number?"

"No," I responded.

"If you know the name or color of his cab, I can go to the airport tomorrow to get that money back."

"What if he refuses to give back the money?"

"I will haunt him until he gives it to me."

"There is no need for you to do that. It's not necessary. We gave him the money. It was a gift," Maria intervened. "In fact, we became friends on the road," claimed Maria.

"Mapofu, *muroora*, you don't give a person you don't know that much money. You gave him a fortune. If you don't want the money, I can keep it."

"Oh, I see. That's where it's going? You don't need to do that, aunt. After all, you won't find him. We are glad that we gave him something valuable for his family. He sounded like an honest guy," I tried to calm her down. "By the way, who is Mapofu?" I asked.

"Your wife, my son. What can we call her? We can't just use her first name."

"Why not?"

"It's disrespectful."

"Why, Mapofu? You can just call her daughter-in-law."

"We were told that all white people have one totem—*Shava. Mhofu yemukuno. Zienda netyaka. Ziwewera.*"

Everybody in the house laughed.

"Who told you that?" I asked.

"One of our priests told us. We all call him, Baba Museyamwa."

"What's *Shava*?" Maria asked.

"It's an eland," I responded.

"You can call me Maria. That's my name." That was directed at my aunt and her kids.

"Never. We don't call married women by their first names. That's not right."

"Then just call her, daughter-in-law," I said.

She agreed.

We spent two days at my aunt's home while recovering from jetlag. The two days of rest did not completely heal us of our jetlag, but they helped a lot. We needed more strength because the journey was not over yet.

Two days after our arrival, we had to proceed with our journey to Nyajena, where my parents lived. We woke up early in the morning, and went to Mbare Musika, which is the main agricultural produce market, and long-distance bus station, in Harare. We purchased vegetables and potatoes, and then boarded the bus to Masvingo. Maria was so amazed to see so many black people in one place, each minding his own business. The market was like a beehive, with each trader loudly inviting customers to her stall. There were different shades of black skin, ranging from very light skin colors to pitch-dark skin colors. All were black except Maria.

"I have never felt so white all my life. It looks like I am the only white person in this market."

"You are the only *murungu*, here, sweetheart. Enjoy the monopoly."

"Are there no white people in Zimbabwe?"

"Of course, there are white people in Zimbabwe, but you don't find them at places like this. This is a marketplace for the poor."

"Where are they?"

"Who?"

"The whites."

"You find them at low residential areas such as Borrowdale or Glen Lorne. They have a shopping center called Sam Levy Village, at Borrowdale."

"They don't allow blacks there?"

"No. Sam Levy shopping mall is open to anyone. You will see blacks there, but since it's in the white residential area, you find many white people, there."

"Very interesting."

We were quiet for a moment as the bus conductor was loading our suitcases into the bus luggage compartment. As soon as we boarded the bus, we continued with our conversation.

"Are you feeling lonely already?" I asked.

"Not quite. It's only that I have never been so conscious of my skin color and otherness like this before. I never realized that I was so white." She paused. "Have you ever felt the same in the United States?" she asked.

"Most of the time; when I was in college, at my workplace, and at the church."

"I am so sorry, Peter. I never knew that you sometimes felt lonely in the United States. Even if you had told me, I wouldn't have understood it. Now, I don't only understand it, I also experience it."

"Thank you. You don't need to apologize. It's not your fault. In fact, it's normal to feel lonely in a new place. What makes it worse in America is that most Americans keep to themselves. If they don't know you, they leave you alone. It's different here. In Zimbabwe, if people don't know you, they are likely to be more friendly to you.

They always seek ways of making you feel comfortable and welcome."

"I think you are right. I am getting a little tired of being greeted. Everyone who gets on this bus looks at me, and talks to me like she has known me for a while."

"That's part of our African hospitality."

"I need to get used to it."

"You will. It takes some doing."

Inside the bus, there was much hustling, the likes of which Maria had never seen all her life. Traders constantly got on and off the bus until the bus left the bus terminus. Each of them was advertising and selling his own wares, and had a different way of doing it. Most of them stopped by when they came to our seat, which was in the middle of the bus.

"Ah, *mukoma*! Is she your friend? Is she a tourist?" One of the informal traders asked me.

"No. She is my wife," I responded.

"*Hehehe*. My brother, you are advanced. You can't be done. You have taken marriage to a new level. I am pleasantly shocked. Are you serious?"

"She is my wife. What's so special about it?"

"She is very special, my brother. Very, best specialist wife. Don't you see that she is white?"

"I know that," I responded, "but that doesn't make her more special than others. All women in this bus are special."

"My brother, don't say that. You know that it's not true. If God blessed you, you must thanked him with full heart. Buy the car, my brother. Best wife don't climb bus. It's us poor in the bus, not special wife." The trader spoke broken English, but I perfectly understood what he meant.

"You are right, my brother. She is special, not just because of her skin color, but because she is a woman. Also, she is special because she is my wife, and I love her wholeheartedly."

"Awesome. Very awesome. If she is my wife, I carried her in my back every day. I doesn't agree her to walk. No. She is the best."

"Thank you, my brother."

"Hello, *maiguru*. I welcomed she at Zimbabwe. This is Mbare Musika. I am the *sabhuku* of here. Do you know what *sabhuku* means?" Another trader asked.

"No," Maria responded.

"It means village head."

Maria thanked him.

"What do you want to eat, my brother's wife? I have delicious beef sausages. I have candy cakes. I have roasted and salted peanuts. What do you want to try, my beautiful *maiguru*?"

Maria looked at me.

"Not today, my brother. Try some other day," I responded.

"My brother, please, let her buy something. I wanted to feed my family. I have poverty. Many poverties. My children is very sick."

"You look very young. How many kids do you have?" Maria asked.

"Many kids. You see me small you think I am children; no, I am family. Much wives. Some kids, I don't know their names."

Everyone around us laughed except Maria.

"What are you laughing?" It seemed his ego had been hurt. "I talk nice English. Ask my brother's wife. She is the most English people here. She is the only one who can judge me. It's only two people, who talk best English here. Me and her. Ah, no. And my brother, here."

Maria nodded her head in agreement.

"*Maiguru,* if your stomach is full, you can buy something for those childrens." That is what Maria did. She bought a few sausages and handed them to the woman in the seat behind us. Both the trader and the woman wholeheartedly thanked us.

"Thank you very, very much, my brother's wife. You have a very big and beautiful heart like your face," said the trader. "Let me look for your change."

"Don't worry. Keep the change," Maria said.

"Really? *Maiguru*, really?"

"It's yours."

"Thank you, *maiguru*. Thank you very much. Can I shake your hand? Can I do it, my brother?" Maria responded by stretching her hand. The trader gently shook Maria's hand. As soon as he released Maria's hand, he started jumping up and down in ecstasy. He looked at his hand as if it had turned into gold.

"Thanks, my brother. First time, I am touched the white hand. I was not washing my hand in two weeks because I touch a white person. I am very blessing."

We all laughed as he hastily left, rejoicing over the change, and having touched a white person for the first time.

Many other traders came by, advertising their wares vigorously until we all got tired of them. Maria fell asleep, perhaps because of the fatigue caused by trying to make sense of their broken English. It also gave me a break from the traders. Of course, they did not go away. They still stopped by, trying their luck, and I just ignored them. Unlike Maria, I knew how to ignore them.

"I have very big bananas, my brother. If you eat them, you will have all the vitamins in the world," another trader said. "Your belly will be full for the next two days."

I ignored him, concentrating on reading my book.

"I am talking to you, my brother. Why do you ignore me? Why do you look at me as if I am selling snakes?"

"Hello," I greeted him.

"How are you, brother? That's what we do. We greet people, even if we are sitting next to a white woman."

"Ok."

"How about the bananas? Buy a few for your white friend. When she wakes up, she will be hungry."

"She doesn't eat bananas."

"What about oranges?"

"No."

"Ok. You are proud of yourself."

I ignored him, and he started walking away. He stopped and looked back at me.

"Do you think that sitting next to a white person makes you white?" He sounded offended.

"No," I responded.

"Then buy something from me."

"Why?"

"To support my business."

"I will do that some other day."

I then went back to my book.

"Why do you read your book when I am talking to you?" The trader was becoming more confrontational.

"Why shouldn't I read the book?"

"It's rude."

"I didn't know that."

"Yes, it's very rude. This is a bus, not a library. If you want to read, please, go to the University of Zimbabwe. They have a big library there. This is a public place, and we should socialize here."

"Thank you. I apologize."

"Apology accepted. Are you going to buy my bananas?"

I ignored him until he left for other customers.

Soon, the bus left Mbare Musika, and within three hours, we were in Masvingo. We got on another bus from Masvingo to Nyajena, where my parents' home is. Most of the people in the bus already knew us, or had heard about us. The word of our marriage had traveled far and wide. Everyone on the bus came over to our seat to greet the white daughter-in-law. Some passengers gave Maria some small gifts. Some offered her food, which she politely refused to take. Some spoke to her in good English. Others struggled to make sensible English statements. But they all had one thing in common; they looked happy and friendly.

Maria was completely astonished.

"How do they all seem to know me?" She asked.

"No. They don't. They know my parents. They may have heard about you. That's why they are happy. You are their daughter-in-law. You are everyone's daughter-in-law."

They kept flocking to our seat to greet Maria, who responded to their welcome messages with smiles, hugs, and handshakes. Some small kids came over to Maria to just look at her at a close range. Many of them had seen white people on television, but never at such a close range. If they were Catholic, they might have seen the Swiss priest, who lived at Renco Mine. Even if they had seen a white person, most of them, if not all, had never ridden on the same bus with a white person. The little children were more perplexed than the adults. Maria patted the kids on their shoulders and stroked their hair, and they loved it. Some of them giggled and ran away in utter ecstasy. Others just stood there, as if petrified, staring at Maria in utter silence. At long last, they had touched a white woman's hand. They had touched a white woman's hair. Some women sitting in the back seat of the bus started singing.

"*Tauya naye nemagumbezi, muroora, tauya naye*," which can be translated as, "We have brought the daughter-in-law in blankets."

It was funny that they claimed to have brought the daughter-in-law, merely by virtue of being in the same bus with us. They had their destinations, and we had our own. They even did not know that we would be in the same bus on that day, but they felt that their presence in the same bus had contributed to the arrival of the white daughter-in-law. Of course, we could not deny them the pleasure of making that erroneous claim.

Soon, we arrived at our bus stop. We bade farewell to our friends in the bus, who still had not arrived at their destinations. Outside the bus, under a big Musasa tree, the whole Masika clan was waiting for us. Baba had brought a scotch cart with which to carry our suitcases. That was very thoughtful of him because the suitcases were heavy. He also insisted that Maria was supposed to ride in the scotch cart on our way back to the village, which she politely refused to do. Her refusal could have been a result of her fear of the two beasts that were pulling the scotch cart, or she just might have felt that she was being given some unwarranted preferential treatment because everyone else was walking. Baba was just trying to offer hospitality to the family's guest, and his new daughter-in-law as per tradition. In the Shona culture, guests receive preferential treatment. They are offered special, delicious food, and a nice place to sleep.

Maria was different. She insisted on walking like everyone else was doing. There were about twenty people, all related to me, in one way or the other. Many of them stampeded to walk next to Maria since the path was narrow.

Everybody was very friendly to both of us. They introduced themselves in a manner that really confused Maria. Some said they were my mothers, sisters, or nieces. Others said that they were my fathers, uncles, brothers, or nephews, which was very confusing to an outsider like Maria. She had read about extended families and relationships in African societies, but had not anticipated it to be all that complex.

One of the women came over to Maria, and informed her that she was my real mother, and that Mother was not my real mother.

"This is confusing. How many real mothers do you have?" Maria was bamboozled.

"Only one?"

"Which one? Because about five women claim to be your real mothers?"

"I see. Don't worry about that. You know my biological mother. The other two women are my mother's sisters. They are my "mothers" as well. The other two younger women are my mother's nieces, the daughters of her brother. They too are my "mothers." In fact, many of my other "mothers" are not here today. All of them call me their "son." It's our kinship system, and we are all related in one way or the other."

"What about sisters? I thought that you were only two in your family—your brother and you."

"You are right. My biological mother had only two kids. All these "sisters" of mine are what you would call cousins in America. They are my uncles' children. So, they are my sisters and brothers. I call their parents, my parents too. Likewise, all of them call my father, 'Baba,' and my mother, 'mhayi'."

"That's very interesting," said Maria.

"And confusing too," I admitted.

As we were climbing up Chitakai mountain on our way home, Maria was impressed by the scenery. There were giant trees on both sides of the path. Unfortunately, most of the bigger trees had shed their leaves, for it was winter. Birds were chirping as if to welcome the new wife from the ancestors. Maria admitted that she had never heard so many birds singing at the same time, each with a different but melodious tune.

As we approached Chitakai Primary School, we came across a troop of daring baboons. They followed us for a while thinking that we would offer them something to eat, but we did not. Maria started taking photos of the ugly animals. No one else had thought about taking pictures of the baboons. Our people saw them every day, and never thought that they were special animals. When I was growing up, during the rainy season, the baboons were the most hated animals in our village because they were thieves. They would come to steal maize cobs from our farms. Our people had to watch their crops lest they were destroyed by the baboons. Although we did not hate them with a passion, we did not like them at all. We did not hold it against them because we knew that it was their behavior to steal, and they could not help it.

For Maria, baboons were just innocent animals, and she proclaimed that they were beautiful, which utterly surprised the delegation. Our people had always known baboons as ugly animals, and were not so happy to see them stealing attention from their daughter-in-law. What everyone wanted was for the new daughter-in-law to have a selfie with them, and not with the baboons.

In about one hour, we were home, where we found more relatives waiting for us. The moment they saw us arriving, they started singing. There was dancing, ululating, and whistling. Then more introductions followed. Maria met many more of my mothers, sisters, brothers, and fathers. By then, Maria was accustomed to it, so, she did not panic. When she thought she had met all my relatives, my young brother, Ben, who had gone into the nearby bush to fetch the cattle, arrived. After greeting us and a few other relatives who had arrived after he had left for the cattle, he came to sit closer to Maria. Mother took it upon herself to introduce Ben to Maria, who I thought she had recognized from his pictures that she had seen when we were in Texas.

"*Muroora*, this is your husband, Ben." Maria was petrified. Before she recomposed herself and regained her speech, Mother had already moved on.

"Ben, this is your wife, from America. *Murungu*."

Ben stood up and walked closer to greet Maria again. "I am very glad to meet you, my wife. I have been waiting for you for a very long time. Welcome home, sweetheart."

Maria was petrified, and I could see her cheeks turning red.

"What? No. I am not your sweetheart. My husband is Peter. I have only one husband. Ben, why do you call me your wife?" Maria was infuriated.

We all laughed, except Maria who was becoming noticeably frustrated.

"Why is everyone laughing?" Maria asked.

"My daughter-in-law, in our culture, your husband's brothers are also your 'husbands.' Of course, not literally. If you are going to have children, they would call your husband's many brothers, 'father.' If your husband dies; God forbid, one of his brothers is entitled to inherit you as a wife. Of course, our tradition gives you an opportunity to choose from the many brothers and nephews your husband has."

"What if I don't love all of them?" Maria wanted to know.

"First, it's not about love, my daughter-in-law. It's about family obligation. If bridewealth has been paid for you, and you are still a young woman, you have the obligation to bear more children for your deceased husband. Of course, with one of his relatives of your choice."

"So, a woman can't refuse to be inherited? It doesn't sound right to me."

"She can. She can choose her firstborn as her guardian to show that she is no longer interested in conjugal relationships. However, if she goes that way, she has to remain chaste as long as she lives in the home of the deceased husband."

Maria nodded her head.

"Yes, daughter-in-law. You don't need to worry about this because Peter isn't dying yet. All of his 'brothers' and nephews are obliged to respect you as their *maiguru*, which means, bigger mother. You call them, *babamunini*, meaning, junior dad or husband. That's our culture," Father explained.

"It's enough, Baba Peter. This isn't a good time for a cultural lecture. It's a time to celebrate the arrival of our daughter-in-law," said Mother. "The wife inheritance practices were crucial in pre-colonial Zimbabwe, when our economy was basically agrarian, and most, if not all women were not gainfully employed. Once the husband died, most widows needed someone to help them take care of the children of the deceased relative. Things have changed now because many women are gainfully employed, and can take care of their children after the demise of their spouses."

Maria said, "Thank you, Mother."

"And now with the advent of deadly infectious diseases, it has become increasingly dangerous for our people to adhere to wife inheritance rituals. Those who insist on inheriting spouses of the deceased may end up contracting the same disease that would have killed the relative. You see," Baba explained.

"I see, Baba," Maria responded.

"*Vakoma*, Mai Peter, why do you continue to call her daughter-in-law? She is our mother. Welcome home, Mai Masika." One of my many 'mothers' corrected Mother.

There was ululation and dancing.

Drinks and juices were served. Before we finished our drinks, one of my 'sisters' brought a live chicken to Maria, and knelt before her.

She said, "*Maiguru*, Mother asked me to offer you this chicken for your relish today." She then extended her hand to hand over the chicken to Maria. Maria was startled. I had not prepared her for this one. She looked at my sister and at the live chicken in utter astonishment.

"Please, take it, and hold it in your hands for a moment, and then, hand it to me," I instructed Maria. "It's called *kushuma usavi*."

She complied. After a moment, she gave the chicken to me without saying a word.

"*Tatenda*. We have seen our relish. Now you can process it." It was me.

I handed the chicken back to my 'sister,' and she took it outside.

"Do we eat it alone? The two of us?" Maria asked.

"No. Others will help us consume it. The ritual is symbolic, and it means that the chicken is intended for the visitors' consumption. If we were not here, it wouldn't have been slaughtered."

Maria nodded her head.

In about five minutes, my 'sister' came back into the kitchen holding a dish, and the headless chicken was in it, very much dead.

"What happened?" Maria pointed to the chicken in the dish.

"She has slaughtered it. Now, it's time to remove the feathers, and cook it," Mother explained.

"Oh my God. You didn't need to kill the poor chicken. It was so cute. That's not right. The poor chicken didn't deserve to die."

Maria looked sad. Everybody laughed.

"There is no need to be sentimental, daughter-in-law. We have many chickens here. We will slaughter another one for you tomorrow. We will also slaughter a goat. We should rejoice." Mother explained.

"Oh, no. Did he die peacefully? Was it traumatic?"

We all looked at Maria in utter amazement.

"He died stoically like a martyr," I said.

"That's so sad."

"It's okay, Maria. Here, we process our own meat. We don't have large grocery stores and meat markets, here, like you have in the United States. It's not that we are heartless, but we must do what we need to do to process our meat. The chicken died peacefully and painlessly. Soon, you will be processing your own chickens, Maria."

"No. No. I do not want to be involved," Maria objected.

"Don't worry, sweetheart. I will do the processing for you," I assured her.

"Thank you," Maria said.

Within an hour or two, the food was ready. There were lots of different meats. There was goat, beef, and chicken meat. There was *sadza* and rice. People were seated in groups of four, and each foursome had two plates of food: one for *sadza* and the other for meat. All the four sitting together used their hands to eat from the same plate. We were three in our group. Mother had thoughtfully provided us with side plates in which to put our individual food. Although a fork and knife had been provided for Maria, she tried her hands, and discovered that she was not bad at all. She seemed to be enjoying her newly discovered skills.

We all enjoyed the food.

After supper, most of the relatives went back to their homes, except a few who spent the night at my parents' place.

We were tired. We retired to bed in the boys' round hut. Ben had to spend the night at my uncle's place. We had brought some form rubber to use for bedding, and it was very comfortable. Since it was winter, the night was so cold that we used a pile of blankets.

Maria was impressed by the sincerity of everyone and the simplicity of the village life.

"This is a wonderful life. It's like we are camping," Maria remarked.

"You love it?"

"I do."

"That's why I don't like going camping in America. I have lived most of my life in this camp."

Maria laughed. "You are right. Where are the shopping malls?" Maria asked.

"We have a township. It's beyond the mountain. People go there when they need some basic items such as sugar, cooking oil, salt, and flour. There is also a grinding mill at the township. Otherwise, the villagers are self-sufficient. They have their own vegetable gardens, chickens, goats, milk, cattle, firewood, fruits, and so on. Here, we have fourteen mango trees, three orange trees, five avocado pear trees, and many others. In addition to that, there are countless indigenous fruit trees in the bush. The people have almost everything that they need, and almost everything that they eat is organic."

"It's a wonderful life. I never knew that people could lead such a simple life, yet lacking nothing, and being so happy and generous."

"It's possible."

The following morning it drizzled a little bit. Maria, who had planned to wake up early in the morning to sweep the yard, like a good daughter-in-law was expected to do, failed to wake up. It was too cold to wake up early, and the blankets were enticingly warm. I guess the people who had tipped her to wake up early in the morning were disappointed because a good *muroora* should follow instructions.

Eventually, Maria woke up, and still served the warm water for washing faces, and the body lotion to the family members, as she had been instructed to do. It seemed that other people had woken up late too. She was assisted in performing that task by other daughters-in-law of the family. Maria also assisted other daughters-in-law in preparing breakfast. Of course, she had a hard time in learning how to cook using firewood with the pot balancing on three stones. Her eyes occasionally teared up because of the smoke. Despite those pinpricks, Maria enjoyed working with other family members, assisting them whenever asked to.

When it was time to milk the cows, I invited Maria to the kraal to watch me doing it manually. She, in fact, took a video of me milking the cows. She also tried milking the cows herself, but could not squeeze out even a drop of milk.

"It's not as easy as it seems," Maria admitted.

"No. It's not easy at all, but with more practice, it becomes simpler."

"Are you not robbing the calf? What will it drink?" Maria asked.

"There is always enough milk for both the calf and us. Also, the cow can always produce some more milk for the calf if humans take more than necessary. Sometimes, the cow can hide some milk in its system for the calf if it feels that humans may deprive the calf of its daily sustenance."

"Cows are very generous animals."

"Yes, they are. I think it makes them happy to be able to provide nourishment for humans too."

"I am not sure about that. I guess if they could sue human beings for stealing their milk, they were going to be successful."

"Maybe. Unfortunately, they can't sue us."

"You are lucky," Maria said.

"We are. We also have milk in the United States. Where do you think it comes from?"

"I don't know. I have never thought about it."

"Sweetheart, this trip gives you an opportunity to reflect on life, and our relationship with nature. Milk comes from cows."

"I agree."

Everyone loved the new daughter-in-law. By midday, more villagers and relatives had arrived at our home to welcome the new daughter-in-law. Most of them were impressed by Maria, but some were skeptical.

"She looks fragile. Can she even carry a baby in her womb for nine months?" One of the women asked.

"Maybe a baby she can carry, but I don't think she can carry a twenty-liter tin of water or a bundle of firewood on her head," another villager responded.

"Can she take charge of an ox-drawn plough?" Said the first woman.

"Why would she want to do that?" Another villager asked.

"Why not?" Said the first woman.

"She is white, and has got money. She can buy a tractor," said another woman.

"I see," said the first woman. "A tractor, she can buy, but she has to carry her own pregnancy, and has to push out her own baby when the time comes."

"Who said, white women can't carry their own pregnancies?" The other woman asked.

"I am just saying," said the first woman.

The conversation went on.

There was more singing, drumming, and dancing. One of my uncles brought a radio with huge speakers, which he said was bought for him by one of his sons who works in South Africa. Music started, and there was more dancing. Maria was amazed to see so many people being so happy, just for her. She said that she had never felt so loved like this before, outside of her family. Everybody wanted to talk with her. Everybody wanted to dance with her. Some just wanted to look at her. Others just wanted to touch her hair. It was not that they had never seen white people before; they had, but only from afar. The only white person they had seen at a close range was the local Catholic priest, who lived at Renco Mine. Some villagers could not remember the last time there was a white person in the village. Some said it was during the war of liberation.

When night came, most people retired to their homes.

The following day started well, but changed later. Something that we had not anticipated happened. About ten, in the morning, Baba summoned me into the kitchen, and told me that the village head, popularly known as sabhuku, Mr. Jokonia, wanted to meet the four of us at his homestead. Baba did not know why Sabhuku wanted to see us at his home. Normally, he should have come to our home to greet us. The summoned four included, Baba, Mother, Maria, and I. Baba just said that there was something sabhuku wanted to discuss with us, and he was not aware of its nature. I sensed that something was not okay. One was not just summoned to sabhuku's home unless something was wrong.

The four of us walked along the path that led to Mr. Jokonia's homestead, and when we arrived, four other villagers were already there. Later, I learned that three of them were sabhuku's assistants or councilors, and the fourth was his police officer and messenger. Mrs. Jokonia, who looked very much advanced in pregnancy welcomed us, and led us to where the men were sitting around a fire, under a tree, behind the big round kitchen. Mrs. Jokonia brought a reed mat, which she spread for Maria and Mother to sit on, and she sat beside them for a moment. No one talked for a while.

We exchanged greetings in the traditional way. After the greetings, Mrs. Jokonia immediately left the gathering for her kitchen. We talked a little about the weather and politics. Then, the officer, Fatso, which is the short form for the name, Farai, asked us to introduce ourselves to the people who already knew who we were. I guessed that he wanted us to introduce Maria, which I did. Sabhuku welcomed Maria, talked a little about America, and was silent again. I could easily sense that the atmosphere was tense with negative energy.

Mr. Jokonia broke the ice. "I have summoned you to my court so that we can deliberate on an issue that is very sensitive, not only to us, but also to our ancestors. As you know, our ancestors can see, hear, smell, and talk. They see everything happening in this village right now. They know the people who strictly uphold our traditional moral standards. They also know the people who frequently and contemptuously break the laws of our land." He paused for a moment, and then continued, "Mr. Masika, VaSigauke, word has come to us that your son, Peter, who is here with us, brought a woman from America. If the woman in question were an ordinary woman, we would not have concerned ourselves with their marital affair, but your daughter-in-law is not an ordinary person, for she is a white woman. It's unprecedented in this village, and perhaps, the whole of Nyajena, for a black man to marry a white woman. We have never heard of something like this before. No black persons marry white women. This is not only new, but also weird." Sabhuku paused, and unblinkingly looked at me without saying a word.

He then continued, "I guess, this is his wife, as your son has already told us during the introductions. Congratulations, young man! Marriage is a good thing, and should be a cause for great joy and celebration. It makes our community fecund, and our ancestors happy. It perpetuates the names of our families, and the identity of our clan. However, I am referring to a normal marriage between a black man and a black woman. I am talking about an ordinary daughter-in-law, not a white woman. Your son's marriage to a white woman is very strange and disturbing to our community. I really don't know what to say, or how to accurately articulate what I want to tell you. I do not want to appear as if I am xenophobic. Maybe I am, just a little. If I am a little xenophobic, I should be justified because marrying a white woman is out of the ordinary. I have no doubt that it is against the moral norms handed down to us by our progenitors. Do you understand what I am trying to say, young man?"

"No, Sir. I don't. Perhaps, you can be more direct, Sir," I responded. "Please, don't just beat about the bush."

"What I mean is this, your marriage to a white woman makes our ancestors angry."

"How do you know that our ancestors are angry, Sir?" I asked him.

"I know it. Don't you know that I am the custodian of our traditions, in this village?"

"I know that you are, but I would like you to tell me how you know that our ancestors are angry. In other words, I am asking for the evidence that you have."

"I have evidence, young man. I had a terrible dream last night. I saw my grandfather, walking towards where I was standing with other men whose names I cannot recall. We were having a conversation whose subject I cannot remember. When he was about to arrive where we were standing, he hesitated a little bit. I started walking towards him to welcome him. When I reached where he was, I extended my hand to greet him, and he refused to shake my hand. In fact, he never looked at me, at all. Although he tried to hide his face from me, I had a glimpse of his countenance. He was very angry. He walked past me without saying a word. I ran after him, calling him to stop because I wanted to talk with him. He didn't stop, for he seemed not to hear me.

He kept walking past this kitchen without saying a word. I then woke up. I was sweating and shivering. The ancestors are angry."

"Sir, I see no connection between your dream and my marriage. What has your dream to do with the issue at hand?" I asked.

"Our ancestors are angry. Do you know the consequence of upsetting the soil?"

"No."

"Severe chastisement."

"Let's say that you are right that our ancestors are angry; how do you know the cause of their anger? You said it yourself that in your dream, the ancestor didn't talk to you. So, how do you conclude that the anger is caused by my marriage? We all know that there are many issues that can infuriate ancestors, so, how do you know that the cause of their current anger is not any of the other causes?"

"Young man, I am not your student, and this is not a classroom. You can't teach me nothing about these things." Sabhuku was getting irritated.

"You have heard what I said, Sir. If you believe that ancestors are angry with me, then, let them punish me. Why do you want to drag the whole community into it?"

"Ancestors don't just punish you alone, but the whole community, and we can't wait for that to happen. We need to do something about it."

"Sir, you said it was a dream?" I asked.

"Yes," sabhuku responded.

"Then it was a dream. What has it to do with angry ancestors?" I asked.

"My son, I wasn't born yesterday. They didn't make me sabhuku because of any other reason besides my knowledge of the ways of our ancestors, and my prowess in interpreting their will. Our ancestors are angry. There is no question about it," sabhuku insisted.

"Excuse me, sabhuku. We have heard your point, but I don't think that you have answered my son's questions, satisfactorily. What has that anger got to do with us? Are ancestors angry because of my family?" Baba asked.

"You have said it yourself. It's because of your daughter-in-law. They have never seen a white woman in this village. They have every reason to be upset." It was sabhuku.

"Okay. Let's say they have never seen a white woman in this village before. Let's say they are angry. So what?" I was getting irritated, and struggling to control my temper.

"There will be pestilence. There will be diseases. There will be misfortunes. There will be a severe drought. Our greatest challenge is that the whole community won't be spared from the tribulations that you have brought upon us. We will all perish. Those who will survive the pestilence and disease will succumb to starvation. I see death knocking on our doors." Mr. Jokonia spoke with the intensity of someone seeing a vision of those things already happening.

"I am wondering why the ancestors are angry. My daughter-in-law is a human being, just like all of us. She is a woman. She wears a dress, like our women do. She speaks Shona, just like all of us do. She cooks *sadza*, just like all our women do. I strongly believe that she, like all our wives, came from the ancestors. She indeed is a wife from the ancestors." Father was getting upset.

"No, Sigauke. Let us not play with fire. Ancestors don't give you a white woman," one of sabhuku's councilors said. "Ancestors don't give you a white woman. That's a lie," he repeated.

"What do they give you?" I asked.

"A human."

"Are white people not humans?"

"They are not. They are white people, not *vanhu*."

"How do you know that?" Mother jumped in. She was annoyed. In fact, she was shaking a little bit. I could see that she was struggling to keep her voice under control. "Please, don't exhibit your lack of knowledge. It's always wise to shut your mouth, if you don't understand the topic under discussion. White people are as human as black people are."

"They are not people," the councilor stubbornly repeated.

"You are ignorant and uneducated. It's not your fault, because you have never traveled outside this village. You erroneously think that this village is the world. I don't want to waste my time debating an ignoramus." Mother had given up.

"*Mbuya*, you are now insulting me. Sabhuku, did you hear what she said? She just insulted me," the councilor complained.

"*Futseki*. I said, *futseki*. You are a fool. You are jealous of my daughter-in-law. Poverty makes you crazy. You have nothing. You smell of poverty. Shame on you." Mother stood up threateningly.

"Please, please, it's enough. Sit down, we have heard you, Mai Peter," Baba intervened. "Let's hear from sabhuku."

"It's tabooed. You can check the whole area of Chief Nyajena, and see for yourself. Who has ever married a white woman?" Who? Please, give me a name." Mr. Jokonia was becoming impatient. "Tell me one couple that you know of."

"If nobody in the whole of Nyajena has ever married a white woman, then how do you know that ancestors are aggrieved? Maybe they are happy to have such a gift on their land," I said.

Mr. Jokonia was angry. "There is nothing you can teach me about ancestors. You are a mere kid. You have some milk on your nose. I was not born yesterday. Look at my grey hair! Don't you see it? I am the guardian of our traditions. I know what infuriates ancestors, and what doesn't. I know what the soil wants, and you can't teach me nothing, son."

"Well, Mr. Sabhuku, we have heard your concerns. I think they are misdirected. We live in a new Zimbabwe. It's a democratic society, which is not run according to the whims of ancestors, who appear in a dream. The new Zimbabwe has a constitution that binds all of us. That constitution allows men and women to marry whoever they want. It does not segregate people according to their skin colors. After all, my wife and I don't live here. We just came to visit. We are Americans." I was getting impatient with sabhuku.

"Are you trying to denigrate our ancestors?" Sabhuku asked, shakingly, while pointing his finger at me.

"Please, Sir, don't threaten me."

"I didn't threaten you."

"You did. Why are you pointing your finger at me? That's a threat."

"It's not. This is my court, and I do whatever I want with my fingers."

"Please, keep them to yourself because I don't eat threats."

"Don't try to divert me. The issue is about the anger you have caused our peace-loving ancestors."

"Ancestors are more intelligent and tolerant than being worried about the race of a person. Ancestors see the heart, not the color of our skin. In fact, they are celebrating because another mother of the clan has been added." I tried to rationalize with sabhuku.

He was unfazed. "Peter, you are just a small boy. There is nothing you can tell me about racial segregation. Do you know that blacks were not allowed to walk along First Street in Harare? Do you know that we were not allowed to drink European liquor? Do you know that blacks were not allowed to even look at a white woman? I mean just looking at a white woman. There is nothing you can teach me about skin colors and racial segregation. We had to go to war to have rights of freedom of association and movement in this country."

Sabhuku was right. The war of liberation was fought. I was a kid, but I could still remember some of the incidents. I recalled how the freedom fighters used to dance at the meeting places called bases. Some of my friends had died during the war. I still recalled the independence celebrations in 1980.

"You are right there, sabhuku. Yes, you went to war. Indeed, you won the war, and you got independence from the British, and you could walk along First Street. You could drink European liquor. Then, what became of you ever since you attained independence? Have you been drinking European liquor since 1980? What did you get out of it? You have been walking up and down First Street ever since you attained independence, and what did you achieve from walking along First Street? Nothing. No production. Just drinking European liquor, and walking along First Street. Drinking liquor, my foot."

"We got back our land," said sabhuku.

"Yes, you did, but why are people hungry? Why is it that most of the arable land lie fallow even in this village? Why are the young people crowding the cities in search of jobs that are not there, while abandoning the land that our brothers and sisters died for?"

"I don't know. I am not the government. Go and ask the government. I am the custodian of the traditions of my people, not a politician," sabhuku said.

"You started it. You are the village head. It's your responsibility to convey our sentiments to the government. Also, it's your job to teach young people to appreciate and to work the land," I said.

"Why are you in America, yourself? Why don't you stay here and work the land?" Sabhuku got me.

"I went to America to learn their farming ways so that I can teach you how to increase your agricultural production. Now, I try to come back, and you tell me nonsense about my white wife. She is here to help, not to destroy your culture."

Sabhuku ignored me. He wanted us to focus on the issue at hand.

It was one of the councilors who spoke, first. "Sabhuku, we didn't gather here to talk about Ian Smith's racism. Times have changed. I worked in Bulawayo for many years, and I had friends who were married to white women. I also knew black women who were married to white men. Mixed marriages are no longer a big deal. They are allowed by the law of this country. There is nothing wrong with marrying a white woman. In fact, it unites whites and blacks."

Sabhuku was quiet for a moment and he then said, "Our traditions are one thing, and the constitution is another. We don't mix things. I am speaking in my capacity as the guardian of our traditions, and the living representative of the ancestors of this land. We can't have a white woman in this village. We don't even know her totem. If she dies, who would mark her grave? We don't want to invite *ngozi* into this village. You can do whatever you want in America. You can marry as many white women as you want, in America or Harare, but not here. You don't bring them here to desecrate our land. You don't bring them to my village to turn our ancestors against us. We don't want a drought. We don't want pestilence."

Sabhuku stood his ground.

Fatso, who had never uttered a word until then, joined the conversation. "Excuse me, sabhuku, and all the officers of sabhuku's council. You are wasting our time here. Some of us are educated. We went to school. You sent us to school so that we can advise you accordingly."

Sabhuku laughed. "You are educated? You? Where were you educated?"

"At Saint Joseph Secondary School. I have an ordinary level certificate of education, Baba. Let me educate you. The constitution of this country says that, a person can marry whoever he wants to marry provided the person is of the opposite sex, and has reached the majority age. Your customary laws can only be relevant if they are in line with the constitution of this country. You can't give people laws that violate their human rights or constitutional obligations. If you are reported to the police, you can be arrested for violating Peter and his wife's rights. You don't just do whatever you want. This court is important, but it is merely ceremonial. The real deal is at the Magistrate's court, or the High and Supreme Court." Fatso sounded erudite.

"You are lying. You think we don't know that you failed all your subjects, including the Shona language? If you passed your ordinary level examinations, why are you not working? Why are you not a teacher like other intelligent young people? Why are you not in America like Peter? Why are you not married to a white woman?" Sabhuku's questions were absurd.

"Who told you that I failed my ordinary level examinations? Can you speak good English like I do?"

"Whether you are more educated than I, or not, you don't tell me what to do in my village. You are just a police officer, who serves at my pleasure. I can relieve you of your duties today. Right now. Challenge me." Sabhuku was shaken. He looked like a man who was not used to being opposed at his own court, and by his own subjects.

"I don't care. You can fire me right now. Do you pay me even a cent for my duties? You say that I am not educated, what about you? Where did you go to school? If you want to be a good judge over the people, you better listen to our learned advice. You are illiterate. You can barely write your name. You were not interviewed for this job, but you inherited it. Unfortunately, you cannot inherit education."

Mr. Jokonia did not respond.

"Thank you, sabhuku for sharing your sentiments with us. We perfectly understand your concerns. However, Peter is my son. He is married to this beautiful woman. If any ancestor were to be angry because of this marriage, it should be my own ancestors, not yours. Your ancestors have nothing to do with my son's marriage. If you are not happy with my daughter-in-law, it's your own problem. She doesn't live in your home. She doesn't consume your food. She is my daughter-in-law, not yours. She wouldn't have come here into your homestead, hadn't you summoned us. I don't want to hear this issue again. If your ancestors are not happy with my daughter-in-law, they can go hang. One thing I know for sure is that my ancestors are happy. They gave us a beautiful woman. We are celebrating, and you can join us when you get over your jealousy." Baba said this as he was standing up to go home. Mother told him to sit down a little longer.

"Baba Peter, you don't talk like that to our village head. Don't you know that he represents the ancestors of this land?" Mother tried to pacify Baba.

"I don't care. He should not talk like that. He should have some respect for other people. He should congratulate my son for marrying a beautiful woman, and should stop this nonsense. It's time to celebrate, not to make enemies. When he is done with his dreams, he can come over and join us at our home." This was directed at sabhuku. "Please, bring your gift for the bride from the ancestors," Baba shouted.

One of the officers, Dhoba, said, "Mr. Sigauke, can I say something? Are you listening? You are missing the point. Sabhuku isn't saying that your daughter-in-law is not welcome in this village. No. Our tradition says that you should pay a small offering to propitiate the ancestors. A beast should be sacrificed to the ancestors to pacify them. It's our tradition. We will all be protected, including your daughter-in-law. Just a beast."

Mother jumped in. "Now you are talking. It's about money, not the ancestors. It's about money. I sensed it from the beginning. You know that my daughter-in-law is American, and you think she has a suitcase of American dollars. You are corrupt. Are you not ashamed of robbing people?"

Sabhuku did not answer.

"If you want some money, you should have told me. When I told you that my son and his wife were coming to visit us, you said nothing. Now you talk of ancestors being angry, yet what you want is some easy money. You are a hypocrite," Baba said.

Fatso jumped into the conversation. "Yes. I knew it from the beginning that it was about money. I know my people. You were just using ancestors to get some free money. You shouldn't have summoned our new daughter-in-law. This is shameful. Truly, I feel embarrassed by your unwarranted shenanigans. She is going to tell people in America about you, and how you tried to con her husband of their hard-earned cash."

"No. It's not about money. Even if it's about money, I won't benefit anything from it. It's for the ancestors. They should be appeased, and it is for our own good. How dare you call a white woman, a wife from the ancestors? She is not a wife from ancestors. We all know that. Ancestors have nothing to do with white people. We have to introduce her to them, lest we perish." Mr. Jokonia was smiling now. He knew that his point had been understood.

"How much money is needed? How much does a goat cost?" I asked.

"No, Peter. Don't give him even a cent. He is a crook. He shouldn't treat us like garbage. If he doesn't like white people, he shouldn't use their money. He mustn't scapegoat his intolerance and hatred for white people on the ancestors. Our ancestors love visitors. They love life, and there is nothing that promotes life more than a marriage." Baba was adamant.

"Peter, my son. Don't listen to your father. He is very argumentative. He knows our traditions. I think that sabhuku is right that the ancestors of the land have to be appeased. There is nothing wrong with it," Mother said.

"How much is needed?" I asked again.

Dhoba responded, "Just give us fifty American dollars. The council is going to share some of it, and the rest will be used to purchase a goat to be used for a sacrifice to the ancestors."

"Who sells goats in this village?" I asked.

"Dhoba responded, "Sabhuku has very good goats."

"You see what I was saying? This is corruption. You are the prosecutor, judge, and supplier, at the same time. You claim that ancestors want a goat, and you are the one selling the goat. Don't you see that there is a conflict of interest?" It was Fatso.

"A goat costs fifty American dollars? You are habitual thieves. Are you not ashamed of yourselves? Let's go home, Mai Peter, Peter, daughter-in-law." Baba stood up and grabbed Maria's hand and started walking. Maria, who hadn't quite understood what was going on smiled and followed the lead.

"Masika. Masika. Are you trying to disrespect this court? I don't want *murungu* in my village. She has to leave today or tomorrow." That was sabhuku.

"What if she doesn't leave? What are you going to do?" Baba was coming back pointing his finger at sabhuku, threateningly. Fatso jumped in front of Baba to block his way.

"I will burn her in the hut," sabhuku said.

"What? What? Try it. I will beat you up thoroughly. I will thrash your back like a bag of millet." It was Baba.

"I swear to God, you can't beat me. Even if you use the *zvidhoma*, which you brought from America, I would beat you together with your evil spirits." Sabhuku said this while walking back to the fireplace. "You will see. I will deal with you severely."

"See what? Witchcraft? You are a witch. You rely on witchcraft, but I rely on my stamina. I will beat the stupidity out of you. You are a witch. My daughter-in-law is going nowhere. She belongs here. She has her rights. Who told you that white women don't have human rights?"

"Baba Peter, please, keep quiet. You are embarrassing us in the presence of our daughter-in-law." Mother tried to calm Baba down.

"No, Mai Peter. Are you with us, or you are with sabhuku?" Baba asked.

Mother did not respond.

Sabhuku stood with arms akimbo, and shouted, "Go away. You will see. You are proud of your son. What is so special about going to America? What is so special about flying in an airplane? You are just pompous for nothing."

Baba stood still, and shouted, "Have you ever been in an airplane yourself? Have you ever been even to Harare? Yes, I have been to America. I will go back again whenever I want. You will never go there. Leave me and my family alone. If you are so desperate for money, you must ask for it civilly. Leave my family alone. Goodbye."

We left sabhuku's home unceremoniously. Sabhuku was visibly angry. His plan to get easy cash had not worked as he had anticipated. Mrs. Jokonia was standing outside her kitchen, watching the drama from afar. She knew better not to interfere. Her baby bump looked dangerously big as she stood with one hand holding her waist. She begged us to wait for the breakfast, which she was preparing for us. Nobody listened to her invitation.

"Please, don't go. I have prepared some food for you," she pleaded with Mother and Maria.

"We have visitors at home. We will eat your food some other day. Please, come and celebrate with us," shouted Mother.

Mrs. Jokonia did not respond. She just looked at her husband, and walked back into her kitchen.

We walked back home in silence. When we arrived home, I explained to Maria most of the things sabhuku had said in Shona. Of course, she did not understand the gravity of the issue. She just laughed it off, much to my greatest relief.

All day long, villagers kept coming to our home to celebrate with us. I went to bed late while discussing sabhuku's concerns with Baba. We decided that we would give him nothing, and that was our resolution when I went to bed. I had no idea what the following day had in store for us. I never thought that our ancestors would intervene on our behalf, but they did. Our conviction that Maria was indeed a wife from the ancestors was remarkably confirmed through the tragedy that almost struck that night. The tragedy did not strike, but it almost did. Perhaps, it is an over statement to call it a 'tragedy,' but just an incident. The incident could have been prevented if sabhuku and his wife had taken appropriate preventive measures. It could be that the ancestors, who had seen sabhuku abusing his power, thought of intervening on our side. They wanted to show him that they indeed were the owners of the land, not him.

It was almost dawn when there was a wild knock on my parents' bedroom door. I heard the door squeaking, and I knew that Baba had opened it. Inaudible voices followed. I heard footsteps coming towards our bedroom, and there was a feint knock on the door. I quickly dressed up and went outside. Mother, Baba, and a third person, who I later recognized as sabhuku, were standing near the kitchen, whispering to each other.

As I walked to where they were standing, I felt that something was wrong. At first, I thought it was about Maria, but I heaved a sigh of relief when I was told that it was about sabhuku Jokonia's wife.

"What's going on?" I asked.

"We have a big problem at Mr. Jokonia's place. Did you see his wife when we were there yesterday?" Baba asked.

"I did."

"She is pregnant. She has been in labor since about 7:00 pm yesterday. Now, the village assistant midwife thinks that the baby is breeched. Both the mother and the baby are getting tired. It looks like we are going to lose both," sabhuku fearfully explained. He was sweating profusely, and his voice was shaking. His eyes were moist, perhaps from suppressed tears. He was in big trouble.

"That's very sad. Why don't you take her to Morgenster Hospital right now? You shouldn't waste time," I said.

"We tried. The only person who has a vehicle in this area is the headmaster of Chitakai School. We went there, but he has no fuel for the car. We need to send someone to Renco Mine to buy petrol for the vehicle, but we don't have the money. And we could use the bus to take her to the hospital, but the situation is dire. She is in labor."

"I can give you the money for the gas, but if the situation is as you tell me, then it will be of no use. You need to walk for about three hours to get to Renco Mine, and another three hours back. Six hours in total. If your wife's condition is as dire as you say, then that would be a waste of time."

Sabhuku looked at me, and I realized how vulnerable he looked. Indeed, the mighty had been cowed by nature. He was crying silently. The mighty had fallen. That is how life chastises people. It has a way of humbling the untouchables. Seeing him crying like a baby, you would not think that he was still the same guy who had threatened us with arson the previous day. No one had thought that before the sunrise of the next day, he would be standing at our homestead begging for money.

"You are right, but we need to do something. I can't just sit and wait for their demise." Sabhuku was now sobbing. The bravado of the previous day was gone. He was back to humanity. He had become as vulnerable as any of his subjects. That is what life does. It reminds you of your humanness and finitude in the most dramatic manner.

I told them to wait for me as I went back into our bedroom. I woke Maria up, who was soundly asleep, and I explained Mrs. Jokonia's situation to her. Withing five minutes, she was ready to go outside. I held a flashlight in one hand, and Maria's medical kit in another, as we walked to sabhuku's home. I explained to him that Maria was an intensive care unit nurse, who was now studying midwifery. I told him that she could help his wife and unborn baby. At first, sabhuku couldn't believe it, or it was just a lack of trust, but he had no other choice. All the odds were against him.

Upon our arrival, we entered the round kitchen in which the midwife was sitting with a few other women and the beleaguered woman. The village midwife quickly blocked my way, grabbed me by the hand, and pulled me outside.

"You can't be in the hut. She is in labor," she said.

"I know, but I must be in the hut to translate for my wife. She is a nurse, and she is going to assist Mrs. Jokonia."

The village midwife relented. "But you should look aside all the time lest you become blind. Men cannot look at a birthing woman without being struck by some misfortune," the midwife said.

"I won't look at her," I assured her, but I do not think that I intended to keep the promise.

I went back inside the hut, and stood alongside sabhuku. I had my flashlight in my hand. When I told Maria that she had been permitted to assist, she quickly sanitized her hands, and put on her disposable gloves. She told me to bring the flashlight closer, which somewhat scandalized the women who were sitting in there. One of them quickly stood up, and snatched the flashlight away from my hand. I took two steps backwards, but I still could see what was happening. I could see the tiny butt of the baby protruding through the mother's birth canal. The mother was tired and pale, and was almost unresponsive. She looked like she was dying.

"It looks like a frank breech. Let me see if the baby is still alive," Maria said.

She assured the birthing mother that she would do everything she could to save her and the baby, as she inserted her fingers into her birth canal to check the baby's pulse or heartbeat.

"Yes, the baby is alive. I can feel the heartbeat. Now, can you give me two pillows or a blanket?"

A blanket was brought. Maria slipped it underneath the birthing woman's back waistline to elevate her hips. She then gently grabbed the protruding bottom of the baby and turned it to face downwards. She reached underneath the baby and slipped one of the legs out. She did the same with the other leg. Now, both legs were out. She waited a little bit while the mother was trying something that resembled a push, but she was too exhausted for any kind of meaningful pushing. Maria grabbed the baby gently, and rotated it back and forth until we could see the hairline on the baby's head.

She did some more maneuvers until the baby's head was out. We could see that the baby was not moving or crying. Sabhuku panicked. "Is the baby dead?" He whispered.

Maria rubbed the baby's back gently.

"It's asphyxia," Maria said.

All of us did not know what she was talking about.

She briefly rubbed the baby's feet, and nothing happened. Sabhuku and the other women inside the hut started crying. Maria then shook the baby a little bit, and the baby breathed through his mouth and cried for the first time. Everyone jumped up and down rejoicing.

"The baby is alive. The baby is alive. She is alive." Sabhuku was ecstatic.

The mother smiled a little bit, and weakly stretched out her hands to receive the baby. Maria placed the baby on her belly instead.

"Thank you. Thank you so much." Sabhuku embraced Maria, who told him to wait, for the job was not yet finished. She was already dealing with the placenta, which she safely delivered. There was joyful noise in the hut. Everyone was happy.

When Maria was done with both the little baby and the mother, she stepped to where sabhuku was standing. He quickly knelt down, and sobbed like a baby.

"Thank you. Thank you. You saved my wife and baby's lives. I was wrong. I was very wrong. I am very sorry. Now, I know, you are indeed, a wife from the ancestors. You are a gift to our village. The ancestors sent you to us at the right time."

"You don't need to kneel down, Sir. I am happy that I was able to assist. I am a nurse, and I am trained to save lives."

"I am very sorry for what I said yesterday. I was wrong. Peter, Mr. Masika, and Amai, I earnestly ask you to find somewhere in your heart, where you can forgive me. Something overshadowed me. I don't know why I couldn't realize that your daughter-in-law, our daughter-in-law, is indeed sent to us by the ancestors." He begged us.

I responded, "No big deal, Sir. That's what life does. It teaches us lessons. We would be fools if we fail to learn something from experiences like this." I paused to wipe off a tear or two. "We are created to help each other. That's what your daughter-in-law has just done. It's a lesson to all of us about our interdependence. Perhaps, the ancestors wanted to show us that what you said yesterday was wrong."

After Maria had given instructions to the village midwife about the care of Mrs. Jokonia, we walked back home. It was almost daybreak.

At about eight o'clock that morning, Mr. Jokonia came to our home. He said that he wanted to officially ask for forgiveness from all of us, and to thank the new village midwife, Maria, for her assistance. After we accepted his apologies, he offered a gift to Maria—a heifer, which she refused to accept, initially.

"My daughter, you must accept sabhuku's gift because that's the way of the elders. A midwife gets a heifer for her work, and that's what our culture prescribes. The gift is not only for you, but also for your ancestors. Our people believe that you can't become a midwife unless your ancestors have called you to do the job. So, it's also a gift for your ancestors. Please, accept it, lest you aggrieve your ancestors and ours," Mother explained.

Maria accepted the generous gift not because she wanted it, but just to fulfil the cultural obligation. That gesture of gratitude seemed not good enough for sabhuku and his wife, who also named their baby, Maria Shamiso. Shamiso means something that strikes awe in people. We were all happy about the sudden turn of events. Maria, who, the previous day, was considered a villain by sabhuku, had become the latest heroine of the village.

Like always, the word of Maria's assistance to Mrs. Jokonia traveled far and wide. Villagers with sick children started bringing their sick kids to our home so that Maria could examine them. They always brought a chicken or two as a gift for Maria's services. We tried to explain to them that Maria was a nurse, and not a medical doctor, and was not registered to work in Zimbabwe, but they did not care about that, for they had heard about the miraculous save of sabhuku's wife and baby. They argued that the proof of the pudding was in the eating. They also said that they were not concerned with job titles, but with the job done. Hence, they kept bringing sick children to my parents' home for Maria to examine them. She gave painkillers to most of them, and recommended that some of them had to go to the hospital. Some children were not sick at all, but just came to see *murungu* or receive some candy. Maria always had time to play some children's games with them, and they liked it.

The news of how Maria had saved Mrs. Jokonia and her baby from death took different shapes depending on who was retelling the story. The story was retold so many times that it ended up acquiring new elements that were not accurate, but only a result of our people's imagination. One version of the story said that by the time we arrived at Mr. Jokonia's home, both his wife and the baby had already died. This version of the events that unfolded that night said that Maria just rubbed Mrs. Jokonia's womb, and she started to breathe again. The same version had it that Maria did the same to the baby's butts, and she was resuscitated. A second version of Mrs. Jokonia's ordeal said that Maria had breathed into both the mother and baby, and they were revived. A third version said that Maria was in a trance as she assisted Mrs. Jokonia. Her skin color was said to have transfigured into black as she facilitated the birth of the baby. A fourth version claimed that during the ordeal, Maria's countenance and voice had changed to that of Mai Zhezha, the most skillful midwife of the village, who had died more than three decades ago. It claimed that Maria was possessed by Mai Zhezha's spirit, which enabled her to assist Mrs. Jokonia. Maria was believed to be Mai Zhezha, who had come back in the form of a white woman to save sabhuku's wife and baby.

Luckily, I was present when Maria assisted Mrs. Jokonia, and I witnessed what actually happened. If I had not been there, I would not have known the truth about what transpired on that night. Those of us who had witnessed Mrs. Jokonia's labor, knew exactly what had happened. There was nothing extraordinary about Maria's assistance. She just did what any other ordinary midwife could have done under such circumstances. She was lucky that both the mother and baby survived the ordeal. It is true that her skills helped, but it is also true that the giver of life was not ready to take home both mother and daughter. It is true that medical practitioners play their part, but as for who survives or perishes, it is the creator's decision to make.

The baby was growing, and our relationship with sabhuku was restored. When we thought that we had seen all the ups and downs of the village life, another incident happened. One of the villagers called Mudha, almost did something that shocked all the villagers. It is not that what he did was against the people's culture, but because that cultural practice had been abandoned by the people, and had also been outlawed by the government of Zimbabwe.

This is what happened. Mudha and his wife had five children. The oldest child was a girl, who was about twelve years old, and could have been in Grade Seven if she had not dropped out of school. It was said that her dropping out of school was caused by her father who did not quite care about his children's school attendance. He never paid the nominal school fees required from each parent for the school's infrastructural development. His children who still attended school never wore school uniforms to school as per school regulation because Mudha did not care to purchase any. The children never had any writing books or pens. They went to school hungry and tired. Even though it was said that Sarah, Mudha's first born, was very intelligent, persistent, and responsible, she eventually dropped out of school. Her mother, who always spent most of her time working in other people's fields for a little money or some grains, took advantage of the girl's dropping out of school. She now had a helper both at home and on the fields. The two spent countless hours toiling in other people's fields while nobody was working on their own field.

We were told that the woes experienced by Mudha's family were not a result of a drought, ill health, or bad luck, but of his own making. Mudha was not only lazy, but also a drunkard who scarcely set his feet in his field. Instead of working in his field, like other men in the village did, he spent his time binge drinking. Some villagers believed that Mudha was in fact, an alcoholic. He pursued beer parties from one village to another. There were times, he would go beer hunting for almost a week without ever setting his feet in his own home. He was the kind of man whose manhood could only be authenticated at night, in the bedroom, when being busy procreating more children. Hence, every year, the Mudha family never harvested enough crops to last for about four months. It was a sad situation, but the villagers had ceased to worry about the Mudhas because everyone knew that they would never starve. In fact, they never starved, for they had mastered the gimmicks of averting starvation. The villagers, who at first, reprimanded Mudha, got tired of advising him to work harder. He always listened to the person offering him unsolicited advice, but would never attempt to put it into practice. Hence, the villagers got tired of advising him, and left him to himself.

What Mudha had done or was about to do, this time, was different and abusive. It was said that Mudha had gone to one of the nearby resettlement villages, and this time, not to beg for food or look for work. He had gone there to find a husband for his daughter, Sarah. He had offered his daughter, Sarah, as a wife to a wealthy old man who already had two wives and numerous children and grandchildren. It was said that the wealthy man had promised to provide grains and cows to the Mudhas to ward off hunger. Of course, Sarah would not join her husband immediately, but was expected to go there as soon as she reached puberty. It was said that the Mudhas had already received grains to save the family from starvation, but the cows would come as soon as Sarah was delivered to her husband.

For the readers who are not privy to the Shona traditional forms of marriage, this type of marriage was known as pledged marriage (*kuzvarira*). Traditionally, it was an acceptable form of marriage though very unpopular with many families. A family, which was besieged by poverty or starvation would offer one of its daughters to a wealthy man in exchange for a food bailout. Usually, the pledged girl would be a minor who could not be legally given away in marriage at the time of the pledge. A gentlemen's agreement would be reached between the would-be husband and the father of the girl, that she would be escorted to her husband at the onset of puberty. Most of the time, the man would be advanced in age, and married to one or more other women already. Hence, some pledged girls were reported to have run away from their parents to avoid the arranged marriage. Others were reported to have eloped with some young men of their choice before they were escorted to their husbands. Whenever that happened, the girl's parents would get into trouble since they were expected to refund the food bailout that would have been received, which in most cases, would have been consumed. Sometimes, the new and youthful son-in-law would ransom the bride's parents from the wrath of the jilted lover.

Although the government of Zimbabwe did not outlaw this type of marriage at independence, in 1980, it just faded away. Of course, the government stipulated the majority ages for both boys and girls, but some people could still get away with marrying underage girls if the girls' parents supported it. During the time I am writing about, the government of Zimbabwe had raised the majority age for girls to eighteen to match that of the boys. Only girls and boys aged eighteen could give valid marital consents. So, what Mudha wanted to do shocked the villagers because the practice had long been abandoned by most people, and outlawed by the government. However, like any other cultural practice, this type of marriage was still being practiced by a few people, clandestinely. Some practiced it in the name of religion, particularly some members of the African Independent Churches.

This issue was brought to sabhuku Jokonia's attention by his police officer, Fatso. Soon, the whole village was awash with the rumors, which prompted sabhuku Jokonia to summon the Mudhas to his village court. Maria and I were also invited as assessors and advisors to the grateful sabhuku. The invitation was an honor for us because I had never sat at sabhuku's court in that capacity. I could not think of a more convincing reason that could have compelled sabhuku to invite us other than his trust and respect for the wife from the ancestors. It was payback time for him.

When we arrived at the court, sabhuku and his councilors were already there, talking about this and that. They were glad to see us. As we were exchanging the elaborate greetings, the Mudhas arrived. I could easily tell that Mr. Mudha was upset because he did not greet anyone, and barely returned any greetings. He just mumbled back something that sounded like a response without looking at the person who would have greeted him. In addition to that, he did not smile. He also refused to sit down for a while, even though he was offered a stool. Mudha's wife and his daughter were the opposite of him. They were cheerful. They greeted all the people who had gathered at sabhuku's compound. They also smiled at us, graciously.

As soon as everyone who was supposed to be present was seated, Mr. Jokonia opened the case.

"Good morning everyone. Thank you for coming. The issue, which we would like to deliberate on today is a sensitive one. It is sensitive because it involves a minor—Sarah, who is here with us. The issue came to my attention through the chairperson of the woman's league, who is here with us."

We thanked sabhuku.

"Mr. Mudha, the issue for which we summoned you here, is about your daughter. I am reliably informed that you have pledged your daughter in marriage to a certain man who lives in the resettlement areas. Is it true or false?"

"Who told you that?" Mudha asked.

"Please, answer the question. Is it true or false?" Sabhuku insisted.

"She is my daughter, and I can do whatever I want with her," Mudha responded arrogantly.

"Yes, we all know that she is your daughter. We all know that, but you are wrong in saying that you can do whatever you want with her. You can't. This country has laws to protect children, particularly minors. So, please, answer my question."

"What does the white woman want here? Is she also a council member?" Mudha wanted to know.

"I invited my friends, Peter and his wife, Maria, so that they can advise us accordingly. These two are Americans. They have another worldview that we do not have. They will only speak when we ask them to. They also know that our deliberations, here, are confidential. So, don't worry about them."

"But she is a woman. Women don't attend meetings like this one unless they are on trial or are witnesses. Is she on trial?" Mudha was not taking any of it.

"I want her to learn our culture. She is our new daughter-in-law, and she should know how we do things here. Now, can you tell us about your daughter? Can you answer the question I asked you?" Sabhuku was getting impatient.

"I already told you that she is my daughter."

"We all know that. How old is she?"

"I don't know," Mudha responded, contemptuously.

"How old are you, Sarah?" Sabhuku asked.

"Twelve," she responded.

"You see. She is a minor. You can't pledge her for marriage. You will be arrested. The husband or rapist will also get arrested. In fact, if you don't want to cooperate with this court, we will send you to Renco Mine police station. I am certain you wouldn't come back home today. Not tomorrow. Not even the day after tomorrow. You will certainly go to jail. You better answer our questions so that we can advise you accordingly."

"She is my daughter."

"You have said that already."

"I did, and I say it again."

"You will go to jail."

"I don't care."

"Do you know that prison is not for old men like you?"

"Is that a threat?"

"No. It's the reality."

There was silence.

"It's true, Mr. Jokonia. We already got five bags of maize, and we expect more to follow from our son-in-law. Sarah won't go to her husband until she becomes a woman," said Mudha's wife.

"Thank you, Mai Mudha. However, the man is not your son-in-law but a rapist. When will that be? When will you send your daughter to that man?" Sabhuku asked.

"Who knows nature's way? Maybe this year. Maybe next year, as soon as she begins her monthly periods."

"You can't do that," said sabhuku.

"Why not?" Mrs Mudha wanted to know.

"It's against the law of the country."

"It's our culture, Baba," Mai Mudha responded. "There is nothing wrong with it?"

"Some of our cultural practices have been superseded by the new laws, which are enshrined in the constitution of Zimbabwe. You can't force your daughter to marry anyone. You can't do it. Not anymore. Yes, it used to be our tradition, but it has been outlawed in modern Zimbabwe. You can't give away a twelve-year-old girl for marriage. She is a baby. If you do that, we will report you to the police. Both of you and that man will be arrested," sabhuku explained.

"If I may ask you, Mr. Mudha, why is your daughter not in school?" One of the councilors asked.

"You don't tell me what to do with my children. If I don't want them to go to school, that's none of your business. Or is it also against the law? Is it against the law to be poor? Is it against the law to fail to get school fees for your kids?" Mudha was angry.

"You are wasting our time, Mudha. We have other fish to fry," said Fatso.

"I don't care about your time. It's you who summoned me here." Mudha pointed his finger toward Fatso.

"You don't disrespect my court by threatening one of my officials. Don't point your finger at anyone here," sabhuku warned Mudha.

"What can you do?"

"You will be sorry."

"You can't do anything. She is not your child."

Sabhuku ignored Mudha, and turned to us.

"What do you think, my advisors?" Sabhuku was referring to us.

Maria spoke. "I think it's not right to force a little girl into a marriage of any kind whatever the reason. In America, a man who tries to force such a minor into a marriage will be arrested and charged with rape. The father and the mother of the girl will be charged as accomplices. They also will go to jail. This little girl is beautiful, and she deserves to go to school like other girls of her age. Do you want to go to school, Sarah?"

"Yes," she responded.

"Or do you want to get married?" Maria pursued her.

"No. No. I don't want to get married to an old man. I want to go back to school." Sarah started crying. Maria walked to where she was sitting, and embraced her to comfort her.

"Don't touch my daughter," Mudha threatened.

Maria ignored him. I walked to where Maria was comforting Sarah, fearing that Mudha would try to attack her. Fortunately, he never did.

Fatso also jumped into the conversation. "Even here in Zimbabwe, it's now called statutory rape. You get into deep trouble for facilitating a child marriage. You should return whatever you have taken from that man. Please, take it back. We will be monitoring the situation closely. Don't make a mistake. If you ever send this child to that man, I will report you to the police."

Another councilor joined the chorus, "We want this child to go back to school. If you have accepted anything from this man, please, return it as soon as possible."

"He will be arrested. At Musvovi's village, someone was sentenced to fifteen years in prison for marrying a minor. It's rape case." It was Fatso.

"Ok. Let me end this session by saying; Mudha, you won't force this girl to marry anyone. In fact, she can't validly give her consent to marriage until she turns eighteen. You, as parents, can't give marital consent on her behalf. We tell you this, Mudha and Mai Mudha, not because we hate you, or because we want to interfere in your family affairs. No. It's because we don't want both of you to go to jail, and to leave your kids without anybody taking care of them. If that happens, it would be a burden to me, as the village head. Maybe you should learn to work on your fields like all of us do. You can't just drink beer, and think that you will harvest enough food for your family."

"You are now insulting me. I have never come to your home begging for food," Mudha sounded angry.

"It's shameful. Don't do it," one of the councilors told Mudha.

Although Mudha never apologized or showed any remorse, everyone knew that he got the message. He unceremoniously left the court, but his wife and daughter remained a little while to thank everyone for their support. I could see that Maria was warming up to Mrs. Mudha and her daughter. They were talking and laughing together like people who had known each other for a long time.

The meeting ended, and we all returned to our homes. Although Mudha seemed unrepentant, he had perfectly understood the message conveyed to him. I thought that he would take the warning seriously, and indeed, he did.

The following day, Mrs. Mudha and Sarah came to my parents' home. Maria was waiting for them since she knew that they were coming to see her. She had talked with them the previous day about the possibility of Maria going back to school, and they had made an appointment with Maria for the following day. Maria had suggested that she would find a way to finance her education. She had also promised them some money for their food provisions.

Mudha arrived at my parents' home a few minutes after Sarah and her mother. We had already agreed on the money that we wanted to give them as a gift so that they could buy some food. We also gave them a little money to recompense the man who had given them some food bailout in anticipation of getting a young wife in return. Mudha and his wife were profoundly touched by Maria's generosity and kindness. Mudha cried, and confessed that nobody had ever been so kind to his family. He went a step further by promising that he would change his ways. He also said that he would work in his field and produce enough food to feed his family like other men were doing.

Maria promised that she would buy school uniforms for Sarah, and pay her school fees so that she could go back to school the following year. She told the Mudhas that the fees would be sent through Mother, who would be responsible for paying the fees, and then bring the receipts to Mrs. Mudha. Sarah was also thankful. She really loved school, and confessed that she was so glad to be able to go back to school. Maria and I were glad to hear that.

The word about Maria's generosity to the Mudhas traveled fast. When we woke up the following day, our homestead was full of people asking for all kinds of help. Initially, Mother was a little upset.

"You see what I was telling you?"

"What?" I asked.

"Don't give money to people," Mother commanded.

"It's just a little money, Mother," I responded.

"I don't care whether it's little or much. Some of these people are witches. They will bewitch us thinking that we have a lot of money. When that happens, you won't be here to suffer with us. You will be back in America. Please, don't give people money," Mother pleaded with us.

"We came prepared for this, Mother," Maria said.

"Prepared for what? Giving money to the whole clan? Has any of these people given me even a penny? They have children in South Africa, Botswana, Namibia, and all over the world, and they come home all the time. Did they ever give me even a cent? You are wasting money. Please, give it to me, if you don't know what to do with it."

"We will give you your share, Mother," I responded. "We should do something for the community. It's you who taught me that our *hunhu* demands that we assist the less privileged. They too assist us in their own ways."

"They are not less privileged, my son, they are lazy."

"That's your perception, Mother, but we do have a different perception."

"Alright. It's your money, but be careful, how you give it away. Some people are not grateful."

I knew that Mother did not mean what she said, but I thanked her anyway.

We stayed in the village for a week after which we left for the Great Zimbabwe Monuments. From there, we proceeded to the Victoria Falls.

Our delayed honeymoon had begun. The Victoria Falls was fantastic. We cruised in a boat, which was very refreshing, although very scary. We did bungee jumping from the Victoria falls bridge, which was not an easy feat for me even though Maria enjoyed it immensely. I know why it was not a good fit for me; I am afraid of heights. I only consented to Maria doing it when I was assured of the safety record of undertaking such a dive. We watched some white-water rafting, which was thrilling and scary at the same time. We flew in a helicopter to see an overview of the Victoria Falls, and the sight was breathtaking. We watched high wire activities. We swam in the Devil's Pool. Of course, I must admit that I did not partake in it, for I deemed it too dangerous to swim in there. Maria insisted on doing it, and I let her be, but only after I was convinced that the life savers were thoroughly trained. I was tense the whole time she was in there, and I felt relieved when she finally got out. We watched other visitors skydiving, which I thought was extremely risky. Maria wanted to try it, but I begged her not to, and she gave in.

The Victoria Falls was awesome. Maria enjoyed every aspect of it, and I did, too. We watched the game in Zambezi National Park. We saw some animals, but we were told that if we wanted to see big game, we needed to go to other national parks.

There was good music, delicious food, and breathtaking traditional dancing.

From the Victoria Falls, we went back to Harare where we intended to meet Maria's parents. We were already in Harare when we found out that they had canceled the trip because of an emergency that had happened at their home, back in Texas. A powerful tornado had destroyed their home, and they had to cancel their trip. We called them, and we were glad to know that no one was injured. We also asked them to go and stay at our home if they needed a temporary shelter. We had two spare bedrooms, which they could use while their place was being repaired. Initially, they refused to take the offer, but we insisted, and they agreed. Since they already had the spare keys to our home, it was easy for them to relocate. We were glad that we could assist them in their time of greatest need.

After four weeks of Maria's intercultural immersion, we returned to the United States. Maria took every opportunity to talk about her experiences in Zimbabwe, and the Shona culture. She was impressed by everything. She loved the extended family relationships, and how everyone was related to everybody else. In addition to complex relationships, Maria was impressed by the spirit of togetherness that resided among the people. The people helped each other whenever necessary. She was also impressed by the respect the people had for each other, even during disagreements. She loved to see the fruit trees that were growing at the villagers' homesteads. She had mountains of news to share with her family back in San Antonio.

7

A Time to Confess

The news came to us during the July 4th holiday, about a year after we had visited Zimbabwe. Maria and I had planned to go to Texas' popular beach, Port Aransas, a plan which never came to fruition because the tone of the news that we received compelled us to postpone the trip. The message was sent to us by my brother, Ben, via social media—WhatsApp, to be precise. The bad news was about Mother's illness. By the time we received the news of her illness, it seemed that she had been unwell for a while, but no one seemed to know the name of the disease that had stricken her. The doctors who had medically examined her on numerous occasions had failed to diagnose or had misdiagnosed the cause of her illness. Hence, some of them had prescribed some medication only for symptoms, which was said to have not helped her much to regain her health. The symptoms included, but were not limited to an on and off fever, a drastic weight loss, fatigue, scars, and cracked skin.

At the time I received the call, Mother could barely walk. At first, Baba is said to have taken her to the nearest clinic, but they did not have any medicine, hence she only got pain killers, for which we should be grateful. I was not surprised to hear that the local rural clinic did not have medicine because at that time, all of Zimbabwe's hospitals and clinics were undergoing some serious funding constraints. To worsen the matter, the medical practitioners in Zimbabwe's Ministry of Health were poorly remunerated, and many of them were leaving the country for greener pastures. As if that was not bad enough, there was not even a single state-registered nurse at the local clinic to which Mother went for medical attention.

Ben explained that Mother's health was deteriorating fast, and he was scared. Things were not looking good at all, but Baba hoped that

Mother's health would improve, perhaps through divine intervention. When Mother's health did not improve as had been anticipated, Baba took her to the nearest general hospital, where they ran all kinds of tests, but could not find out what was wrong with her.

Ben said that he had delayed telling us about the illness because both Baba and Mother thought that it was something that would pass. In fact, Mother did not want to worry us unnecessarily. Despite those hopes, the illness did not go away. As a matter of fact, Mother became worse.

Later that day, I called Baba who told me that when he felt that Mother was not going to get any meaningful help from the Western medical practitioners, he took her to the Christian 'prophets,' where he was told that there was a *ngozi* spirit tormenting her. However, the 'prophet' did not tell them the identity of the avenging spirit, and what it wanted, and how it should be appeased. The 'prophet' is said to have tried to exorcize the *ngozi* by prescribing the use of sacred water, fresh milk, and a white chicken. The prescribed ritual was meticulously performed at the nearby crossroads, at dawn, with the 'prophet' presiding over it. The sacred water was sprinkled unto Mother, and her body was drenched with the fresh milk. The live white chicken was held by the legs by the 'prophet' while being swirled around Mother's body. The man of God is said to have slaughtered it, smeared a little blood on Mother's forehead, and took the carcass to his home to properly dispose of it. However, Mother's health did not improve as had been promised by the man of God, which caused a great deal of anxiety to both Baba and Ben.

Baba could not just sit and watch while Mother was slowly fading away like mist. He decided to take her to traditional healers, where they were told that one of their neighbors had bewitched her because of jealousy. Father claimed that although the healer had refused to mention the name of the witch, he suspected one of their neighbors to be the culprit. The healer also mentioned that Mother was too proud of her children's success, which I think was not true about Mother. She was a humble and generous woman, who would never try to show off her successes in life. The healer prescribed and provided all kinds of herbal concoctions for Mother to drink, which Mother is said to have faithfully done. He is said to have promised that Mother would be healed within a few weeks, but still, several weeks after starting the treatment, there was no improvement.

When she did not heal, Baba took her to another traditional healer who claimed that the ancestors were not happy with my marriage. They were said to be angry because I had married a white woman. The aggrieved ancestors demanded a sacrificial goat and some traditionally brewed beer to appease them so that Mother would regain her health. Baba unwaveringly followed all the instructions prescribed by the healer. The beer was brewed, and the sacrificial goat slaughtered and offered to the ancestors, but Mother remained ill. In fact, she became worse.

Another traditional healer told them that the illness was caused by *zvidhoma,* which were drinking Mother's blood in her sleep. They were advised that the mother of the *zvidhoma* was angry that Mother had a good life, home, livestock, children, and a good husband. It was said that the *zvidhoma* were now resident at my parents' home, and they would not go away unless they accomplished their mission. In other words, they would not go away without causing Mother's death. Baba brought the healer home to drive away the *zvidhoma* and other evil spirits. The *zvidhoma* were chased away, but the evil spirits were placed on a black scapegoat, which was then driven into the bush. The healer then drove into the ground, around my parents' home, some medicinal pegs that were intended to keep evil spirits, *zvidhoma,* and witches at bay. The pegs acted as an invisible electric fence that would prevent the deleterious witches and their evil forces from entering the premises. Sadly, Mother's health continued to deteriorate.

Finally, Baba instructed Ben to notify us about the illness. I blamed Baba for having taken so long to bring Maria and I into the loop about Mother's ill-health. After talking with Baba for almost half an hour, I called Mother, and we had a long phone conversation. Her voice was barely audible, and I could tell that she was in both pain and fear. Our conversation went as follows:

"Hello, Mhayi."

"Hello, my son."

"How is your health? I was told that you are not feeling well."

"I am ill, my son. I don't know if I will survive this time."

"What's wrong, Mother?"

"It started like skin rash, which was on and off. Then, I had small cracks on my skin, a problem which was not new to me. It's a problem I have had all my life, but this time, the cracks became more visible and bigger, and would not heal as quickly as they used to do. Then, I had joint inflammation and fever. I started losing hair at a few places on my head. I am always very tired as if I have worked hard. I have lost a lot of weight, which started gradually, and then intensified as time went by. Last night, I couldn't sleep because of chest pains."

"What do the doctors say?"

"They don't know what it is. I have been tested for everything you can imagine, but I was found negative. They just give me medicines to treat the symptoms."

Mother was sad, and it made me so sad. I explained to Maria the symptoms that Mother had described to me. Maria then called Mother, and they had a long conversation, in which Maria asked her questions about her health. Maria did a good job because as a medical practitioner, she knew the right questions to ask. After the conversation, Maria told me that she suspected some kind of thyroid disease, or lupus caused by some autoimmune disorders. I did not know what lupus was, for I had never heard of such a disease before. Maria explained to me that it was an inflammatory disease caused when the body's immune system mistakes its own tissues for enemies, and begins to attack them. It is thought to be an inherent disease, which can be triggered by one's environment, food, mental disposition, and many other factors.

The following day, I called Mother, and carefully explained what Maria had told me. I then suggested that she needed to come to the United States to undergo medical examination by experts, and to receive the appropriate healthcare. At first, she was enraged by my suggestion.

"No. Why should I come to America. You know very well that your wife caused this, and you want me to come over there. No."

"Mother, you know that it's not true. My wife is a nurse, and her primary job is to save lives. If you follow what your fake prophets tell you, you will go crazy."

"Maybe your wife bewitched me."

"Excuse me."

"I don't want to come to America. I don't want to die away from home."

"Please, never say that again. You know very well that Maria is not a witch. She doesn't even know what a witch is. If that is your game of accusing people who love and care about you of witchcraft, then, you are beyond redemption. If you and I are going to maintain our relationship, you should learn to respect my wife. I don't want to hear that again."

"Peter, you don't speak to me like that. I am not your kid," Mother sounded upset.

"You also don't speak to me about my wife like that, I am your son. The respect should be mutual. We will send you some money to apply for a visa. We want you to be seen by a specialist. We know that you will be alright. Just be strong enough to fly."

"Why do you want me to come over there? I have been to the doctors here, and they don't see what's wrong with me. It means that my illness has traditional causes."

"You should come over to the United States because Maria and I love you very much. We want to have an opportunity to care for you. We don't want you to die of something that can be treated. We want you to be well so that you can go back to your normal life."

"Okay. When do you want me to arrive?"

"As soon as possible."

Mother thanked me. Later that week, she applied for a visa to visit the United States, and she got it. We were all relieved that she now could come over and be medically examined by medical specialists here in the United States. We purchased her flight ticket, and enlisted the services of the airport wheelchair since she was so frail to walk. Even if she were strong enough to walk, the airport wheelchair service would help her to find her way through airports easily. We just hoped that she would not become seriously ill before her travel, or on the plane.

Her travel was without a hitch and was on schedule. I went to pick her up from George Bush International Airport, in Houston. When she emerged from the baggage collection area, I could barely recognize her. She looked frail and skeletal. She had become a shadow of herself. Her face was dark, and her cheekbones were protruding as if they could pierce through her skin. She struggled to pull the only suitcase that she had brought, and swerved from side to side as if she would fall at any time. I shed a few beads of tears as I greeted her.

"Why are you crying? Is everything okay?" She asked.

"I am alright. It's about you. You look very tired. How was your flight?"

"It was good. I didn't have to worry about getting lost because the wheelchair people took good care of me."

"How are you feeling? You look so frail, Mother."

"I am better now, my son. I nearly died last month. Now, I have regained some strength. I can walk. I eat. I am alive, my son. Don't cry, Peter."

"Can I hold your hand to give you support?"

"No. I can walk."

We took the nearest elevator to the car garage. Within a few minutes, we were on the road to San Antonio.

"I am glad that you arrived safely. You will receive first class healthcare here, Mother. Maria has already made appointments for your care at the hospital where she works."

"Thank you. How is she doing?"

"She is doing good, and she is very much pregnant. She wanted to come with me, but she is working today. She will be home by the time we arrive."

"She is pregnant?"

"Yes."

"That's good news, my son. I don't think I will die before I see my first grandchild. God and our ancestors wanted me to live to see my first grandchild. I just want to live to be able to hold her or him in my hands." Mother was excited.

"It's a boy, Mother."

"How do you know?"

"Technology, Mhayi."

"I think that they shouldn't tell people the sex of a child before it's born. That information should only be known to God and the ancestors."

"Why not tell the parents?"

"It takes away the element of surprise when the child eventually comes. Every child is a gift from God and the ancestors, and its sex should be discovered and announced by the midwife. Also, in the same announcement, the child gets to know about its sex, when the midwives first pronounce it to the parents. A gift makes the recipient more curious when it is wrapped than when it is open. Having foreknowledge of the sex of an unborn child takes away the curiosity and surprise that should accompany the birth of a child and the announcement of the child's sex."

"It's very interesting. Anyway, things have changed now. We already know, though the midwives can still announce the sex of the child to us. Many people think that having some foreknowledge of the sex of an unborn baby helps the parents to buy the right kind and colors of the baby's clothes."

"It sounds reasonable, although I would prefer not to know."

"I understand."

"When do you expect the baby?"

"In a few weeks."

"Let's hope I will be strong enough to be able to welcome the baby, and to assist in caring for him. I am so happy. This is good news."

"It's good news, Mother. How are Baba and Ben?"

"They were doing very well when I left. Of course, they were worried about me. Baba wanted to come with me because he thought I would get lost."

"I explained everything concerning the airport wheelchair services to him, and he pretended to understand it. I will call him when we arrive home."

We drove to San Antonio, mostly in silence. Mother was tired, and slept most of the journey. When we arrived home, Maria was waiting for us, and had already prepared supper. She was as shocked as I was to see Mother in that skeletal state. Mother was ecstatic to see Maria advanced in pregnancy. She jumped up and down, and tried to make some noise that resembled some ululation, but she was too weak for that. Maria, fearing that Mother would fall to the ground, firmly held her by the hand and assisted her to sit on the sofa. She was exhausted.

"What's that, my daughter-in-law?" Mother asked while pointing at Maria's baby bump.

"It's our boy, Mother. His name is David. Would you like to say hello to him?"

"Yes," Mother said. "Hello."

"Please, touch him. Feel his legs. Oh my God, he is kicking, He is greeting you. He heard your greetings," Maria shouted.

"Touching your belly?" Mother was petrified.

"Yes, Mother. It's okay. Please, feel the baby," I encouraged her.

Mother touched Maria's baby bump, reluctantly. Her eyes lit with joy. "Yes, I can feel the baby. He is moving. I am so happy. I can't wait to see my first grandchild. Even if I die afterwards, it would be okay with me. What else can a person ask for?"

"You won't die, Mother," I assured her.

"We gave him Baba's name," Maria said.

"Why? Couldn't you find a better name for the baby?"

"Mother, what's wrong with the name David? It's a good name. I guess Baba is not all that bad that we can't give his name to our baby," I said.

"I am not saying it's a bad name. There is nothing wrong with it. It's just that I didn't expect it. Most people no longer do it in Zimbabwe."

"How do they name their kids now?" I asked.

"They give them Christian names, such as Kumbakwashe, Anotidaishe, Tawanigwanyashanashe, Tadiwanashe, and so on."

"I think there is something about "*ishe*" that drives people crazy."

"They are not crazy. They want to honor, our Lord, Jesus Christ."

"That's not bad," I responded.

"What about my name?" Mother asked.

"It's a boy, Mother," I said.

"I know. Won't you have another baby?"

"Ask Maria."

"I heard the question, Peter." Maria looked at Mother and said, "We will have many more children, Mother. You will truly find a namesake."

"Thank you, daughter-in-law."

"We will cross that river when we come to it, Mother. Are you a little jealous?" I asked.

"No. I was just kidding," Mother replied.

"I don't think so, Mother. I felt some jealousy in your voice."

"Maybe I am a little jealous," she admitted.

"I got you."

"So, that woman was lying?" Mother asked.

"Which woman?"

"Mother JK. She said that white women don't like to have kids."

"Let's not talk about Mother JK, today."

"Okay."

Soon, after supper, Mother retired to bed. I was happy that all the appointments and payments for her blood tests had been made. I just hoped that she would not become seriously ill before she could be examined by a rheumatologist or an endocrinologist.

The following morning, I gave her a ride to our family physician, who after subjecting her to a thorough physical examination, ordered Mother to have blood samples taken for further tests. The results for the blood samples were out the next day, and Maria's fears were confirmed. Mother had an autoimmune disease, which had caused lupus and hyperthyroidism. Hyperthyroidism had caused a goiter to develop, and had led to her drastic loss of weight and energy, and numerous other health complications.

Maria quickly booked an appointment for her, first with an endocrinologist, and second, with a rheumatologist. Mother was lucky because the endocrinologist squeezed her into his schedule the following day because somebody had canceled her appointment. She was examined and some medication to reduce the secretion of the thyroid hormone was prescribed. The medication was just a small pill that she was supposed to take once per day. The doctor said that the quantity of the medication would be reduced as time went on, and would be stopped when the normal thyroid hormone level was achieved.

Just a week after Mother had started taking the prescription medicines, her health improved, significantly. She claimed that the lethargy disappeared, and the nocturnal fevers stopped. The joint pains lessened, and the skin lacerations started to heal. By the end of August, about two weeks into the medication, her goiter started to dissolve.

She came out of her bedroom, one day and said, "Look at my neck. The lump is gone. I cannot feel it when I touch my neck."

"It's a miracle unfolding," I replied.

"And the miracle worker is Maria," Mother replied.

"It's not, me. It's the doctors," Maria answered.

"It's you, my daughter-in-law. You knew exactly what was troubling my body. You even said so when we talked on the phone when I was still in Zimbabwe. Thank you for the insight and diagnosis."

"You are welcome. I am glad that we could assist you to regain your health. Just follow the doctor's advice, and you will be good."

"Thank you, my daughter. My family is lucky to have you as a member of the family. People in Zimbabwe are still talking about you, and how generous and kind you are."

"Thank you, Mother. How is baby, Maria Shamiso?" Maria asked.

"She is no longer a baby, but a toddler. She is very beautiful, and the villagers say that *inhodzera*."

"What's *nhodzera*?" Maria asked.

"The Shona people believe that an unborn baby can resemble the things or people that its mother sees during her pregnancy. The resemblance is not a problem, when the person is beautiful, but it is undesirable if the person is ugly. So, pregnant women should not look at ugly animals such as monkeys and baboons, lest the unborn baby resembles the animal. Now, since you facilitated the birth of Maria Shamiso, people say that her looks took after you." It was Mother who explained.

"But the encounter was too late to have effects on the baby's looks," I said.

"That's what I told the people, but no one listens. Now, she has a nickname."

"What do they call her?" Maria asked.

"*Murungu.*"

"It means, white person," I explained to Maria.

"That's funny," Maria replied.

Every other week, mother had to go for a review with her doctor. In her second review, the results of Mother's blood tests showed that her thyroid gland was still overactive, and she had to continue with the same quantity of medication. During that visit, the doctor suggested something to which we all objected. He advised that if the thyroid gland were not responding to medication as quickly as he expected, an operation to remove it altogether or a procedure to dissolve it would be recommended. What that meant was that Mother would have to rely on medication to perform the job of the thyroid gland hormone. Since, she would be returning to Zimbabwe, where there was no such medication, we told him that it was not an option for her. The doctor understood our predicament. We just hoped that the symptoms would be reversed using medication.

In the meanwhile, baby David came, and our joy was indescribable. We were lucky that Mother had started recovering, and had already regained considerable strength to be able to hold the baby. We celebrated the arrival of the baby together. There were no surprises because we already knew the sex of the baby. Mother assisted us in taking care of baby David, and before long, the pair became inseparable. Mother carried him on her back whenever she could. We complained about it, but she did not listen, and baby David seemed to like it very much.

At first, Mother vehemently objected to David sleeping in his own court. For her, it was neglect of the baby, and she offered to sleep with him in her bedroom, and on her bed, to which Maria and I objected vehemently. We explained to her that the doctor had recommended that the baby should sleep in his court, and their advice was to be taken seriously. Mother got used to it.

In the first few days after Maria and baby David had been discharged from the hospital, Mother would wake up early in the morning, waiting for David to wake up. She was always disappointed when David did not wake up until breakfast time.

"Why don't you check on David? Is he still sleeping?" She would ask.

"He is still asleep," Maria would answer.

"Why don't you wake him up? Don't you think he is now hungry?" She would suggest.

Maria would get into the bedroom to check if David was okay. Sometimes, she would find him already awake, and would bring him into the sitting room. Mother would quickly take him from Maria.

When Maria went back to work after her maternity leave, Mother took full responsibility over the care of baby David. The two loved each other. We persuaded her to always talk to the baby in English to which she tried to object.

"He should learn the Shona language," Mother said. "He is Shona, and should be able to speak and understand the language."

"I agree. We will teach him some Shona, later, but not now. We want him to be bilingual, but he must start with one language so that we don't confuse him. When he begins to speak English, we will introduce him to Shona, but he has to master English first."

Mother agreed. So, whenever we were home, she spoke to baby David in English, but I do not think that she did the same when we were not home, which did not bother us much.

Within two months of commencing treatment for hyperthyroidism and lupus, mother had fully recovered, and had already started to gain weight. Her doctor kept reducing her medication until she stopped taking it altogether. Since, she had planned to go back to Zimbabwe by the end of August, we thought that it would be a good idea for her to stay with us until December. Mother did not need any persuasion to extend her stay because she loved to be with baby David. Her stay with us was also a big blessing for us in many ways.

During that time, the Webers visited us frequently to see the baby. Whenever they were around, Mother would be always worried about how they held the baby. The Webers also complained about how Mother always held the baby on her lap, and was carrying him on her back.

One day Andrea said, "Mrs. Masika, thank you so much for all you do for David. We are all grateful for your assistance. However, you need to teach him to lie in his court so that when you are gone, he will be accustomed to playing alone with his toys."

"You are welcome, Mrs. Weber. Since I am still here, I should do everything that a mother should do for her baby. As to what happens when I am gone, I can't control it."

"I understand that, but you should think of the person who will be taking care of David when you are gone. She will be a person from a different culture, and may not understand your babysitting techniques."

"What techniques are you talking about?"

"Like cuddling the baby all the time."

"Please, say exactly what you want to tell me."

"I already said what I wanted to tell you. Baby David belongs to all of us. He has two parents, who belong to two different cultures. I think that he should benefit from both cultures. You are trying to monopolize him, which I think is not good for all of us and the baby. I don't like the way you look at me whenever I am holding David. You make me feel as if I am too incompetent to hold or feed him. He is my grandchild too. I love him as much as you do. Please, give me a little space with him." Andrea was upset.

"This baby is black. He is Shona just like his father. He has a totem. I should teach him how to be a Shona man," shouted Mother.

"You are wrong."

"What?"

"I said, you are wrong, Tendai." Andrea paused a little, and continued. "David is both black and white. You can't run away from that fact. He belongs to all of us."

"I agree, but I don't think that putting a baby in a basket is a good thing. It's cold. I can't just leave him alone in a lifeless basket. He wants others. He needs friends. He wants to be loved. I can't allow you to mishandle or neglect him when I am around."

"Who the hell, do you think you are?"

"I am his paternal grandmother."

"I am also his grandmother. I deserve some time with him."

"David is a Masika, not a Weber. I will be leaving soon, and he will be all yours."

"Are you saying that your culture is better than ours?" Andrea was becoming confrontational.

"No. I never said that. I just want to take care of my grandson without you hovering over me like an eagle. He is still too young, and he needs motherly care and warmth. He will be able to adjust to the new babysitter when I am gone. He doesn't need to be trained for that now."

"The baby might be a Shona like his father, but he has a mother too," Andrea said.

"And a grandmother, too," Mother responded.

"Two grandmothers, not one, if I may correct you," Andrea answered.

"I know."

"You are a good grandmother, but there are certain things you overdo," Andrea complained.

"I have heard them already," Mother responded.

"I haven't told you everything. For instance, you over bath the baby," Andrea said.

"What do you mean?" Mother was curious.

"You give David a bath every day, which is not recommended at all."

"What is the recommended number of baths he should have per day?"

"One per week."

"What? One bath per week?" Mother was dumbfounded.

"Yes."

"Why?"

"Because if you bath the baby daily you will irritate or dry out his skin," Andrea explained.

"It is very surprising to hear this from a white person. A baby is a human being, and should take baths every day. That's what we do in Zimbabwe. After every bath, we apply baby lotion to the baby's body."

"It's different here. Now, that you have made it a routine for David, it will be difficult for Maria not to give him daily baths."

"No mother should ever complain about giving her baby a bath."

"I just wanted you to know how most mothers bath their babies, here."

"Mother, I think that Andrea was making a suggestion," I said.

"You are right, Peter. It was just a suggestion, and your Mother doesn't need to do it. I just wanted her to think about David when she is gone back to Zimbabwe. He will miss her. He should begin to learn some American culture now, lest he has a culture shock when all of a sudden, Tendai is gone. I also wanted her to know how I feel when she monitors me when I hold the baby. I, too, had children. I know how to care for babies. Your mother doesn't have a monopoly over that knowledge." There was concern in Andrea's voice.

I had to pacify them. "I think both of you have to understand that David has two cultures, and it should be to his advantage. Both of you need to respect each other's culture. You should give each other an opportunity to play with the baby. You can teach the baby your different cultures without denigrating each other's culture. Otherwise, you will end up confusing the baby."

I continued, "When Mother is gone, the baby will be all yours, Andrea. And we appreciate that you will be here to assist us. I think that Mother is sad because she is leaving soon. She loves David. If we had two babies, we would distribute them between you," I said jokingly.

Andrea did not respond.

Baby David loved both his mother and grandmother equally, for he seemed to yearn for them equally. Whatever was going through the baby's mind, I did not know. However, I thought that the presence of both a black woman and a white woman as mother figures at such an early stage, provided the best intercultural learning for him. I felt that later in life, he would remember that at the beginning of his life, there were two mothers—one white and the other one black. Both cared and loved him whole-heartedly. Perhaps, that will help him to grasp the fact that his parents belong to different cultures. Genetically, David had inherited something from both of us. His skin would pass for a white kid, but his hair was black, curly, and almost kinky. His nose was straight and thin, but his lips were full. He was very handsome, for he had inherited from the best of both worlds. I am not saying that I am very handsome, but that, David was.

The news of Mother's recovery was celebrated by Baba, Ben, and our relatives back in Zimbabwe. If Mother's visa allowed, Baba wanted her to stay in the United States a little bit longer, so that her health could be monitored by her doctors. Unfortunately, that was not possible because she had been granted a six-month visa. She needed to go back to Zimbabwe by the end of December. She would look for a specialist in Zimbabwe to continue monitoring her health. In fact, I had talked to a doctor in Zimbabwe, who would do her medical reviews, and the blood tests would be processed in South Africa. We also arranged that if she needed the service of an endocrinologist, she would have to go to South Africa or come back to the U.S.

A week before Mother departed for Zimbabwe, we threw a party for her. In fact, it was a combined belated Christmas and Mother's farewell party. Most of our Zimbabwean friends except Mother JK, who could not make it from Corpus Christi, attended the celebration. That evening, the Webers overstayed to bid Mother farewell privately. Then, something that we had not expected happened. I am still grateful that the Webers decided to stay until all the invited guests had left because the conversation that we had that evening was not for public consumption, though extremely transformative to all of us.

Mother made a public confession. As a matter of fact, Mr. and Mrs. Weber also confessed. It happened after supper, when everyone else had wished Mother a wonderful and safe journey back to Zimbabwe. It was started by Mother. "I would like to take this opportunity to say a few words that I have always wanted to say in the presence of you all. I would like to thank, Maria, my daughter-in-law from the ancestors, for her generosity and kindness. She saved my life just like she saved sabhuku's wife and baby, in Zimbabwe. I was sick, and was almost dying, and I could smell death, for it was just around the corner, and Maria whisked me away from the fangs of death." Mother paused, and then tapped Maria on the shoulder and continued. "My daughter-in-law, I owe you my life. You invited me here, and sent me to the right doctors. Look at me now. Look at me." Mother stood up to show herself to all of us. "I cannot remember myself being as healthy as I am right now. Thank you, my daughter."

That was not enough.

"I also would like to thank you, Mrs. and Mr. Weber for allowing your daughter to marry my son. Thank you, for all the support you have rendered them. At first, I doubted your sincerity of heart, but I now know that I was wrong. You are people of honor. You stood by your promise, to love my boy as your own. Thank you for your kindness. Thank you for raising your daughter, Maria, well. I must admit that I was misled by some people who said that my son could be hurt by this marriage. I strongly believed that you would dehumanize my son, and make him feel like a subhuman. I would like to apologize for having entertained such erroneous thoughts. I judged you wrongly." Mother paused, and everyone looked at her in silence.

Andrea recovered first from the effects of what Mother had said, and jumped into the conversation. "You don't need to apologize, but we accept the apology, anyway. We are in the same boat with you, for we are also not perfect. We have our own biases and prejudices just like everyone else. So, we may also need to apologize to Peter, for doubting his goodness, in the first place. Maria and Peter's marriage has taught us many things about blacks that we did not know. We never dreamt that one day we would sit on the same table with a black person, in our own home. Never. It's not that we were racists, but blacks were not in our orbit. Our encounter with Peter increased our horizons, and changed our mindset. It was an encounter that we had always dreaded. Even when we got the courage to encounter Peter, we had hoped that he would assimilate and be like us. We had hoped that his skin color would be a little lighter, and when we met him, we were disappointed. We thought that it would be shameful to accept him as our son-in-law, as he was, for he was too black for us and some of our friends. His heavy accent did not help the situation. But when we decided to open our hearts and home to him, reluctantly though, we could not avoid being transformed by that encounter. We discovered that most of our ill-conceived perceptions were wrong. We erroneously thought that his otherness was bad and harmful—a big mistake. In fact, his otherness has brought something new into our family. Although some of our cultural practices and perceptions cannot be changed, we now have a second culture. We look at issues from another cultural perspective. We are also comfortable with our cultural differences. Peter, we love you dearly. We have said this before, and we reiterate it now."

Andrea started crying. Mr. Weber handed her a handkerchief with which to wipe away her tears. Mother and Maria embraced her and patted her shoulders to comfort her.

"Thank you, Mrs. Weber," Mother said. "So, our fears and suspicions were mutual. I am glad that time and love have proved us wrong. To Maria, I would like to say, I love you with all my heart. You are the daughter that I so much wanted but couldn't get. I could not have asked for a better daughter-in-law. I am sorry that I doubted your sincerity. Some people told me that white people could not be trusted. That they hate blacks. I believed what I was told. I now know that human beings are different. We can't just stereotype people. We should give everyone a chance. I am sorry, my daughter, for doubting your love for my son." Mother hugged Maria.

"Thank you, for giving us baby David. I will miss him so much. I will miss his giggles and beautiful smile. I will miss his irresistible gaze. If I could take him home with me, I would, but I know that I can't. Please, bring him home to Zimbabwe, whenever you can so that we can introduce him to our ancestors. I am taking his umbilical code home, and I will bury it in our yard, where all the umbilical codes of my children are buried. It will connect him with the ancestors and God. Thank you. Thank you." Mother hugged Maria, and would not let go.

It was Maria's turn. "Thank you, Mother, for being with us and taking care of baby David. You are so kind, honest, and generous. You have wisdom and a certain understanding that we the youth don't have. We will miss you. David will miss you. You have shown him some kind of love and commitment that we may not be able to replicate. He loves you. I can see it in his eyes when he looks at you. In fact, he thinks that he has two mothers, one black, and the other one white. I am jealous because he seems to favor his black mother. I hope that one day, we will be able to sit down at your homestead in Zimbabwe, and narrate to David how in his first six months on earth, he had two mothers. We have pictures of all of us that we will keep for him. Perhaps, we will have more children, and we will need your assistance again. So, please, come back again. Anytime. This is your home. *Nuestra casa es tu casa*. Please, don't forget to take your medication. We want you to live longer."

"Thank you, my daughter-in-law," Mother said.

Mr. Weber, who up to now had said nothing, decided to join the conversation. "Can I say something?" he asked.

"Please, go ahead. This is your home and family, and you do not have to ask for permission to speak," Mother responded.

"I, too, have a confession to make. I have said this before, but I think that today is the right time to repeat it. When I got to know about Maria's relationship with Peter, I was angry. Very angry. I cried all night long. I lost my appetite. I felt that my only daughter had betrayed us by falling in love with a black person. It's not my fault, but my upbringing. I grew up in an area where there were no blacks. I went to schools were there were no black people. The things that I heard about blacks were not nice. Of course, some of the things said about them were true, but the rest were imagined, generalized, and blown out of proportion. We were taught that blacks were violent, angry, lazy, and dishonest. We were taught to fear and mistrust every black person. That's why I was angry. Indeed, I don't blame others for my own prejudices. I just wanted to give you a background to it." He paused for a moment.

"I was very angry. Then, my anger turned into anxiety. I was anxious about my daughter's wellbeing. I was worried about what my family and neighbors would say about us. I was worried about many things. Then, my anxiety turned into blaming others. I blamed Andrea. I told her that she had failed our daughter. She had not guided her properly. She had not taught her anything about the need for racial purity and separateness. Then, I stopped blaming my wife, and started blaming myself. It was my fault that I had not instructed my daughter about the dangers paused by falling in love with a black man. Of course, I had told her, but I hadn't emphasized them enough. My self-blame turned into the hope that they would break up. Soon, I realized that I was wrong. Eventually, reality dawned on me that their relationship was more serious than I imagined." Mr. Weber paused and wiped his eyes.

"When I realized that I wasn't going to win, I started reading books written by blacks about blacks. I also read books about Zimbabwe and African cultures. Something happened to me. I didn't see a vision, but I felt that something happened. I was transformed. It was not sudden, but gradual. I started giving Peter the benefit of the doubt, and allowed him to enter our home. I started asking him questions about his culture and his family. The more I listened to him, the more I liked him. In fact, I was surprised about how my encounter with Peter changed my worldview about blacks. I started to have empathy for them. I know that they are not perfect, just like I am not. We are all not perfect. My encounter with Peter made me realize that there are bad and good people in every culture." Mr. Weber paused, and sipped his water.

"By the time of the wedding, I was a changed man. Now, I am happy that Maria married Peter, for my horizons have been enlarged. I see things that I never thought existed before. I eat food that I never knew before. Now, I tell stories that I never heard before. I have a vocabulary that I didn't know before. And most of all, I have the most handsome grandson in the world. Look at his curly hair. Look at his handsome face. He is not black and not white. Maria and Peter created something new and unique out of their different ethnical identities. We are grateful to you, Tendai, for raising Peter to be a gentleman. He is a caring and kind father. He is hardworking. He has taught us how to be human again. He added a piece that we never realized was missing in our lives. We are now in touch with our common humanity. We are similar in many ways. We need each other. We need each other."

I was dumbfounded. I did not know what to say after all these speeches. My eyes were moist. I went to the bathroom to wipe them. When I came back, Mr. Weber proposed a toast.

"To happiness, friendship, good health, prosperity, and longevity," he shouted.

We all raised our wine glasses.

"And to the wife from the ancestors!" Mother shouted.

And everyone said, "cheers."

The End

A Glossary of Foreign Terms and Phrases

Amai: mother
Amigos: friends (Spanish)
Baba: father
Babamukuru: older brother, your father's older brother, woman's older sister's husband
Babamunini: younger brother, woman's young sister's husband, husband's younger brother
Babangu Moyo: my father, Moyo
Chigutiro: proverbial person's name
Chinonzi chirungu: it is called English
Chivanhu: tradition
Danga: wooden enclosure in which cattle sleep, cattle given to the father-in-law as part of bridewealth
Egusi soup: Nigerian soup made from fish, vegetables, and other ingredients
Futseki: Shona derivative for the Afrikaans word, *voertsek* (cursing word)
Hazvina hunhu: it is not ethical
Hunenge usahwira: it is like friendship
Hunhu: good character and morals
Hunhu hwedu: our morals
Ishwa: edible winged insects/ants
Kongonya dance: Zimbabwean traditional dance
Kupfumba: a clearly marked path, getting used to a nickname
Kushuma usavi: a ritual of offering meat to the visitors
Mababes: young unmarried women
Madora: edible caterpillars with spikes
Mai: mother
Maiguru: older sister, mother's sister, father's older brother's wife, older brother's wife
Makadiniko, Shumba: How are you, Shumba
Makorokoto: congratulations
Mandipedza mate mumukanwa: You astonished me
Maningi sitereki: so much/extensively

Mapoto marriage: unofficial live-in marriage

Masivanda: Totemic name for married women belonging to the Lion totem

Mbodza: half cooked *sadza*

Mbuya: grandmother, uncle's wife

Mhai: mother (Karanga)

Mhayi: mother (Karanga)

Mhofu yemukono, zienda netyaka ziwewera: totemic saying for people belonging to the Eland.

Mufushwa: dried vegetables

Mukoma: brother

Muroora: daughter-in-law

Muroyi: witch

Murungu: white person

Mutimwi: talisman/protective traditional medicinal band tied around the waist.

Muzukuru: Nephew, grandson, granddaughter, niece

Mwanangu: my son

Ndichadzidza zvakawanda: I will learn more (broken Shona)

Ndizvo zvakaita bush *sezvino*: does a bush look like this

Nhaiwe, Peter: You, Peter (calling)

Nhodzera: resemblance

Nuestra casa tu casa: our home is your home (Spanish)

Nyavhe: popular Zimbabwean indigenous vegetable

Nzungu: peanuts

Pero en vivo: but, live (Spanish)

Rine manyanga hariputirwi: (Shona proverb, which means that some things cannot be hidden

Roora: bridewealth

Rugaba: part of bridewealth, which gives the groom exclusive sexual rights over the bride

Rupfumbidzo: money paid to make a nickname official

Sabhuku: village head

Sadza: Zimbabwe's staple food made from corn meal and boiled water

Sekuru: grandfather, uncle

Tamba wakaguta: dance after eating

Tatenda zvakawanda: thank you very much (broken Shona)

Tinofara kana muchifarawo: we are well if you are also well

Ukamai: What kind of a relationship is this
Unoda kushamisira: You want to show off
Vakomana: boys, young men
Vanhu: people
Vanyarikani: respectable people
Varoora: daughters-in-law
Varungu: white people
Vasikana: girls, young women
Vatezvara: father-in-law
Vuroyi: witchcraft
Wagona: well done
Zambia: piece of cloth used to wrap over women's dresses in Zimbabwe
Zveusiku: witches' invisible and nefarious children used to harm other people
Zvidhoma: see *zveusiku*
Zvikara: see *zveusiku*
Zvitupwani: see *zveusiku*
Zvokwadi: true

www.ingramcontent.com/pod-product-compliance
Lightning Source LLC
Chambersburg PA
CBHW050341030726
47503CB00008B/2552